SOME OF THE PARTS

a novel by T Cooper

SOME OF THE PARTS

a novel by T Cooper

AKASHIC BOOKS
NEW YORK

This is a work of fiction. All names, characters, places, and incidents are the product of the author's imagination. Any resemblance to real events or persons, living or dead, is entirely coincidental.

Published by Akashic Books
©2002 T Cooper

Design and layout by Sohrab Habibion
Cover images by author, friends, and booth

ISBN: 1-888451-36-X
Library of Congress Control Number: 2002106360
First printing
Printed in Canada

Akashic Books
PO Box 1456
New York, NY 10009
Akashic7@aol.com
www.akashicbooks.com

ACKNOWLEDGMENTS

I am indebted to the following people
for a variety of reasons.

Diane Baldwin, Kate Bornstein, Chase Byron, Scott Conklin,
Karen Covington, Michael Cunningham, Jeni Englander,
Ken Foster, Alexis Gannon, Will Georgantas, Johanna
Ingalls, Ari Kelman, Murray, Sigrid Nunez, Spencer Presler,
Lauren Sanders, Helen Schulman, Elizabeth Stark, Johnny
Temple, James P. Withers, and my parents. And mostly,
Kathryn Greta Welsh.

Perished. Alone. The gray-green light on the wall opposite. The empty places. Such were some of the parts, but how bring them together?

−Virginia Woolf, *To the Lighthouse*

"When I was a kid I used to think about which of my parents I'd let the Nazis take to the ovens if I could only save one of them. Usually I saved my mother. Do you think that's normal?"

−Art Spiegelman, *Maus*

CONTENTS

1

ISAK

I WAS THE NEWEST ADDITION to the freak show. And don't think it was easy getting the job. I got it purely on account of the geek's misfortune. Once the animal protection laws went into effect and actually started being enforced, the geek was rendered pretty much useless and couldn't get good enough at anything else to stay with the show. Sure, he tried sword-swallowing, but soon after discovered that his gag reflex wasn't as persistent as most people's, and thus he couldn't get the swords out of there when needed. Then, I think, he tried lifting heavy objects as the strong man but ended up with a slipped disc in his spine.

Anytime you asked one of the old-timers what happened to the geek, they'd cast their eyes down and shake their heads. The snake charmer invariably crossed herself and muttered something softly in Latin even at the mention of the geek's name, which I was told not to utter or pass on in any way, shape, or form. It was apparently something more than the animal protection laws that plagued the geek.

But the geek's misfortune became my fortune. Although you can't really call it a fortune, or even a small fortune–in that I made about fifty dollars per shift, and one shift could sometimes entail five or six performances. Plus, this spot vacated by the geek was supposed to be cursed, and ever since he left, it never quite has been permanently or even comfortably filled by anybody else. According to legend, nobody in modern Coney Island freak-show history has been able to exist peaceably in the geek's place.

The first person to fill the geek's spot was a youngish bearded lady. But after her husband died in a tragic motorcycle accident on the Brooklyn-Queens Expressway, the bearded lady went to San Francisco and opened a gay men's leather bar called, well, "Beard." The bearded lady after her was stricken with an aneurysm that left the right side of her body and face paralyzed, and so she became a psychic with her gypsy family in a storefront in Queens instead. No one would say what happened to the snake lady who came after the second bearded lady (apparently she got into penetrating herself with the snakes, and then the act–and her life–went straight downhill from there). Then the woman with a tail protruding from the base of her spine found that she could make much more money as a prostitute, and so with no notice, up and left the show for Atlantic City.

And finally, before I came on board, there was the hermaphrodite whose family came and rescued her from the freak show one balmy summer night. So there I was.

I happened to be at Coney Island, hitting some balls in the batting cages, on the night the hermaphrodite's parents came to take her away. I saw it all happen. It was the kind of night where you go out knowing something's going to change, but you're not quite sure what it is. So you blow twenty dollars smacking the shit out of little, yellow imitation baseballs in the medium-speed baseball cage and sit around and wait for the something to come your way.

I was taking a break from batting with some French fries and a Coke, when I wandered through the flashing lights of the midway and over toward the freak show. I stopped in front of the Whack-A-Mole and considered giving it a try, but my shoulders were too sore from swinging the bat.

"You're doing this to hurt your mother," I heard someone yelling, though in a somewhat controlled fashion. I became immediately interested. "Look at your mother; this is killing her."

I looked over at what appeared to be the hermaphrodite's mother. She was wearing pleated khakis and a flannel shirt tucked into them. She looked like she was from New England. And it seemed as though the father was right; she did in fact look like she could've been dying, or at least dealing with the death of someone very close.

The tattooed man crossed his massive, colorful arms on his chest and firmly placed himself between the hermaphrodite and her approaching father. The tattooed man looked back at her protectively, though I could tell by the look in her eye that she wasn't letting her parents go home empty-handed that night. (I say "her" because that's what she was calling herself. Later, I found out that she had never had what passed as testicles and a penis removed from her body, her parents having decided at birth to "make" her a boy.)

"Why didn't you tell me?" she screamed around the tattooed man at her father.

"We did. We did tell you . . . Who the hell is this guy?" her father asked, clearly annoyed. "Can't we have a family discussion without this, this *Neanderthal* around? Jesus H.!"

"He's not a Neanderthal. He's my friend, Daddy," the hermaphrodite said. "And anything you have to say he can hear."

"Listen, please come home. We can talk about this later. Look at your mother. Your poor mother."

The hermaphrodite stepped around the tattooed man and reached for her father's outstretched hand, but just before she made contact, the boss came out, screaming, "What the hell's going on out here? Not in public!"

"I am just trying to have a conversation with my—" and here the hermaphrodite's father stumbled on his words, for when he last left her, she was most likely a man, or as much of a man as she could manage. "I'm trying to talk to my *daughter* here, sir, so if you'll just give us a few seconds." The father's bald spot revealed its true magnitude when a cool Atlantic breeze blew over the boardwalk and through the midway. A row of pennants flapped loudly above us. The wife looked as though her knees were about to collapse under the burden of her body.

"Aw, Jeez, we got a show to put on here. She's up in a few

minutes," the boss whined, pointing up to the painted wood sign advertising "Henrietta Lee, the Herm-Aphrodit-E."

"Oh honey," the mother cried. "My baby!"

"She is not going on. She's coming with us," the father protested. And then everyone, the tattooed man, the boss, Linus the Menacing Midget, even the small gathering crowd, all of us looked to the hermaphrodite for the answer to what would happen next.

You could see it in her eyes: "Daughter" had been the magic word, and she was about to give in.

Still, her mother added, "You have a college education!"

But it was a superfluous final plea. The hermaphrodite hugged the tattooed man, whispered something into his ear, and stumbled into the circular embrace of her mother and father, who wrapped a feminine cardigan of sorts around her shoulders and guided her off in the direction of the train station.

As I watched the reunited family amble off, I heard the boss say, "What the fuck are we gonna do now?" and the tattooed man respond, "Give it a fucking rest, huh? Just once."

And then I knew my something had happened. I hated office-temping, needed money, and hell, I had a college education.

"Sir," I said, poking the boss on the shoulder. "Sir, I think I can help."

"Who the fuck are *you*, asshole?" he responded, which I took as a favorable response, since strangers usually reserve "asshole" for men they are trying to insult, while saving "bitch" for women.

"Hire me," I said, holding my arms up in front of him.

"Are you kidding me? You're the most boring looking asshole I've ever seen. You look like you should be hawking cologne on a billboard." I shrugged my shoulders. He continued, "What the fuck can you do? And don't say 'card tricks,' cause I don't need any more girls who can pull a good trick. Wait, what the fuck *are* you?" He actually made eye contact with me, and I saw the light bulb in which both confusion and a good idea flickered behind his dull eyes.

14

"So, hire me," I said again, nodding toward the show. "I can do something like she did."

"I'm not paying you a cent," he said.

"Fine."

"Right this way, then, uh, what's your name?"

"Isak," I answered, and waited for a response. When none came, I added, "See, you don't know which I am either, huh?"

"I don't really care what the fuck you are, just so the folks out there can't tell," he said, taking me past the fairly empty bleachers to the backstage area. "It's a tough crowd. And I told you I'm not payin' you, right? Not 'til I see if you can do something."

"I understand."

"No monkey business or dirty stuff, nothin' like that. Just a good show where you keep them guessing, right?"

"Right."

"And you keep your pants on the whole time, right?"

"Right. Pants on."

"Don't fuck with me."

"I won't."

15

"Ladies and gentlemen, we have a special treat for you now," the tattooed man began. He had just taken a turn in the "high voltage" chair before I was set to go on, and thus had the task of introducing me to the small but eager audience. "It's appropriate I say 'ladies and gentlemen,' folks, because, well, it's hard to tell which is which when it comes to our next act. Please welcome Mr., Ms., well, you can decide for yourself."

The small, muffled applause sounded bored from my spot backstage. My chest tightened up, and my sinus cavities started pulsing. I could feel sweat pooling in the crevices between my fingers. The boss pushed me off the barrel on which I was sitting, and the next thing I knew, I was on stage in front of about twenty people on bleachers, not ten feet from where I was standing.

The first thing I noticed was the smell. It was so damp in there. Just a damp, wood smell. Dark, and creaking. Every time an audience member even so much as shifted his weight, it sounded as though the entire set of bleachers was going to come down.

So I just stood there in front of them. A few people coughed. One guy in the front row started picking the top of his head and examining his fingers in between picks. Still I stood there.

I then tried to recall everything I'd ever heard or seen or read about freak shows: the genius Siamese twins, the smallest woman in the world, the goat with two heads, the world's strongest baby, the woman with the tiniest feet. It smelled as though they had all passed through this space at one point or another during the past couple hundred years. And now it was my turn, though I was admittedly just my boring self, and had no claim to being up there other than that I either fulfilled or didn't fulfill others' expectations of what I was supposed to be–which is truly no different from what most people do anyway.

This thought twisted between my ears for the first few minutes up on stage, and I kept coming back to that ancient, sodden smell. Still I stood, rocking back and forth because blood wasn't sufficiently traveling to and from my legs. Whose expectations was I playing on, I wondered. Theirs or my own? And then I heard, "Aw, Jesus, come on!" from the direction of backstage. It was the boss, bemoaning his crisis involving the runaway hermaphrodite and a fill-in stiff up on stage. A second audience member got up to leave the show, tossing his program under the bleachers behind him; it fluttered noisily to the dirty ground below.

This woke something in me. All the disappointment I'd ever experienced from both myself and others came rushing at me, like in that Munch painting: all of it swirling around in all sorts of colors and old, rotten smells of termite-infested wood, wet ketchup-soaked paper plates, crumbling corn dogs, stale funnel cakes, and bent cigarette butts spinning in every corner. And I just opened up my mouth, not as wide as in *The Scream,* but wide enough to be heard. I lowered my regular talking voice and started to speak.

16

"When I was in the fifth grade, I was scared to use the bathroom because once a substitute teacher yelled at me for using the wrong one, and she called my parents to intervene and make me use the appropriate bathroom." The head-picking guy stopped his endeavor and looked up at me.

"Since kindergarten, I'd just always used the boys' bathroom, and no one cared or knew the difference until that teacher saw me walking out of there that day, and all hell broke loose. Problem was, the girls wouldn't let me into their bathroom because I had been using the boys' for all that time, and there was nowhere else for me to go."

A lady in the front row smiled at me. At least I thought it was a smile. "And this was before the time of family bathrooms," I added. But no one laughed, so I went on.

"Well, I developed bladder infections that year, and they lingered throughout high school. But after that, I was free to go out there and use either, or both. Or neither." I could tell the audience was somewhat interested, although that interest was on the verge of waning.

"I'm not telling you this to gain pity. Just your understanding that when you look at me, there might not be one answer to the question you all are asking, but rather, many answers to that one question. And also, many other relevant questions. Like, 'Why is it so important that you know?' and, 'What do you think would make me a woman? And what would it take to make you think this same body is that of a man?' You start asking these kinds of questions, and it becomes blurrier and blurrier as to what a freak really is in this world—" At this point I'd blown any audience interest I'd gained in the first place.

"Folks, folks," the boss said, waving his arms as he rushed out on stage—which I later learned was a true rarity. "Folks, what our friend is asking is, what do you think? Do you think you know which he or she is?"

Nobody in the audience so much as stirred, perhaps out of shyness, or horror at the possibility of being picked out of the crowd. But after a few uncomfortable seconds, a tough guy in

17

baggy jeans, a Mets cap, and a blinding gold necklace around his thick neck tried to impress his girlfriend: "I think it's a she because her voice isn't that low."

"Ah, maybe so," the boss said. "But I can talk like this," and he raised his voice an octave, managing to sound quite natural doing so. "Anyone else?"

I heard a kid whisper to his mom, "Can I say what I think, if it's a boy or a girl?" The mother shushed him, but he was just a few months past allowing her such a privilege.

"I think he's a boy," he continued, standing up adolescently in the bleachers. He was the kind of kid who would've been acting quite differently had he been with three or four of his friends instead of his family, who were visiting New York from Columbus, Ohio or some other place like Missouri or maybe Kentucky. He would've been much more threatened, and thus more obnoxious, around his friends.

"Well, young man, tell me why," the boss prodded, grabbing my arm to ensure my silence.

"Mostly his clothes," he started. "But no, like, there's something else. Like his haircut; it goes down more than a girl's," he said, pulling at the skin just in front of his ears, where sideburns would've been if he could grow them.

"Interesting. Anyone else?" the boss asked.

A woman stood up in the back, clutching her purse. "Well," she started, "that story she just told, that would seem to indicate that she is a she, because the teacher bothered her about going into the *wrong* bathroom."

The audience was silent. A small drop of sweat fell from the tip of the boss' nose onto his potbelly. (He wasn't used to being under the lights.) Nobody had been listening except for this woman, and I hadn't thought out the implications of sharing my childhood with the audience.

"Am I right?" she asked, expecting some sort of a prize for the correct answer.

The boss looked at me, also not quite sure of the answer, also not having listened to my story.

Then chaos broke out in the stands, a state which the boss

18

frowned upon severely. Audience members started whispering and talking to one another, and the boss appeared unsure as to where to go from there, probably kicking himself in the ass for having let me go on stage with no plan. And me, I was comfortable just standing there, happy for once to see tangibly all of the confusion that my mere presence was capable of engendering in the world.

"Ma'am, a fine observation. But might not the story just be another part of the act?" the boss asked suddenly, pulling the rug out from under my cathartic moment. "And that is the mystery and intrigue of the freak show, isn't it?"

The audience quieted. Blood returned to my legs.

"Would anyone like to get a closer look before making a decision?" the boss proposed. "For a small extra donation, you may come up one at a time and shake our friend's hand, look into his or her eyes, and go away with your own knowledge in order to make your decision. We ask only that you come up one person at a time, and please, no donations smaller than a dollar."

Much to my surprise, the good listener came up, paid her dollar, and shook my hand rather limply. She smiled right at me. She was my first customer in a new occupation as someone who sells his body in some way. I had been selling my mind for years, lending it to useless endeavors like alphabetizing files upon files of unidentified *things,* and taking an infinite number of useless phone messages for an infinite number of useless people calling me both "Sir" and "Ma'am" in the same sentence. But this was the first time my body was exchanged for money. It was a little creepy–a *dollar* to shake my hand?– but I liked it.

Another audience member came up, planted another bill in the boss' hand, and grabbed mine with the fervor of someone who just sold you a fucked-up used car that was going to blow its transmission three days after the sale. There were no more takers, though I could tell I was a success of sorts. Two audience members left the show after my act, and the boss said, "Ladies and gentlemen (and I use that term lightly around here), please give our friend a hand, and join me in welcoming our next act, Sharon the snake charmer."

I found myself being ushered off stage by the boss' hand, pressed firmly into the small of my back. Sharon passed us on her way to the stage with a thick, yellow boa constrictor wrapped around her neck. She wore torn fishnet stockings with a leather garter belt holding them up. She had enough tattoos to be the tattooed lady, and I started seeing how so many of these jobs overlap so beautifully. Which is why the tattooed man was also the man who could lie on a bed of nails with an audience member standing on his gut, but then also get jolted in the electric chair just five minutes later.

I couldn't actually see the snake charmer's face as she passed me; she had to strain her eyes upward because her head was forced so far down under the weight of the massive snake around her neck. "Good job," she grunted. Or at least that's what it sounded like she said.

I was going to have to come up with some sort of a spiel. It was all so simple when you made it into a game like that. Is he, or isn't she? Black or white was much easier than a whole life lived somewhere else in the gray. And yet they weren't even peddling right answers at the freak show.

As the few claps died down and Sharon started talking to the audience, the boss turned to me and put a five-dollar bill into my palm. "At least you can get home and get a drink with it."

"Thanks," I said.

"And you can, uh . . . come back again tomorrow if you want," he started. His stage voice was entirely different from this normal speaking voice. "But no more of that bullshit story about the bathrooms and the kidney infections, all right?"

"Bladder infections."

"Whatever. What the hell was that shit anyway?"

"I don't know, it just came out," I said, pocketing the five-dollar bill.

"Yeah, well, the less you say, the better. You hear?"

"Yes."

"And no more bullshit philosophy out there, okay?"

"Okay."

"Don't fuck with me." A fat finger in my face.

"No, I won't. Never again."

2

TAYLOR

SAND BLEW ACROSS THE ROAD like it had somewhere to go. It scattered the way pedestrians do after "Don't Walk" begins to flash at a crowded intersection. Taylor had to get to Provincetown soon or Jules was going to kill her. The ceremony was at six-thirty, and Taylor was supposed to pick up the flowers by five and then get the booze by five-thirty. Or was it booze by five and flowers at five-thirty? Either way, the traffic was horrendous, and Taylor wasn't used to having to follow through on anything for Jules. But this time she had promised. It was Jules's little brother's second wedding. Third, if you counted the girl in Thailand.

Taylor mouthed lyrics along with the radio, tapping words out on the steering wheel as though it were a keyboard. She had to hit the dash a few times to get the gauges to register and the radio to kick in, but when she did, her old Corolla was fine. Best $450 she ever spent. Come to think of it, the *only* $450 she ever spent. It came with a faded "Free Tibet" sticker with red and black sun rays behind the letters. Taylor had eaten lunch across from the Dalai Lama once when he came to speak at her college in Michigan. He looked suddenly plain and less compelling there in the cafeteria, sitting in front of a cracked, brown plastic tray filled with limp greens, she had thought.

She swerved to the shoulder to look at the line of traffic snaking ahead. Friday evening wasn't the best time to be driving out to the Cape, but Taylor's mother had kept her late at

the store, where they unpacked and tagged the latest shipment of crap. Arlene kept stacking invoices in front of Taylor.
She was so anxious about the upcoming summer season,
Taylor thought it better to help out and risk being late for the
wedding, rather than listen to more of her mother's whining.
Arlene's Artifacts: her mom's store in Providence. It was a
wonder the place was still in business. A wonder any of the
Providence tourists and locals still had blood left to suck. How
many charming wicker baskets and arty little frames did a
family need, really?

"Fuck, *fuck*," Taylor said, the second "fuck" much louder
than the first. She fished around the floor behind her seat,
found a plastic water bottle and took a few big swigs. Some
water splashed out either side of her mouth and landed on her
shoulders, across her breasts. Taylor hated her breasts. They
rode too high on her chest, one considerably smaller than the
other. But no one else ever seemed to care or even notice.
Taylor realized she was sweating, even though both windows
were rolled all the way down. Traffic wasn't moving over fifteen miles an hour.

24

Taylor looked down and wondered why she wore that particular dress. It was yet another detail–though minute–that
came about without Taylor's really having decided upon it.
She didn't even remember standing in front of the guestroom closet in her mother's house and staring at herself in the
mirror. She didn't remember pulling the dress off a hanger
and slipping it on over her head, thinking, *Yes, this looks good
on me.*

There was no way she'd make it in time to pick up the flowers and liquor. Taylor decided to pull off the highway and
phone Jules to let her know. She dialed her cell phone number from a pay phone.

"What?" Jules asked.

"It's me. I'm a little late," Taylor said.

"Clearly."

"Traffic's a bitch. I don't think I'm going to be able to pick up
the stuff."

"It's covered," Jules said. "No, over there. Over *there*." It sounded as though Jules was telling someone else what to do. "Anyway . . ."

"So, will you make it for the ceremony even?" Jules asked, doing her best to sound thoroughly exasperated.

"I just hit Orleans."

Huge sigh from Jules. "Great."

"What?" Taylor asked. "Jules, what?"

"I have to go. People are starting to show up." Jules hung up, and for a moment Taylor looked back in the direction from which she came. Nothing in either direction, really. So she got back into her car and kept driving toward Jules, or more accurately, back to Jules.

It was six thirty-seven when Taylor first got sight of the pilgrim tower in Provincetown. It looked like a fork, stuck into a plateful of dunes. The sun was already going down behind it, and Taylor was officially late. She checked herself in the mirror yet again, bit her bottom lip, and smiled at herself. She tucked her short, dark hair behind both ears. It was her favorite ritual—tucking the hair. She did it when she was pretending to listen to someone intently at a party, when she was flirting. She had used it when she walked into The Sun, the Moon, and the Stars Bed and Breakfast and asked Jules for a job—any job—a few summers back. 25

Taylor kept her hair a perfect length—long enough in front to make it just behind the ears, but short enough so it'd keep falling and she'd have to tuck it back again. The back could be short, but the front had to be just right; it was practically a gold mine of its own. Lovers always touched Taylor's dark hair first, dutifully tucking it back behind her ears before moving on to something else. Older men liked doing it most, a caretaking ritual of sorts, Taylor guessed. It happened like this invariably.

When Taylor pulled up to the hotel, Jules was in the parking lot, stacking bags of ice into a caterer's arms. Taylor thought she looked worn—more so than usual.

"Wasn't it supposed to start at six-thirty?" Taylor asked.

"The J.P.'s not here yet," Jules said, stacking a fourth bag of ice and motioning back up toward the bed and breakfast. "Okay, I'll get the rest," she said to the caterer, and he headed up through the gate in his too-tight, thrift store tuxedo, balancing the huge stack of ice. "I knew I couldn't depend on you–"

"Come on, Jules. You know how bad traffic is on Fridays."

"Right. Which is why *I* would've left earlier." Jules's suit was wet from the ice. Her salt-and-pepper hair stuck to her cheeks with sweat. *I let this touch me?* Taylor thought.

"Well, I'm sorry, but–" Taylor started.

"Forget it, the flowers were taken care of, the caterers brought the wine. It's fine. Just go get cleaned up. The guy's supposed to be here in ten minutes."

"I am cleaned up," Taylor said, smoothing out the front of her dress. Jules looked at Taylor and stopped. Then she reached over to straighten one of the dress' thin straps, resting her fingers lightly on Taylor's tan shoulder.

26   "You look great," Jules sighed. "I'm just stressed out with this party."

"I'm sorry," Taylor said, pecking Jules on the cheek. Purely out of habit.

They climbed the long staircase leading to the property. "So what happened to the J.P.?" Taylor asked.

"Stuck in traffic," Jules said, without even a hint of a smile. With this, Taylor knew–finally–she couldn't stand Jules anymore.

Taylor remained in her seat after the brief ceremony, in the very last seat of the last row. All of the other guests stood and began the requisite though excruciatingly uncomfortable chitchat that follows all rituals. They all seemed to know one another. She didn't know anyone there, except of course the groom. Taylor had fucked Kurt at the end of the previous summer, in the hotel's sunny laundry room. She made him swear not to tell Jules, ever. Taylor said she'd tell his fiancée (now wife) if Jules ever found out. He was a bad lay anyway, Taylor remembered. Predictable. And too easy, which was why Taylor was finished with him even before he came on the side of the stackable dryer beside her.

After, Taylor had pulled her shorts back up and finished taking the hot, stiff sheets out of the dryer. She told Kurt to leave, and that Jules was coming back soon. But Jules wasn't coming back until late that night, from a day trip to Boston.

Taylor also saw Catherine skulking about the party, and Marlene hovering around the bar–both women Jules's partners in the business. Catherine ran it with Jules, and Marlene financially backed them. Both ex-girlfriends of Jules, too. Or, technically, when Taylor wasn't around, Catherine and Jules were still together. Taylor was so sick of this little world she'd stumbled into. Everyone who knew everyone else. Everybody who had slept with everybody else. And Taylor had played the prize possession for Jules for so long. Kind of made her sick when she thought about it. It was only now, after the fact, that Taylor could ask herself what the hell she'd been doing there in the first place. She did that with a lot of things, but mostly relationships, or what passed as relationships in her life.

It's funny how people can just be exchanged, one for the other, like that, Taylor thought. They always had been.

Marlene spotted Taylor and began to make her way over, with her stiff walk, the shoulders too large for her frame. Marlene, who'd been enamored with Taylor from the day she brought Marlene that first drink out by the pool when Taylor started working for Jules at The Sun, the Moon, and the Stars. Marlene had left Taylor a twenty-dollar tip that day, and Taylor had spilled the first of several margaritas on Marlene's white towel. The woman could put them back, all right.

With each of Marlene's slightly slurred steps toward her, Taylor felt herself disconnecting from the place. By the time Marlene sat next to her in the last row of seats, Taylor could almost make herself feel as though none of it had happened in the first place, that she was a complete stranger in this foreign world.

27

"I don't know anyone here," Marlene said.

"I was just thinking that," Taylor replied.

"Bartender pours a mean Martini, though."

Taylor looked over toward the bar. There were a few younger people in their twenties, but a seemingly larger, older bunch of folks from out of town predominated. Women were in white and cream colored skirt suits, the men in basic boring khakis and blue blazers. And it seemed as though this party was for the sole benefit of the bride's family. Taylor wondered whether they thought it strange that the groom's parents did not attend this, their son's third wedding in as many years.

"It was a nice ceremony," Taylor offered.

"Please. I hate these things," Marlene said. "I give them three months."

"That's not very nice," Taylor said. "Would you excuse me, I have to go to the bathroom."

Taylor headed up toward the upper deck of the hotel. Once upstairs, she felt a sweaty hand on her shoulder. Kurt stopped her just as she slid open the glass door to the office.

"Thanks for coming."

"I came for Jules."

"Laundry room, fifteen minutes?" he suggested quietly.

"Funny," Taylor said. "Enjoy married life. I hear three's charming."

"You mean 'three's a charm,'" Kurt corrected her, and then: "You look really beautiful." Boring.

"Well, thank you," Taylor said, sighing. Briefly, she thought it might be fun to play with him. "No."

"No, what?"

"Nothing. I have to go," Taylor said, placing her hand softly on his lapel without the wilting flower attached to it. Taylor turned and slipped into the office, trying to enter quietly. Catherine was sitting at the computer, entering data into a spread sheet.

"Oh, hi," Taylor said, crossing to the file cabinet. Catherine ignored her. Taylor opened the drawer and found the hanging file with "Taylor" written in red. She shuffled through it.

"What are you doing?" Catherine asked, pushing back from the computer table in a rolling chair. The wheels made an annoying scraping noise on the plastic pad beneath.

"Just getting my last paycheck."

"You haven't worked here in months," Catherine said, laughing. "Why would you have a paycheck?" Taylor noticed two empty glasses on the table. It looked like the remnants of maybe Scotch.

"I've been doing some freelance stuff for Jules."

"Oh, some freelance stuff. I see," Catherine said. "Well, you're not going to find anything in there."

Taylor didn't know what to say. She could leave. But she wanted her money. Luckily, she could see Jules heading up the stairs toward the office. Catherine returned to pecking at the computer's keyboard.

"What's going on?" Jules asked upon entering the room.

"Taylor was just looking for her check."

"Don't start," Jules said to Catherine, and then to Taylor: "We need to talk."

"What about?" Catherine asked.

"It doesn't concern you," Jules insisted. "I told you, I need to figure this out on my own."

"What's to figure out? I'll do it for you," Catherine began. She picked up one of the glasses and took the last bit of liquor into her mouth, throwing her head all the way back. "Jules, Taylor does not in any conventional way care about you, and it's quite pathetic that you fancy yourself as being even remotely attractive to her. Look at her, Jules. Look at yourself."

"Damn you!" Jules screamed.

Taylor stood there watching the scene unfold. It was strangely unsatisfying to be the center of attention in this situation, the cause of yet another emotional eruption. Taylor usually thrived on situations in which she was the center of attention; she could just leave them as soon as they went bad. But if earlier it had been generally time to leave this one, now it was specifically time to do so.

"I always said, Jules, if you love something, let it go, and it will come back to you," Catherine continued. "But in this case, I think I was wrong."

"Fuck you."

"Fuck me? Very creative," Catherine laughed. "Oh, and Taylor, why don't we start calling those little paychecks what they *really* are?"

"You're making an idiot of yourself," Jules said to Catherine, but Taylor thought that Jules might as well have been saying it to herself. Taylor stepped backwards slowly, one foot after the other. Which was supposed to be simple, really, but wasn't working out so well for Taylor in this case. Taylor had warmed up for soccer games running side-to-side, forward-and-backwards a thousand times before stepping into the goal box and waiting for the onslaught of an opposing team. She could keep her balance while moving in any direction—on a split-second's notice. But this time the ground was falling out from under each of her steps. Taylor fumbled at the glass door's handle.

"Taylor, wait. Come back," Jules yelled.

"Better get used to saying that," Catherine snapped.

"Oh, you're on a roll," Jules said, turning back to Catherine, as Taylor slid the heavy glass door shut behind her.

The pebbles on the steps cut into Taylor's butt through her thin dress. She sat outside The Sun, the Moon, and the Stars, watching the occasional car turn the sharp corner around the property, tires screeching softly.

"Hey, you."

Taylor turned around to see Marlene approaching with two glasses of wine. She had assumed it would be Jules, chasing after her and exhausted from the ensuing fight with Catherine. But it was just Marlene. Again.

"White, right?" she asked Taylor, offering her the glass.

"Yeah, white." Taylor took the glass, and the wine almost spilled over the rim. "How'd you remember what I liked to drink?"

"It's kind of hard to forget." Marlene started rolling up the sleeves of her navy linen blazer. She even rolled up her sleeves stiffly. "So what the hell's going on in there?"

"Yeah. I don't know," Taylor returned, trying to read Marlene, who was sitting close enough to Taylor that she could smell the sweet alcohol and sour nicotine seeping from Marlene's pores. Taylor tucked the hair behind her left ear, and she saw Marlene watching. Changing the subject: "It's a nice night."

"Seemingly," Marlene replied. She was a little drunk. She was always a little drunk. Her words were invariably slurred, no matter what time of day.

"It'll be a nice summer here," Taylor said, glancing at her rusty car in the lot below.

"Same old shit," Marlene sighed, sipping her wine and then taking out a cigarette.

Taylor didn't say anything. The two sat quietly as the breeze from another car speeding around the corner brushed over them. A bit of sand lodged in Taylor's eye, and she flinched.

"Let me see," Marlene said, holding Taylor's head in her hands and gently pulling down the skin under her eye with a thumb. "Stop blinking." She blew suddenly, and Taylor jerked away. Marlene's breath smelled sweet, but fermented, like dried fruit.

"Thanks." The bit of sand was gone, but her eye was still teary.

"So what are you going to do?" Marlene asked, flicking her cigarette onto the driveway below.

"Catherine's pretty pissed off," Taylor said, glancing back up at The Sun, the Moon, and the Stars.

"You could say that."

"I'm not sure I should hang around here anymore."

"If you leave, Jules will have a rough time of it. But she'll be okay. They'll be okay."

"I know," Taylor said. "I feel bad, though."

"Naw," Marlene replied, finishing off her wine. "I can give you some money."

"What?" Taylor asked, genuinely surprised.

"I said, I'd like to help you out, give you some money."

"No, Marlene, that's okay, I–"

"No. It would make me happy. Pay me back in a few years if you want. Or never." Marlene got up, brushed off her butt with both hands. "I've been wanting to do this since last summer. Get me another red wine, and I'll get my checkbook out of the car."

Taylor did, without another word. She left Marlene on the steps and headed to the bar. She thanked the bartender profusely for the wine, smiled, and gently touched his knuckles as he passed her the drink. This clouded world suddenly brightened as Taylor turned and headed back in Marlene's direction. A get-out-of-jail-free card of sorts. On her way back down, Taylor saw Jules, and she could sense that Jules was trying to break away from other guests so she could follow her. Taylor kept going, though, carrying out her mission for Marlene. She had to get there before Jules did.

Marlene stood awkwardly on the staircase, resting her forearms on the railing. Taylor held out the glass of wine for her, checking behind her one last time for Jules. Marlene pressed a check into Taylor's strong, square hand, then pulled her into a hug. Taylor whispered "Thanks" into Marlene's ear. Red wine spilled out of Marlene's glass and onto the steps behind her. The skin on Marlene's neck was thick and leathery, Taylor could feel with her cheek. Taylor could also feel Marlene's attraction for her, even through the smoky haze that surrounded Marlene. Then Jules appeared at the gate above them, and Marlene broke the embrace abruptly, patting Taylor roughly on one of her bare shoulders.

"I'm sorry we never–" Taylor said, softly. "I mean, it was just, you know, Jules and stuff."

"No, no, no," Marlene said. "Jules, hey, we were just waiting for you."

"Would you mind giving us a second?" Jules asked Marlene.

"No, not at all. Not at all. Taylor? If I don't see you, good luck. Keep in touch." Marlene disappeared behind the gate.

"What's that about?" Jules asked Taylor, as soon as Marlene was gone.

"What?"

"'Good luck'?"

"Jules, I think I'm gonna leave."

"What? Where are you going to go?" Jules sat down on the steps, slowly. "Your mother's? I think you're wasting away there. I'll teach you the business. You can decide whether you want in later. You know, see how it goes."

"Not my mom's," Taylor said, sitting down next to Jules on the step. She took off her bulky black shoes and put them to one side of the staircase. "It's not my mom at all."

"What then? What about us?" Jules stepped down and knelt in front of Taylor, on a lower step. Jules moved almost like a child. The last time Jules moved that way, Taylor thought, they had just met at a party and left for a walk on the pier. Jules had seemed thrilled that Taylor left with her. She walked backwards in front of Taylor, playfully balancing as though on a beam. It was windy. Masts ticked all over the bay–thick, oily decks filled up with tons of tangled, flaking, fishy nets.

"What?" Taylor asked, much later than she should've.

"I said, what is it? What about–"

33

"No, it's not you," Taylor interrupted. "It's just, I need to get off this coast."

"Oh, that's profound," Jules said, looking beyond Taylor's head and up at the property. Her property, the one she was offering to Taylor in exchange for what really just amounted to hope.

Taylor shook her head.

"You know, this offer isn't just going to be around forever. This is hurting Catherine," Jules continued, starting to twitch slightly like she did when her monthly receipts didn't add up. "I can't do this to her much longer. You either stay, or, or, I don't know."

"I'm gonna go." Taylor tried to pull Jules's pale, dry hands into her own bigger ones. Again, out of habit. But Jules pulled away and stood up.

"How? How are you going to get out there?" she spat. "Ha, that's a joke. The kid has to borrow money for a gallon of gas,

and now she's flying first class to live in a Hollywood bunga-
low with Lucy and Ricky Ricardo. You're a piece of work."

"Don't be mean," Taylor said, standing up and brushing the
dirt off her butt.

"Oh, right, you probably don't even know who Lucy and
Ricky are," Jules added. Taylor started walking toward her
car, and Jules followed. A convertible came around the corner, screeching loudly. This time Taylor squinted so that her
lashes covered her eyes in the wind. She didn't want to get dirt
in them again.

"What the hell are you going to do?" Jules asked, putting her
hand to her head and brushing back her hair. "You can't even
take reservations at this hotel without me coming in behind
you and fixing up your mistakes."

Taylor didn't respond, just got into the driver's seat and
looked at Jules, whose face was illuminated by the bare bulb
in the car. Jules still wasn't catching on that her little fantasy
of Taylor was petering out. Jules acted superior to Taylor,
pulling age and rank on Taylor whenever she went against
Jules's wishes. But still Taylor was the one who was leaving,
she reminded herself. The ultimate power: taking yourself
away from somebody against her will.

The tiniest amount of light from the car's interior went a
long way in the strange, orange darkness. Jules's face was lit
as though in a spotlight, but it looked unfamiliar to Taylor. She
could forget things very quickly when she needed to. Taylor
looked out into the darkness and saw something else coming.

"Pete!" Taylor yelled, and ran over to an old guy in a red vest
and work pants, limping toward them out of the darkness.
Pete was a familiar face in town. He wandered the streets at
night. He used to have a fishing rig, but somewhere down the
line, he'd lost it.

"I got brushed," he said, staggering even more pronouncedly.
Jules came over then. Taylor reached for Pete's left arm,
which was dangling loosely by his side.

"This is broken," Taylor said, jerking her hand back. But
Pete didn't seem to mind that Taylor had touched it.

"I think I got brushed by that car . . ." Pete said, pointing with his other arm.

"Which car, which way, Pete?" Jules asked, turning to look into the darkness. The fix-it Jules: Taylor's least favorite aspect of her. At one time, when Taylor wanted someone to take care of everything, it was a relief, but now it just seemed excessive. "I'm going to call the police."

"No, no, no, no, I had a little drink. Maybe I didn't get hit, maybe I fell. I'm fine," Pete said, waving his arms, the broken one flopping in impossible directions. He turned to Taylor. "You won't call the police, right? You won't call them. I'm just going to get some rest, take a load off."

"No, we won't call the police if you don't want, Pete," Taylor said, looking at Jules. "We just need to get you to the hospital."

"No, no, no, you said you wouldn't call the police."

"The hospital, Pete, just the doctors to make you better," Taylor repeated, now following Pete, who was making his way back into the dark street.

"I gotta get in bed, take a load off. Enough walking for tonight," Pete said, waving the arm to show that it was okay. "Doctor in the morning. Rest now."

The road was sprinkled with a layer of sand. It was so still, Taylor could hear Pete's shuffling feet on the sandy pavement as he walked away. Jules stared at her, seemingly annoyed by the distraction. Pete started to disappear into the darkened patches of road where the street lamps were not. He shuffled loudly.

"Listen, just stay the night," Jules said, exhaling like a slow air leak. "We'll figure it out in the morning, and then you can go."

"Are you *insane?*" Taylor's mouth hung slightly open. She tried to catch up with her breath. "He needs to go to a hospital."

"He doesn't want to go, Taylor. You can't make him."

Pete was all but invisible as Taylor squinted after him. Squinted both through her indecision and against Jules's prescription for things. Then she slammed the door of her car, and Jules practically vanished when the interior light was

35

extinguished. Just like that, someone can disappear so completely and refreshingly.

"Pete!" Taylor yelled after him. At that moment she thought she knew him better than she'd ever known anyone in her life. She loved his good timing. And yet this was all she could do. Then it was the sound of her feet scratching over the sandy pavement, running after him, calling, "Pete, honey, come on and wait for me."

Every time Taylor shifted gears she became hyper-aware of the tangle that was Pete's arm. He did not speak for the first ten minutes of the ride. Taylor concentrated on blending her foot's pressure on the gas pedal steadily into the pressure she applied on the clutch. Pete didn't seem to notice, but it made Taylor feel better to try to make it a smooth ride.

Once the pilgrim tower was a faint twig lit up in the rear-view mirror, Pete finally looked at Taylor, who was hunched tensely in the driver's seat. Taylor realized she was being responsible here. And that she was also a little scared.

"Jules and Catherine give me towels and shampoos," Pete said. "Sometimes dinner. I sweep the steps on Sundays." He moved his broken arm slightly to show Taylor how he might maneuver a broom. Taylor felt a twinge of nausea surge when she heard what had to be the fractured splinters of Pete's humerus scrape together.

"I know, Pete," Taylor said. "We're gonna get you fixed up down in Wellfleet," she added, as much for herself as for Pete. She kept checking the speedometer. There were no cars on the road. It seemed like hours before they pulled into the clinic's small parking lot.

One doctor was on call. He pushed through the front door wearing green scrubs and a gray M.I.T. sweatshirt.

"Well, what happened to Grandpa?" he asked Taylor.

"He's not my—he's just a friend," she corrected him.

"Mr.—, what's his last name?"

"I don't know," Taylor said, stepping back in that delayed, free-falling way again. "He got hit by a car."

"Do you know if he has insurance?"

"I don't know. Probably not."

Pete remained perfectly still, perhaps afraid for the first time that night, as the doctor put his hands on the arm. Pete's eyes sailed back and forth from Taylor to the doctor. Like a puppy getting its first round of shots. Taylor tried to look as though everything was going to be okay every time Pete made eye contact with her.

"Yeah, we've got a lot of crepitation here," he said. "He's gonna need surgery to set this." Pete looked at Taylor.

"Something for the pain, sir," a nurse said as she stuck Pete with an impossibly long needle. Pete's eyes now twitched in Taylor's direction. He moaned, or maybe it was Taylor. "That's it, sir; just a little something for the pain."

By the time Taylor finally got back to her mother's in Providence, it was two in the morning. Arlene sat by the fireplace, the right side of her face burning orange. A line of blue flames with orange tips skittered the length of a fake log. Taylor placed a callused hand on the back of her mother's head.

A pile of black hairs twisted into small strands lay next to Arlene's thigh on the brick fireplace. Arlene must've been plucking and stacking them there all night, like mini-kindling. Taylor brushed the hairs into the fireplace and sat down next to her mother.

"It's almost summer," Taylor said.

"Oh, well. A fire's nice any time," Arlene mused, looking at her daughter. "The chill's not quite burned off yet."

"Mom–"

"Tay, will you rub my back? I had to unload some of those boxes, and I'm a little sore. Can I go lay down, and you get some oil and rub me a little?"

"Mom. I'm leaving tomorrow."

"Honey, you can just rub me a little here then. Start low." Arlene pointed with her thumbs behind her, turning her back toward Taylor.

Taylor watched the muscles in her mother's neck as Arlene moved her head like a dancer does before exercises. She placed her hands on her mother's blue tanktop, in the middle of Arlene's back. It was warm and dry from the flames.

"Mmm, that's nice," Arlene said, breathing deeply. "Did you see those mirrors that came from the craft center in Vermont? They're gonna sell quick. And you know what? At that price, I can afford to be reasonable on the mark-up. Those babies are going to sail out of the store."

"Yeah, they're nice." Taylor rubbed her mother's back for about fifteen minutes, kneading the back of her arms, forearms, sticking the tips of her thumbs into the grooves of her mother's elbows. She knew the contours and bony crags of Arlene's body like no one else. They both looked into the blue and orange flames, which were beginning to flicker and recede.

When the log finally crumbled in half and fell through the grate, Taylor guided Arlene upstairs to her bedroom, lit a candle, and turned out the lights. "Just sleep, Mom."

38

Taylor watched her mother stretch out, twist, and then curl around a pillow. Did she forget to take her pill before she went to bed? Taylor wondered. She went over to the dresser and picked up a few prescription bottles, examined the labels.

"Tay?" It was like her mother could hear her trying to decide. "Will you mark those mirrors before you go tomorrow? I think forty-five, no—just forty—is about right. Forty dollars for the big ones, thirty for the smaller ones. Okay?"

Arlene curled back around the pillow, this time throwing a leg over it before dozing off, literally in seconds.

"Okay. Yeah, forty dollars."

3

ARLENE

TAYLOR WAS JUST FIVE, finally asleep at midnight, a little later than usual. I tried, but it always got so late by the time we realized it was time for a child to go to sleep. I lay on the bed on my stomach, breathing out of one nostril because the other was pushed into a musty pillow. Just breathing, and trying to read 14-Down in the crossword puzzle folded on top of the nightstand. "Et tu _____." I remember thinking it was a particularly easy one.

I had just moved on to 15-Down when Ken came in. I heard him loosening his tie, the way men say they can hear a woman uncrossing her legs when she's wearing hose. After he got into bed, he rolled on top of me and proceeded to thrash around inside so that he tore me. When he couldn't ejaculate, Ken pulled out and held my face to his. I think he did that so I could see him when he said, "I guess too much pussy in one night makes Kenny a dull boy." That movie was popular then. But I was past getting worked up about his infidelities by that point.

The next day I felt fire when I went to the bathroom, in little streaks, mostly on the outside. It hurt when I rubbed up against myself, even walking. Straddling my cosmetics mirrors, I could see the little red streaks. Some of them oozed clear fluid. My gynecologist told me not to wear panties, to wear a skirt for a week and keep it clean with something non-irritating. Like witch hazel. She asked if I'd ever tried K-Y, if I'd had a problem with dryness in the past.

Ken left something like a month later. He got a townhouse, where else, but in town. I know he might've taken Taylor from me, but it would've been solely on principle. Ken knew that even though he spent a good seventy-five percent of his time telling me how incompetent I was, *I* knew what to do with Taylor and he didn't. I found a job at a boutique by the river. Then the idea to run my own business when that one went under. I kept the house, I kept Taylor. He didn't come around much after that.

So what do you do? You keep on. You wonder how on Earth you were blessed with the most beautiful living creature in the world, and you hope that you didn't ruin her. Even though I knew I was doomed to ruin her. If that's what I did, I don't know.

I know her hands were always big–unnaturally big. And square. They looked like Ken's, except they were on a little girl. It was actually quite strange. She didn't have any friends, but she got along with everybody. We took baths together every Sunday night before school. Afterwards I rubbed her entire body with baby oil, until she turned thirteen and started using the guest shower. She rubbed aloe vera lotion into my skin. She poked my breasts, said once, "I got Grandma's, not yours." I cleaned out her ears with Q-tips–one whole Q-tip, both ends, for each ear. One time she pulled at my wet tampon string when I was toweling off my calves. Then the next thing I knew, she got a waterproof radio and hung it over the showerhead in the guest bathroom and started bathing by herself. Every morning she listened to the traffic report on Providence radio. We didn't even have to drive through town and worry about traffic in order to get Taylor to school.

And so today she moved to another coast. It was the first time I'd called Ken in well over a year. In the many years since the divorce, he wore down just like I did, and he didn't have to be so mean. He asked whether I wanted him to stop by the house on his way home. I said, "No, don't."

I couldn't give her more than a fifty-dollar bill. I know that's odd; no one carries fifty-dollar bills. But one of my regular

40

customers bought an embroidered pillow that said "Honey" for his wife on the way home from work, and he paid with a fifty.

"It could get you to St. Louis," I said to Taylor, handing over the bill. That was all I said. She had come by the store on her way out of town. I didn't even recall her saying anything about leaving in the first place.

I followed her outside, and Taylor rearranged the bags in her trunk. It struck me as the muscles in her forearm flexed under the weight of a duffel bag, that this is the kind of girl who gets pregnant and comes back home. Maybe I got this from watching too many made-for-TV movies, and it had nothing to do with Taylor. But that's what I thought. And at least getting pregnant wasn't really a threat. Or maybe it was. Maybe we'd already been through that with the teacher in boarding school. I think she had an abortion. She made me sign a blank permission slip for March fourth through the fifth, and mail it to the headmaster's office. I think it takes two days for those things; she was away in western Connecticut for two days, then back at soccer practice on Monday. The teacher, he was on leave from dorm duty that weekend too. I telephoned the school and asked.

When I called to tell him my concerns at the time, Ken had said that he didn't want to hear about it. Whatever it was, he wasn't paying for it. His wife had just lost a baby of her own. Their second. He said it "spontaneously terminated because it was genetically unsound." Down syndrome can do that. I liked that. Something's so fragile it just decides what it can and can't take. What it simply is not equipped to handle. Obviously, I lost the ability to do this when I left the womb.

Which is why, for me, and for as long as I can remember clearly, there has always been the store. Buying season, Halloween, Christmas, Easter. Just the coming of a new season necessitated entirely refreshed stock, interesting new displays. It's a little store, but it's a lot of work. The kind of work I can handle.

This company in Vermont, I never went wrong with them. I

swear. Way back, I bought these beautifully carved benches from them for the store. Solid oak. I sold two, never could get rid of the third. I kept it until Taylor wanted it for her house in college. She lived with a bunch of the girls from the soccer team up there, and I guess they had a perfect place for it in the backyard. I never got up to Michigan to see it, but Taylor said it worked out great. She studied on it sometimes when it was warm out. At least that's what she said.

I pulled Taylor out of the local high school and sent her away to boarding school because of that bench. It was the one thing I got Kenny to help me out on, coming up with that tuition. I sent her away because I was losing her. It made sense at the time.

"She's got good hands," is all I heard from this coach of hers. Always calling me at home, dropping by the house to tell me what a "natural" my daughter was. A natural soccer goalie. I don't know what's natural, but soccer wasn't ever it for me. She told me Taylor needed to get involved in athletics "to round out her academic experience." That she'd never seen a player with "such raw talent." That woman worried me from day one. Taylor sat in the car for a whole five minutes when that Jill gave her a ride home from practice the first time. Jill, Taylor called her. Jill, or Coach sometimes, but outside of soccer, always Jill.

It was the pear shape of that woman's body, straddling the carved bench and talking to Taylor about her "technique." And Taylor swinging her legs and playing with her hair, not listening in that way she does, but making you think she only has ears for you. I can see how a person could fall in love with that. Believe me.

I saw that Jill a few weeks back, in the grocery store. She had a mighty empty basket. Looked like she was still shopping for one. Or maybe she had just arrived at the store, to be fair.

They live such lonely lives.

She waved at me down the pet-food aisle. I never went down there; I don't know what I was doing. Well, the coffee grinder was across from the dog food, and mine had broken, so I had to get my beans ground in the store. Jill came rolling down the aisle toward me, more like waddling; she hadn't lost that pear shape, but I did notice she didn't look much older than she had when Taylor was in school. She didn't look half as bad as some of Taylor's other teachers I see sometimes. I don't know. Maybe when you don't have a man to cater to, or kids to pick up after, you don't get that stretched out, pained look. I have it. The others with full shopping baskets have it.

Jill asked me how Taylor was, right away. Where Taylor was. She didn't even ask how I was at all. I didn't give her the satisfaction. I lied and said I was estranged from Taylor, that after she graduated from college and trained hard for a year, she decided not to try out for the national team (I knew that would kill Jill).

I don't know why I did it. It just came out. Well, not all of it was untrue. It probably got me a seat on the express elevator to hell, but the look on that woman's face. It was worth it. She pushed her cart on by the kitty litter without another word.

When Taylor left this morning, and I gave her the fifty-dollar bill, I didn't even tell her about her Uncle Charlie. I still couldn't tell her. I think she already knew. We don't really talk anymore like we used to. And Charlie said that we didn't need to trouble her with any of it until he gets sick anyway. *If* he gets sick. That's how Charlie puts it, but it sounds like a veritable death sentence to me.

One good thing about Taylor's leaving is that there'll be space for Charlie in Taylor's old room. I've been thinking of asking him up. It's something Mom might've done in the time between Dad's death and her own—make him a son again. If Charlie comes to live with me, I think he's got a friend who could help take care of him when he needs it. There are only three bedrooms. And I don't know for sure, but a dying man probably takes up the space of two or three living.

Maybe if I thought it'd make her stay, I'd have told her about Charlie. But I knew she wouldn't stay. And that's not a comment on how she feels about Charlie. It's mostly a comment on me.

43

* * *

In truth, at one point I wanted Taylor's help in the store. I thought it could work that way, mother and daughter running the business together, living life together, all that. She seemed to be going nowhere at the time. The soccer thing was a dead end, and she didn't even seem to care for the girls on the team very much. I always thought soccer was all about camaraderie, but no. In the store, Taylor's good with customers, but her inventory and accounting skills are horrendous. In that respect, I'm kind of glad she's gone. I think she feels obligated to help her mother out when she's in town. But I honestly don't need that kind of help.

I know I maybe shouldn't be saying that about my own child, but it's true. She's completely unskilled. Like the other day, Mrs. Williamson came in with her fifteen-year-old daughter, Elaine, who's, well, at an *awkward* stage in her development. All frowns and limbs. She smelled of that sour, bitter adolescent body odor—like imitation apple flavor tastes.

"There will be eighteen girls at the party, so we'll need eighteen baskets," Mrs. Williamson said, her purse sliding off a shoulder and into the crook of her elbow.

"Seventeen," Elaine piped in, practically inaudibly.

"What?" Mrs. Williamson snapped.

"Seventeen," Elaine whispered, barely louder than she had the first time.

"What do you mean, honey?"

"Jessica's not coming. Her mom's getting a hystericalotomy."

"Oh god. You couldn't have told me sooner?" Mrs. Williamson looked at me apologetically. "And honey, it's hyster*ectomy*."

"Whatever."

"How old is her mom?"

"I don't know: how old moms are," Elaine said, rolling her eyes. Mrs. Williamson shook her head, ridding herself of it all—age, surgery, hormones, everything.

"Okay then. Well, Arlene, I guess that'll be seventeen baskets—minus one uterus." Mrs. Williamson laughed that way that's supposed to be at herself, but is really at me. So much pity for me—no husband, no parties to plan or even go to, a job I have to do, not just want to. No charity work down at the Methodist community center.

"That won't be a problem," I said, laughing along with Mrs. Williamson, at myself. Elaine glared at me, the light from the lamp display reflecting off her braces. Kids never can close their mouths entirely when they've got those things in. Taylor never needed them. "What color ribbon are you thinking? Elaine honey, do you have a favorite color?" I asked.

"Black."

"Elaine!" Mrs. Williamson frowned entirely with her mouth. The rest of her face didn't move. Must've been a byproduct of plastic surgery. I used to want plastic surgery on my nose. It points down.

"We can incorporate black," I said.

"No. We can't," Mrs. Williamson said. "This isn't a funeral. This is a sweet sixteen. We'll have violet and yellow, and whatever else you think goes with it."

"Okay, that'll be nice, a nice mood-setter. Purple and yellow. So the party's when?" I asked. "I think I can have them ready in a couple of—"

"Oh, it's in two days," said Mrs. Williamson. "I was hoping to bring them home today. I have to arrange them with make-up, stuffed animals, and issues of *YM*."

"I guess I could have them for you tomorrow."

"Oh," Mrs. Williamson trailed off. "Not today?"

I didn't really have anything else to do, but I didn't want to give in so easily. "Well, I don't know . . ."

"Please, Arlene. I've always counted on you."

"Agh, okay," I gave in, throwing my hands down in front of me.

"Thank you *so* much," Mrs. Williamson said, disingenuously. The winner of this and all battles in the little, mighty world she inhabited. She seemed proud of herself. I wrote up an invoice.

"Young miss," I said after a moment.

"What?" Mrs. Williamson was confused.

"Young and *modern*," Elaine corrected me. "It stands for *Young and Modern*."

"When my daughter read it, it stood for *Young Miss*," I said.

"Oh," Elaine replied, shooting air through the spaces between her braces, making little squeaky noises.

When I went to count out the seventeen baskets, there were only fifteen. There should've been twenty, according to Taylor's inventory. This was the kind of help she gave me. I tore through the storage room, but I couldn't find any more baskets than that.

Where the heck I was going to find another two baskets, I didn't know. Mrs. Williamson wanted these specific ones. I called the distributor. They could overnight a half-dozen. It would cost me though.

Mrs. Williamson was going to pitch a fit. At least *I* didn't have to worry about where my husband was every night. I knew. I mean, I didn't have to worry *anymore*. I'd seen her husband quite a few times around here with a nurse of his from the hospital. He performed a strange ducking maneuver whenever he kissed her, but people recognized him anyway.

I suppose that to Mrs. Williamson, I reek of misery. I am nothing like Mrs. Williamson. I watch TV. The last time I went out to see a movie was *The World According to Garp*. I don't view shopping as a competitive sport. I've had the same Volvo station wagon for fifteen years. My hands are dry, and cracked around the fingernails. I haven't been out of Providence in two years. My house is still owned by my ex-husband. My brother's a homosexual. My daughter could be one too. I wouldn't know to stuff party-favor gift-baskets for my daughter's party with teen magazines and makeup. I wouldn't think to have party favors in the first place. My daughter gave me a vibrator for my forty-fifth birthday. I never even put the batteries in. It's pink with a pearl-like finish. When I tried to open it, the plastic it came in cut my thumb. That plastic is so hard to pull apart you have to cut it, but then it's razor sharp. I never finished opening the vibrator. It's just sitting underneath my bottles of Tylenol, Nytol, and Ex-Lax in the nightstand next to the bed. Come to think of it, I don't even think the vibrator came with batteries.

I could've given all this up to be Mrs. Williamson instead.

4

CHARLIE

I'M GOING TO DIE. I'm technically already in the process. Maybe three years. Maybe five. Or fifteen.

I have a different TV show I like to watch every night except Saturday. Saturday night TV is for shit. My favorite night is Wednesday, when *Beverly Hills, 90210* comes on. It's a sacred night. The show was supposed to be worse, now that the characters are out of high school and even graduated from college, but I think it's even better. I know the end is near for the kids though. You can tell it's their last season by the skittery looks on the actors' faces.

I also spend a lot of time in therapy. It's kind of all I have. The only place I'm expected each week. In these sessions, I talk about Isak and me and our dog Mary, like most people talk about their wives, kids, and families. The normal stuff a not quite, but soon-to-be forty-year-old guy talks about. Against my better judgment, I sometimes end up talking about the men I've dated since Jack—like Bobby, Dave, Darius, and Sid. Framing my HIV status in the context of my (at one point) voluminous sexual history is a convenient way to talk about the failed relationships I've had with men, without seeming like that's what I really wanted to talk about. It's a game I play. And even though I pretend not to like talking about relationships, it always leads back to the fact that I am somewhat stuck on the demise of myself and Jack. Or on the demise of our relationship, I should probably say.

And I don't really care where I got HIV. It doesn't matter

whether it was Jack for sure. It's not really an activated option in my life. Something akin to when you buy a car from the factory and it doesn't have air conditioning. The skeleton of the equipment is there, if you ever want to hook it up, but you save a ton by not ordering it in the first place. I try to explain the air-conditioning option to my therapist and everyone else who asks—but they don't understand. This culture seems to hinge its very existence on the assertion that we need to want to know where things come from—in essence, how we got here. Just to make "peace within," and to make sure we don't move backwards. But I don't care. And I wouldn't mind going back. I really wouldn't. Anyway, therapists are weird that way. I mean, as a race. Who could sit there listening to that kind of shit day after day anyway? Things are much easier on *Beverly Hills, 90210:* Last week's drug-related shooting becomes next week's promising new dress design. And so on.

I talked to my friend Bryan a few days ago. We used to work together at *Life*—him in edit, me in production. He has brain tumors. Tons of them. Now we are both on disability, but for very different reasons. The tumors are like stars in the x-rays of his brain. They are even named for stars, these tumors, like enemy aircraft in *Star Wars.* Astrocytoma. Red alert! Astrocytoma, starboard right. Secure shield. Fire! Fire!

Bryan took a train to Minnesota for his own personal star wars. He couldn't fly anymore. It took almost the whole year. They planted little seeds of radiation in his brain. Then they waited. But instead of killing the tumors, the seeds started eating the few healthy cells in Bryan's brain. Bryan said he felt special because he was the only person his doctor ever had to remove the radiation seeds from. But this was not good news, special or not.

It took Bryan a considerable amount of time to speak to me. What would otherwise have been a twenty-minute conversation took an hour. He said, "I talk myself into traps, and then it's just best to start over and gather my thoughts." I pictured him with his arms full of firewood, stooping in corners to pick up the brittle chips of words that inevitably keep falling from his arms every time he bends down to pick up another.

"They scooped out the part of my brain that is involved in doing language," he told me. "Well. I should say, they touched on it, rather." Sometimes I waited for ten or fifteen seconds in between his words. On average it was three or five. The most was nineteen. I counted.

It wasn't entirely clear to me how much of him was still there. It had been only six or seven months since we last talked. And now this. The old Bryan was almost too witty and sarcastic to have a regular give-and-take conversation. But now he was almost like a child. Everything a wonder. An exclamation point at the end of every sentence. I thought for sure he was just being a smart-ass, but that was who he was now. If I had to live that optimistically, I think I would just expire.

To the old Bryan I could say: "What the fuck is up? Can you wipe your own ass, or what?" But instead I took a more respectful (and uncharacteristic) tack: "How are you, physically? I mean, can you get around the apartment, get yourself a glass of water, answer the door . . . ?"

"I reached my nadir," he answered. He always used words I had to look up to make sure I knew what they meant. This was why he worked as a copy-editor, while I stuck to production. But I had a feeling–from context clues–I knew what this one meant. He had been, or was still (what do you say in these cases?) a writer. Yeah, yeah, all that. Just starting to get some work published in respectable journals and magazines. At writer's conferences and City College, he was known as a generous teacher with undergrads lining up to fill his workshops. Struck down in his prime, or on the way up. Yeah, yeah, yeah. Who isn't on the way up when the shit hits the fan?

Lucky he hadn't quit his copy-editing job like he'd been planning. He kept sensing success, waiting just around a corner, so like clockwork, every Monday, he threatened to quit when we'd go out for lunch at SoupStravaganza on Seventh Avenue. We went there every Monday because Monday was bisque day. But it's a blessing that he never followed through on any of the threats; he couldn't have afforded to try to keep living without the benefits. Nor, I guess, could I.

Out of nowhere, he said, "Dropping small, colored dowels into a pitcher." I gathered this was his summation of physical therapy. "But you have to be tilting it to get them out. Honestly, I couldn't do it anymore." I assumed he meant it was so fucking inane that he refused to do it anymore. But I think he meant he physically couldn't do it.

"The right side is further and further paralyzed." His sentences kept coming, sometimes related to the ones before, sometimes not. I listened, patient.

At this point in the conversation, I got up to get myself a glass of water, and Isak was in the kitchen gluing little pictures onto paper. I had forgotten she was home. Mary sat next to Isak, his shiny nose touching her knee. I held the cordless phone to my ear with my right shoulder while I pulled the refrigerator door open. Isak didn't look up at me until I spilled a little of the water from the pitcher onto the table, too close to the messy collage she was working on. She intended to be annoyed, but then I saw her face go slack and concerned.

"You okay?" she whispered. "Who is that?" I must've looked dumb to her. It felt like I had an itch deep in my throat, where I couldn't reach with the base of my tongue. I wanted to put my head down on something–the top of the TV, the kitchen counter, the dust-covered coffee table–anything flat and cool. I didn't feel up to the task of holding up my head anymore.

I waved Isak off and went to sit back down on the couch. Sure, everything was great. Bryan proceeded to tell me how he had seizures every four to eight days. That if I wanted, I could come the day after a seizure and we could maybe go to the Met together, take a taxi, stay for an hour, and then go back to his apartment to put him to bed to rest. I wanted to do this more than anything. I would even tolerate the entire Oceanic art floor; I would read each plate's description of every carved bowl, every canoe.

In fact, there was no one I wanted to see more than Bryan.

More, even, than Isak. I found that in the days after we spoke, I was hoping Bryan would have a seizure, like you hope for tiny jockeys to fall off their massive horses. Just to see what would happen. What I would do. How I would take it.

"Well, what's wrong with this month?" Arlene whined over the phone. "New York is so vile in the summer."

"My sophisticated sister," I started. "You've been here what, maybe once in the summer, twice during other seasons? I love that you're the resident New York City expert, Providence division."

"I saw a report on the TV that you can catch TB just from riding the subway in New York," she said. "You laugh, but I know. Providence could extend your life."

"Well then, there it is," I said.

"What? Charlie, what?" She didn't understand. My considering going to Providence had nothing to do with extending my life, more to do with saving it.

"What?" she asked again, but I didn't answer. I'm sure she was twisting her hair up in her fingers, plucking out the occasional strand and tying it into knots with other hairs. She'd been doing it since high school.

She had no idea what to do with me.

"Charlie, honey, I'm sorry," she said. "I just, I think this would be good for you. Don't you?"

"People die. I'm going to die."

"Don't say that."

"Why not?"

"This is different."

"Oh, really. Why?"

She didn't respond.

"Why, Arlene," I repeated, "because *I* did it?"

"No." She was getting worked up. I could tell. She didn't say anything. Nor did I. And then: "Taylor left."

"What? What do you mean? I thought she was going to be there for a while, playing ball." I hadn't connected much with Taylor lately. The last time we spent some time together, she came down to New York for a few days after she'd graduated from college. "Where's she going?"

"L.A."

"L.A.? Why? What's in L.A.?"

"I don't know. She has some agent friend-of-a-friend out there. Said he'd give her a job."

"That's great. You heard from her yet?"

"It's been one day. She's driving. I don't know where she is. Probably in Kalamazoo for all I know."

"There are worse places," I offered.

"Than Kalamazoo or L.A.?"

"Either, I suppose. Both."

She laughed. It had been a long time since I'd heard that laugh. It was a willowy, whispered laugh–as though it were forbidden in the first place. But it was a laugh nonetheless. The sound of it made me recall the smell of the hallway in our folks' old house in Providence: sawdust and warm glue. My father could do just about anything with a nice piece of wood. Arlene was so beautiful then. And like a good little queen, I worshipped my big sister like none other.

"I have to get these picture frames marked," she said, mid-laugh. She wouldn't let herself have too much fun. Or perhaps she could tell I was slipping back into that hallway, that house. How could I, after everything? "The frames are all different sizes and shapes, and I have to go back over the invoices to see what I paid for each."

"It's eleven o'clock."

"Yeah, but it's alumni weekend at Brown," she said, and then paused. "It's going to be a busy few days."

Isak's cheek was already rising with a maroon bruise. She looked smaller than I usually thought of her, sitting there in the ninth precinct's grimy holding cell. She sat on a metal bench with her legs spread wide, firmly planted, elbows resting on her knees. She clasped her hands together in front. It smelled like piss.

This wasn't the first time I'd bailed Isak out of jail. There was the civil disobedience arrest in D.C., another in New York, and then the third Act Up protest in Maine, where I'd actually been arrested too. A lawyer I was sleeping with at the time came up and got us out.

Isak stood when she saw me. She was smiling with her head cocked to the side. I'm sure that's why they brought her in on something that otherwise might've just entailed a summons. She thought it was all so funny, and that pissed people off, especially people in positions of authority.

"What are you going to do when I'm not around to bail you out?" I asked as the cell door slammed open.

"Oh, you'll always be around to bail me out," she said, her jacket stained across the front with spray paint. The officer called Isak over.

Pushed across the desk: her backpack, minus the spray paint bottles and stencil, her wallet, belt, and keys. All emptied noisily from a bag. Like in the hospital when they hang your possessions from the gurney in a swinging plastic bag with blue daisies on it.

The officer behind the counter appeared bored. One of his eyelids sagged more than the other. The left one. It was wrinkled despite the fact that it covered more pupil than the right. It looked like it had been stretched out from his face at some point, never getting the chance to retract fully. He didn't talk to Isak, just pointed to where she should sign her name.

"Honey, I told you I wasn't going to marry you if you kept getting in trouble like this," I said.

Isak looked at me.

"I mean, what kind of a mother goes and gets herself arrested?" I went on. "What will the children think? And lest I remind you . . . You're *breastfeeding.*"

"I'm sorry, cupcake," Isak said, falling in step. "It'll never happen again, sweet cheeks." She kissed me right in front of the officer, who by then couldn't resist looking up. Even his sagging left eye opened some. How could it not, I mean the image of Isak—more of a boy than me—breastfeeding a child?

Tongue and everything, we smacked and sucked, making

55

loud, wet squeaks that echoed against the shiny floors and white, white walls.

"Okay, enough. That's enough, you two," the officer said. "You're free to go." And then his eyelid went back to normal, drooping toward the paperwork on the desk in front of him.

"Vandalism?" I asked, as soon as we exited the precinct.

"It was stupid, I picked the stupidest spot," Isak said, shaking her head. "Second and sixth. Basically around the corner from the nick."

"Oh, we're British now?"

"That's where I was, right there," she said, ignoring my jab. She pointed to the sidewalk in front of an overloaded Dumpster with moldy pink fiberglass insulation spilling out of it.

"Bollocks," I said in a thick British accent.

Isak looked at me oddly and continued, "I got about twelve more done before they nabbed me." She was still buzzed on adrenaline.

"Looks like you took a bit of a beating."

"Nah, not as bad as it could've been. Of course they thought I was a guy at first, slapped me around a little, smashed me into the paint before it dried. My coat's fucked." She looked down at her chest, then surveyed her paint-stained palms as though seeing them for the first time, seeing what hands can do.

We walked down Tenth Street. A skinny brown dog with ribs like a ladder skittered in front of us with a wet brown paper bag in his mouth. It looked like he was clenching a squirrel's hide in his muzzle. One that had been run over a few times in the street. We walked in silence until Isak ran ahead and stopped in the middle of the sidewalk. When I caught up with her I realized she was standing over one of the stencils.

"I did this before the one I got caught doing." It said: *New York = Police State.* Understated.

The stencil looked rushed, smeared on the bottom right. Her activism at one point was inspiring to me, but suddenly the sight of it made me very tired.

"Wow," I said, trying to sound interested.

56

Isak looked proud. She was all beat up, her shirt ripped and jacket smeared with the same color paint as was on the ground beneath her.

"How many did you say you got done?" I asked, unenthusiastically.

"I already told you. Like a dozen," she said, slightly annoyed with me, as though I just wasn't getting it. Which I wasn't, anymore.

The skinny dog was chewing on the paper bag behind us. It looked like the remains of a burrito were squeezing out. He glanced around anxiously as though an enemy were stalking him and his feast.

I could, for once, see why some people move to the suburbs.

"Do you think—"

"What?" Isak interrupted me.

"No, I guess I was just wondering if maybe you were getting a little sick of all this . . ."

"This?"

"Yeah, like nothing ever changing, graffiti—"

"It's political art." 57

"Fine. Political art, getting arrested, being a freak in the freak show, eating Kraft macaroni and cheese in alphabet shapes at the age of thirty. This sort of a thing."

Isak didn't speak to me until we got to our apartment and she came out of the shower. She couldn't find something she was looking for.

"Any more mail than this?" she asked, throwing the pile onto the kitchen table.

"Nope, that's it."

"Fuck. I knew they were fucking me over with that check."

"What check?"

"Nothing. Fucking temp agency."

She sat on the couch next to me. I bounced up slightly when her weight settled into the cushions. "What's on tonight?" she asked. A peace offering perhaps. But something had just switched over—from how it used to be, to how it would be.

"*90210*," I said. "But it's a repeat, of course."

"I'll watch with you," she said. But I knew she'd rather watch something educational on cable. She was like that sometimes, and it only served to underscore the inanity of my television viewing preferences. I mean, if you're going to have your brain numbed to the point where every ounce of creativity has been sucked out of you so that you will choose not to join the revolution, instead remaining seated on your couch, eating processed foods, you might as well go all the way. At least to my thinking.

Isak leaned forward and sat like she had in the jail cell earlier. She just sat, breathing, while the muscles in her cheek twitched slightly. Mary came over and threaded his thick head in between her knees and elbows. She massaged him behind the ears–the softest place anywhere. He was a good-looking dog, silver-colored, but more precious than that even, like platinum. She was good-looking, too, the epitome of handsome. Strong, smart. Aggravating as hell. She smelled clean from the shower.

"I didn't mean anything by that out there," I offered.

"It's okay. You were being honest."

"Actually, no. It was just a pathetic way to bring up my sister," I said, heading into the kitchen as I spoke. "She wants me–us–to come up to Providence."

"For a vacation?"

"No."

"The holidays?"

"No."

"What?"

"For good, actually."

Isak followed me into the kitchen, where I stared into the florescent-filled vacuum that was the refrigerator. And then she said, "So, you want all of your girls to sit around up there and watch you die?"

I slammed the refrigerator door shut, empty-handed. "There's still no milk," I said.

"What?"

"I said, there's no fucking milk. How many fucking Post-It

notes with smiley faces do I have to leave on the front door before you'll remember to do one fucking thing around here once in a while?"

"Fuck you, Charlie. I work."

"Oh yeah, hard day's work, getting hauled into the local precinct."

"And what is it that *you* do again? You're not even sick."

"You have no idea," I said.

"Oh yeah? Tom is sicker than you, and he works thirty-hour weeks."

"*You're* the one to lecture me. When's the last time you brought an actual food product into this house?" I screamed. "Not toilet paper!" I knew I had her there.

"You know what?" Isak asked, and then she stopped.

I don't think either of us knew the answer to that question. Isak turned to go, and I watched the leaves shivering on the branches outside the kitchen window. Bugs had chewed holes through most of them, and I could see right through.

For a moment, I hated her like no other. But then I lost her, right then as she hitched Mary up to his leash and dragged him out of the apartment behind her. He always got so upset anytime people yelled at each other, even strangers. I could hear Isak's keys jingling on the other side of the door, and then the audible certainty of the deadbolt; she had locked me in.

Then I envied her. She would eventually stop suffering so much and grow more comfortable in the world, and I would become less and less effective. It was all very simple.

5

ISAK

I GIVE GOOD HEAD, for a girl. Women can't really give head the way men can. I've been told I give some of the best head, but I didn't start until I was an adult–recently, really. Never did in high school. No cramped neck and bruised knees from sucking off some football player behind the bleachers at the homecoming dance, or in the back of his brother's rusty truck.

I don't do it much, but when you look like me–like a young hustler, it's kind of hard not to. I would be a fool not to. They think they're getting one hundred percent adolescent boy head. So I can even mess up every once in a while, drop it midstroke, shy from the semen–the nuances of being new at something. Over the years, I've watched so much gay porn with Charlie, I can hold my own. I've always been able to pick things up pretty quickly–I'm gifted that way.

I give head like the European boys in the videos–not the Americans. The Americans take as much as they can, and then they take some more. But not the Eastern European boys. They suck on the tips only, letting their smooth, androgynous bodies do the rest. Fingers pulling back foreskin, then back up over the head. This is much more appealing to my thinking. The thought of gagging on some guy's dick that's poking my trachea makes me, well, gag.

"I knew you'd start soon enough," Charlie said, after I came home from the first time I sucked a guy's dick for money in the park. "You are the best looking thing downtown, after all."

It seemed like the next logical step after parading my

freakish self in front of the masses for shitty pay at Coney Island. Plus, there just wasn't much need for handsome escorts for rich women, or even lesbians. Go figure.

"It took four minutes," I told Charlie after that first one. "Forty dollars for four minutes." The bills had been damp and sweaty in my back pocket.

"Keep it up and you can start paying some rent," Charlie said.

I looked at Charlie then, and he looked as though he was reminiscing about a war or something—a particularly gruesome battle. Though I know it had nothing to do with me or even our conversation. He looked at once younger than his thirty-nine years—boyish almost—but then also pained and weathered in this nostalgic way.

"Maybe I will," I said, sitting on the couch and opening a crusty Chinese food container. Dry rice sprinkled the table like the church steps after a wedding.

I clicked on the TV, switching channels rapidly. This was Charlie's most hated quality in a roommate, but I know that from me, he was willing to put up with it. He put up with my bits of paper scraps and glue smudges on the furniture, spray paint stains, the chips of dry packed dirt that dislodged from my thick-soled boots. Then there was the little problem with rent—which his disability covered with change, thanks to rent control—but Charlie let me slide on this sometimes, too. Maybe I should've been giving him jurisdiction over the remote control more often.

On TV: Pandas behind bars in China, chewing fingers of bamboo: *click.* A stunning Cubic Zirconium ring, set off by two real sapphires on either side, fourteen-carat setting, $149.95, only twenty-three, no twenty-two left! *click.* Cops, live from the streets of Los Angeles, pulling a rolled-up dead body out of a car trunk like a late Christmas present.

There was no way I could do it anymore with Charlie. Not like this. It was either that, or watch myself curl up and die right alongside him. His sister could watch us both go.

"There's another new drug, but I don't know if I'll qualify,"

Charlie said then, sitting down next to me. I put the remote control in his lap, the TV radiating blue from the Weather Channel. He scooted toward me, close, with our knees touching–his knobby, bare ones tapping my wider, concealed ones. It seemed to make a hollow sound between us. "I don't know if I can afford it either."

I had nothing to say. I felt nothing. Everything was different since he brought up Providence. I put the food back on the coffee table, balancing the chopsticks on top of the container. But they soon fell to the floor, and Mary came over to lick them. The suction created between his tongue and lips made a truly disgusting sound. My stomach twitched at the thought of eating any more. Mary wiggled up for me to scratch his butt, and when neither Charlie nor I so much as made eye contact with him, he settled back down and licked his penis for a good couple of minutes. "He's just trying to make you jealous," I said.

"No, I can do that too," Charlie said. "I just don't feel like it."

This girl Stacey came over because I promised her she could see some photos of me, and then we would go out. It was what amounted to a date. I was hoping Charlie wouldn't be home, but he was, languishing on the couch.

"Come in, come in, Miss Thing," he said when he answered the door. I could see over Charlie's shoulder that she looked like a quivering chick under a heat bulb.

"Hi. You must be Charlie. I'm Stacey, here for Isak?" She didn't step over the threshold until I came from behind Charlie to save her.

"Charlie, this is Stacey. Stacey, I guess you've met my roommate Charlie."

"Roommates," Charlie said, in his queeny high voice. He sat down on the couch.

I was willing to leave then, and even reached for my keys and jacket, but I could tell Stacey thought it would be polite to sit with Charlie for a spell. Charlie had a way of making you feel as though it would be fortuitous to get on his good side. So we sat down on the couch. Mary was writhing in circles in front of Stacey, banging out a beat on the coffee table with his tail. Stacey tried to pet his head, but kept missing because he was moving so much.

"This is Mary," I said. "Do you like dogs?"

"No, I *love* dogs," she insisted, but this was not convincing, since she still hadn't managed to land a hand on Mary's head.

"So, Stacey," Charlie started, "are you interested in the Fox network's television programming?"

Stacey looked at me, completely perplexed. There was no helping her with this question.

"No? *Beverly Hills, 90210, Ally McBeal?* Nothing?" Charlie crossed his legs and slapped both hands down on his knees. "You're probably more of a *Friends*-NBC kind of person."

Stacey laughed nervously.

"Don't be fooled: Charlie really spends most of his time grappling with Nietzsche and Schopenhauer," I said, confounding Stacey further. "Well, this has been nice, what do you say we go to dinner?" I stood up.

"No, stay a while. Didn't you show Stacey your prints?"

"Oh yeah, I really want to see those, Isak."

"Can I get you a cup of tea, love?" Charlie asked. He was a green sea anemone, coming to life only when something fresh was within reach of his feelers.

Stacey looked at me as I was shuffling through a pile of papers on the table, searching for the photographs. I shook my head, and she said, "No, thank you very much though."

"These are beautiful, really beautiful," Stacey cooed while flipping through the photos. They were mostly of me, taken by my photographer friend Skye. They had been part of a show in Los Angeles that ran for a few months, and now a gallery in New York was going to show them. "Which ones will they be using?"

"I don't really know."

"Where were they in L.A.?"

"Just this place downtown," I said.

"Just a place downtown?" Charlie prodded. He had been watching Stacey fondling the photos the entire time. "Only the Museum of Contemporary fucking Art."

"I don't think it's called that," I countered. They were acting as though I'd taken the photographs myself.

"Isak, you didn't tell me that," Stacey said, slapping my shoulder playfully. "You are such a jerk."

"Yeah, I'm a jerk. Let's go." I took the photos and dropped them onto the coffee table. "You'll walk Mary?" I asked Charlie, and put my arm around Stacey to guide her toward the door.

"Yes, he'll be fine. You kids have a good time. Bring us a doggy bag."

"You are so beautiful, or handsome, or whatever." Stacey looked directly at me across the table as she spoke. It made me slightly anxious. We were having after-dinner Turkish coffees. "I can't believe I'm saying this. Not like you don't already know it."

I couldn't believe she was saying it either. I think it was clear we were going to have sex by that point.

"You are too kind," I said, as a reflex.

"Are you blushing?" she asked, looking up.

65

I wasn't. But I smiled as if to say, *"Yep, you got me; I'm blushing."* I was tired of the same old shit. Different mouths, lips, inflections, but basically the same conversations.

She paid the bill, and I held the door open for her as she walked out onto Avenue A. Stacey poked her hand through the hole between my arm and ribs as we walked. She grasped my elbow lightly, and I left my hands in my pockets. We walked in silence past two new restaurants bathed in oppressive fluorescent light. Ted the Vet was hocking piss-stained paperbacks on the corner of Sixth and A. "Oh, hot date, oh," he said as we passed. I nodded my head at him. Stacey perked up as though Ted's attention wasn't just a random utterance that happened to coincide loosely with reality.

"Want to come upstairs?" We were kissing in the foyer of her apartment building when the elevator came. Stacey pushed me into it (moderately sexy), and then the doors squeaked shut and we went up.

In bed, she tried to take off my tank top, but I wouldn't let her. I didn't want to take my clothes off. She had taken most of her clothes off, and I began pulling the underwear over her knees.

"Those photos—you have such a beautiful body. I wanted to see it." This was not what I wanted to hear. She pushed her crotch up onto my thigh and squeezed with both legs. My jeans were bunched up, and my heavy belt buckle was cutting into my stomach. I wanted to get out.

Stacey relaxed onto her back and spread her legs. I buckled down and did her with my hand, waited for her to come, and then I lay there in her big bedroom with my eyes wide open while she slept across my chest.

She was attractive. Everything was attractive. There were attractive pillows all over the bed, on the floor, attractive curtains over the window, partially covering an attractive view of the attractive park.

After an hour or so, I extracted myself from Stacey's embrace and sat on the edge of the bed, quietly pulling on and lacing up my dirty boots. They seemed out of place even on the wooden floor of her apartment. She stretched her arms up toward the ceiling and looked at me.

"You have to go?"

"Yeah. I have to walk the dog."

"You know you can trust a guy with a dog," she said. "He'll always come home."

"Yeah, guess so."

"Call me sometime."

"I will," I said. And I leaned over to kiss her on the temple. She smelled a little more like me than she had before.

Sometimes when I look at a woman's crotch, I get sick to my stomach. Sometimes the wiry, thick mess is so out of control I don't want to touch it. It's not the smell, no, not the usual stuff about fish. It's the texture, the excess.

This is, admittedly, a little insane. I think it's because women's crotches always remind me of the Holocaust. How's this? How nuts is this? The psychologists loved it. Because I remember clearer than anything else from my childhood, the first thing that came into my consciousness and stayed: the scratched photographs and films of the women in concentration camps. They stand there naked, shivering, in all of their excess. So much black pubic hair, creeping all the way down to their knees, practically up to their breasts. They run in circles, form lines, try to conceal what is virtually impossible to deny.

It was the only way I could hate the images and myself at the same time. I didn't know how to hate them. I didn't know what made me hate them so much.

My born-again Jew friend said I was self-hating when I tried to explain this. It's internalized anti-Semitism, she said. Probably. There's probably a little of that in there. Probably internalized misogyny too, and gynephobia, homophobia, heterophobia, transphobia, balletophobia. I'm sure I have them all.

I do abhor my breasts, don't even really love them on other women either. Mine aren't big. They're actually rather negligible, but I despise them nonetheless. Most people cannot even see them by the time they're hidden by a couple layers of clothing and an already tight jog-bra.

When I came home from Stacey's and took off my tank top and bra, I stood in front of the bathroom mirror and looked at the red lines that had been cut into my body by the jog-bra's elastic. I had bought it a size too small so it would be tighter. I lifted my arms, craned my head over each shoulder, following the whiter strip of skin leading to the base of my neck. I do this sometimes–look at my breasts–but only when the bathroom door is locked.

They itch. They itch so much I cannot scratch them enough. I tried to put lotion on them, but I spent fifteen minutes in bed itching them before I could fall asleep. I know there is something growing in my breasts. I feel for it all the time. More than I ever wanted to touch them. The more I have to touch them, the more I am reminded of them.

67

I cannot find anything though. No tiny pebbles, no attached bundles or clusters. It's just a matter of time. I know they are infused with something toxic–absorbed, I'm sure, by simply wading through this city on a daily basis. New York toxic tits. Everybody has them.

I would not be like one of those women who begs her surgeon to do everything he can to save as much of her breasts as possible. If there was a questionable lump now, and it could be paid for, I would take them both off. I would. As a precaution.

But I would want to keep my nipples. I would want the scars to go underneath, two T-shaped scars where the insides had been cut out. It would be messy. I would go to the gym even more and make new breasts, only these would be sheer muscle tissue and fiber. I wouldn't have to fold my arms over my chest when I wore a tank top in the summer. I could start a round of testosterone to give the new chest a boost. I could probably make even more money in my illustrious career giving head.

I could also stop worrying so much about myself and be happy with what I have. Each year I seem to care less and less.

In the morning, Charlie was reading the *New York Times*. "You got in late," he said.

"It was about one, I think."

"No, it was later."

"Well, whatever."

"Did you have sex with her?"

"I don't like her very much," I said, joining him at the kitchen table.

"She was drooling over you more than Mary." Charlie poured me a cup of coffee. The way I always like it–one sugar and half soy milk. He set it on the table in front of me. Then for a few seconds there was just the light color of the coffee, and the spoon sliding around the edge of the old, chipped porcelain mug we stole from the Ukrainian restaurant on the corner. And it was a sunny morning, the kitchen unusually bright. All these things.

"So that's the last we'll be seeing of the lovely Stacey?" Charlie asked, as he sat down next to me at the table. I shuffled through sections of the paper.

"Charlie," I said, no longer stirring my coffee even though it was still swirling around my spoon in the mug. "Char, you know I'm not going to Providence with you, right?"

"I know."

"No, Charlie, I'm serious. I can't do this anymore."

"Oh, Isak, don't worry about it. We just had a little fight," he said quickly. "We'll talk about it later. But what about this girl, this Stacey girl?"

If he was giving it to me, I would take the out.

"I don't know about the Stacey girl," I said after a long pause, during which something had been decided about the future of Charlie's and my relationship. "She's awful rich. I guess she's into slumming it with me."

"She's kind of cute, no?" Charlie offered a spoon to Mary for a lick or two. His lapping was loud, and Charlie was acting strangely. Normally we talked, but neither of us wanted to this time; there was so much happening so fast, with no time to slow down and take a look at anything.

"Too bad you didn't have sex with the girl at least," Charlie added.

"Oh no, I had sex with her."

Charlie started chuckling, though hesitantly. He laughed harder, making the crooked kitchen table rock and shake. Some of my coffee spilled onto the sports section of the paper, which neither of us ever read. Despite everything, it was astonishingly and pleasantly quiet in that kitchen. And warm.

Later that night I went to the park, warming my hands with a cup of hot chocolate. The trees hissed in the breeze. This skinny old guy in tight jeans came up and nodded at me, cupped one of his hands around my cheek like I was a hot coffee mug. It was the kind of touch that makes you feel like nothing bad can ever happen, even though you know it will.

He held up a twenty and a ten in front of me and then tucked the bills into my back pocket. I put my hot chocolate down on the ground beside us, knelt to unbuckle his belt. His dick, though hard, bent downward like a boomerang. Even when it was completely free, it still bent down.

The old guy in my mouth pushed on the back of my head with his palm, which I normally don't like. But he wasn't pushing too hard, so I let him. He grunted twice, which I assumed meant he was about to come. I took his dick out of my mouth, and he finished himself off while I tried to knead his thigh exuberantly with my hands. In all of his excitement, the guy kicked over my hot chocolate. It soaked my knees.

"You're so good," he grunted again.

On the way home I said this to myself over and over, putting the emphasis on a different word each time: "*You're* so good. You're *so* good. You're so *good.*"

70   My family was falling apart and there was nothing I could do about it. Charlie would die. The first little scare with his lungs foreshadowed that. I always stared at the two of them, Mary and Charlie, wondering who would go first. Mary's already showing signs of arthritis. And many dogs actually die from cancer or something else before old age anyway.

The last time my other family saw me was when I was hung up in a museum in Los Angeles. The photos Stacey wanted to see so badly went up at the contemporary art warehouse in Little Tokyo. My mother always kept a membership and made sure to see new exhibits, even the little ones. "Bending Gender," it was called. To make things palatable to supporters like my mother, you have to name things to death like that– "gender bending" is an asinine term, like we're evoking the luxury that was David Bowie and Mick Jagger. Five of Skye's photos made the show. It was good for her. I guess L.A. was supposed to be a tough market.

There were two photographs of me in the show. One from

the back, just me dressed in tuxedo pants and a fedora, but no shirt. Very '80s. You cannot tell what I am. The next photo was the same, but from the front. And although I am trying to cover them with crossed arms, just enough of my chest is visible through the cracks to show that they are in fact breasts, and not just pectorals.

When my mother called me, she said, "I know this is impossible, but I just got back from MOCA, and—"

"It's me," I interrupted. She passed the phone to my brother, who was apparently at the house doing laundry and eating.

"Nice tits," he said, laughing. I heard my mother struggling to get the phone back.

"You know, we have friends who support MOCA too. It's not just us."

"You can barely tell it's me."

"Oh yeah? Well, I knew."

"You're my mother."

"Allegedly."

"Where's Dad?" I asked.

"He's right here. He doesn't have anything to say right now. You know how he needs to think about things."

Yeah, I knew. But how could he say anything after a warm-up like that?

We haven't talked much since then. They check in once every few weeks or so. It's been three, maybe four years since I've seen them in person—not just me hanging on a wall. I think they still tell their friends and family that I work at the same job I had years ago, in publishing. At least I've moved up in the world. Being a whore is much better than being a freak. And more lucrative too.

"Look: a chick with a dick," a guy on the street said to his buddy.

I turned around, offering the guy at least enough pause to reconsider his original assessment. I got these comments all the time. But there was something different about this one, in that he had a memory.

"Oh, I wasn't talking about you," he offered, as I stared him down.

"I do got a dick, as a matter of fact," I said, stopping in the middle of the sidewalk. It was cold out and I was cranky, otherwise I might've ignored the comment, like I do most others. I added, "A big one."

It was my voice.

"Oh, so you're one of those special people who's both, huh? I saw that on *Ricki Lake*," he said to his buddy. "Come over here and show me that little dick of yours, sport."

I despised being called "sport." An old uncle used to call me "sport." I fucking hated it. Actually, he wasn't really an uncle. More like a neighbor. But I was supposed to call him "Uncle." Once when I went over to his house when his wife was out, he threw me up against the pantry and forced his hand down the back of my pants. His dog barked as though his wife was coming home, or somebody else was coming. Then he stopped. And I went home.

I had decided to go see Stacey again, even though she was so annoying. I was frustrated, wanted to get off, and yet seeing her, I knew, would only frustrate me more. So I called her anyway.

I left the heckling guy outside Stacey's building. The doorman called up while I waited in the shiny lobby. I tried to keep an eye on the guy and his buddy. The two of them skulked back and forth, smiling at me the whole time.

"Isak," Stacey said as she opened the heavy door to her apartment, "you look different. Good, but different."

"Why?" I asked, sinking deeper into annoyance.

"I don't know, did you lose weight or something? Get a new haircut?"

"Nope, it's probably nothing." I wanted to cut through the shit and get into bed.

"Sit down and have some wine with me?" She started flirting. "I just opened a nice bottle of white."

"No thanks," I said. "I'll have some water though."

"Anything you want," she said, and disappeared into the kitchen.

72

I looked around her apartment. There was art everywhere. Even more annoying. Why was I there, again? Right: sex. But it looked as though I was going to have to work a little harder for it this time. Or at least put up with a lot of crap in order to get it. She came back with ice water and a glass of wine.

"Where've you been? I've been trying to call you for a few weeks. Charlie just says you're out," Stacey said. "You weren't avoiding me, were you?"

"No, I've just been really busy. There's a lot going on these days."

"Everything's okay, I hope?"

"Yeah. Fine."

Stacey giggled. "I don't even know where you work. What you do with your time."

"I'm a hustler."

She laughed. "You're so funny. And good-looking. Don't forget good-looking. No, seriously, what do you do?"

"I'm a hustler," I said again. Stacey put her wine glass down on the table in front of us. I took a sip of water and asked, "Do you have a problem with that?"

"No, no, I don't," she began. "It's just—are you serious? I mean, I thought you were temping or something. I mean, I knew about the freak show, I mean, I think that's just *great.*"

"Well, I started fairly recently," I said. Then there was the screeching of brakes, a crash, and then a scream from outside. After that, it was very silent, both in the apartment and on the street downstairs.

"That sounded bad," Stacey said.

I got up to look out the window, but I couldn't see anything on the street.

"Well, I guess I'm glad you told me," she said after a few seconds. I had forgotten what we were talking about. "So, do you do it with men or women or both, or what?"

"Fags, mostly. Or straight guys who want to get it on with a guy."

"Do they know, I mean—"

"What?" I wanted to hear her say it.

"Do they know you're, you know, not a guy?"

73

"Who says I'm not? Or enough of a guy for what they want?"

Stacey was getting threatened. So, finally, she said, "Well, I guess I wish you would've told me sooner."

"Why? You don't have anything to worry about. They don't come in me."

I could tell this didn't make her feel any better. Downtown trash chic went only skin-deep, it was clear. She scrambled for something else to say. She was judging me, but she also knew I knew that she was passing judgment. So she tried to say something to save herself.

"God, it's dangerous, you know?" This was not what she really meant though. "I mean, if I got to a place where I cared a lot for you, I don't know. I'd really worry."

Sirens echoed all up and down the block. It was loud because the windows of Stacey's apartment were cracked open. I could see the red and white lights flashing off the windows across the street from Stacey's building.

"You know, this is probably not gonna work," I said, putting my glass of water on the table and standing up to leave.

74   "Wait, Isak, no. I just, it was just a little surprising, is all," she started. "Please don't leave."

"No, I'm going to go. This wasn't really anything in the first place," I said. I could see how much it hurt her, the way she squeezed her knuckles together. But because I could make it look like she was turning me away, I felt like I could be a little harsh.

"Isak, wait," she said, but I already had my hand on the doorknob.

Downstairs, I turned toward the red and white lights circling the block. The flashing lit up the second-story windows, spilled into the black, naked trees. On Avenue A, I noticed a nice coat crumpled in the middle of the street. It was dark fur, warm looking, maybe worth some money. Then I looked under the coat where all the attention on the street was focused (dead woman, snapped neck), and the coat didn't look very comfortable anymore.

I glanced up toward Stacey's apartment building, as though I might want to go back for some reason, but I didn't. And when I looked down at the fur coat again, it had been covered by a yellow plastic tarp. Black blood spotted the yellow like paint splashes from a messy paint-job. A leather dog leash connected to a frayed, studded collar snaked out from under the tarp.

Then I thought of Mary. He would've probably been sitting in bed watching TV with Charlie right then. Mary loved watching TV. Or at least it seemed like he did. It was over with me and Charlie and Mary, I knew, but I could at least go back and lie around with them for the rest of the night. This one night. So I turned toward home and started walking.

There, on top of a parked blue Celica, what had presumably been on the other end of the dead woman's leash lay bent around the driver's side mirror. It looked like some sort of a small spaniel. Its neck was also snapped. Its entire body was snapped. The car with the dead spaniel was several feet from the woman in the fur coat, under the yellow plastic tarp.

I thought of this old cartoon by Chas Addams: I saw it in a collection of *The New Yorker* cartoons that my father gave me for my thirteenth birthday. Chas Addams was the sick one and, of course, my favorite. I remember flipping through the book and looking at only his cartoons in the collection.

I never forgot the one with an archaeologist in a car: He had a dinosaur skeleton tied to the fender like hunters tie deer they've shot to their cars. I don't think I ever truly got why it was funny. But I never forgot it. The dead spaniel reminded me of the skeleton tied to the fender of the archaeologist's car.

When I started walking again up Avenue A, the guy with the buddy and the "chick with a dick" comment presented himself again. He was wasted, and it was a potential situation. A situation with the potential to turn into a bigger situation. These occurred all the time, but I didn't need to act as cocky as I did this time.

I hadn't stood a chance with two guys going at me. They came from behind.

75

My crotch heated up when they pinned me to the side of Chinese Restaurant No. 5. Nobody on the street looked our way, although I thought I'd grunted pretty loudly as the first blow to my gut separated what I assumed was my liver from my spleen.

I couldn't move because they held both my arms. The more I struggled the more the fire crept from my crotch into my throat. But I couldn't speak. Before dropping me to the curb, one of the guys held my hands behind me while the other pulled down my pants. I didn't even fight it. They just wanted to see for themselves.

The one who held me started laughing, and then the "chick with a dick" one stomped on my head with what felt like a thick-soled boot. I remember hearing the grit of the street grind into my scalp. They fished my wallet out of my pants pocket.

It seemed like a few hours. It seemed like a day.

My head is bashed-in, I remember thinking, and soon after, the red and white lights returned, swirling and flashing. Only this time I was pretty sure all the lights were for me. *At least I'm in better shape than the woman with the fur coat*, I remember thinking. And Mary was safe at home watching TV, instead of wrapped around a Celica's rearview mirror.

My head is really bashed-in, I thought again, or maybe I said it.

I knew I shouldn't have been thinking about it–it wasn't the most appropriate time or place–but my attention was drawn between my legs, where my crotch started aching. Amidst all this, I wanted to get off. On the sidewalk where my blood was mixing with the grit on the street, all I wanted to do was ease the pressure down there. I had gone out that night wanting to get some at Stacey's, and now I wanted nothing more than to finish the deed. I may even have tried to stick a hand down my pants as the ambulance doors slammed shut.

"Do you want me to call your parents or something?" Charlie asked.

"You're an angel," I said.

"You're mumbling."

"You look like an angel," I repeated. My throat was dry. "The light behind you makes it look like you have a halo."

Charlie arrived at St. Vincent's shortly after I was told they wanted to keep me overnight for observation. It was a pretty bad concussion. I was lucky it wasn't worse.

"Do you?" he asked.

"Do I what?"

"Want me to call your parents."

"No. *No.*"

"You're lucky it wasn't worse," he said.

"Oh really? I don't really need to hear it right now."

"Fine." Charlie looked unhappy. "Want some water?"

"No." It felt like every word was lost just seconds after I said it. My head was pounding, like my brain was trying to squeeze out of my eyes and ears.

"It looks like you're an angel," I said.

"I know. You already said that."

"No, I didn't."

"Because of the light above me, I have a halo, right?" Charlie said, now more patiently.

"Oh. I guess I did."

I continued fixating on the ceiling tiles, convinced they were filled with asbestos. I didn't notice Charlie had slipped out of the room until he came back in with a nurse.

"She keeps saying the same things over and over," he told her.

"That's quite normal," she said, flipping through the chart hanging at the foot of my bed. "She just needs to rest, and we'll keep checking on her every hour or so. She'll be set to go in the morning."

"Thank you." Charlie sat back down in the chair next to my bed. He looked over at the other two patients in the room. The nurse pulled the curtain around one of them.

"Well," Charlie whispered, "quite normal."

I wanted him to leave. Every breath hurt, both in and out. I think they said I had two broken ribs. Or three.

"I told Stacey," Charlie said after a moment.

77

"What? Why?" I asked, scooting myself up in the bed. "Why would you go and do that?"

"She called right after the hospital did, and I was worried, so I told her."

"You didn't tell her where I was, did you?"

"I think I did."

"Jesus fucking Christ," I said, slamming my head back into the stiff pillows. "Ow!"

"I'm sorry. She sounded worried about you before I even told her what happened. She said you were supposed to be with her tonight."

It felt like my eyes were uncontrollably rolling up into my head. All I could see were the haloes of light and the asbestos-filled ceiling tiles. I knew that Stacey was going to walk in at any moment.

Maybe taking the focus off me would work, I thought. So I decided to torture Charlie a little with what we were both obviously, though silently, being tortured with this whole time in the hospital.

"It's hard being here, right?" I asked. Charlie knew exactly what I was talking about, although he didn't look up at me or even acknowledge my words. Between the two of us, we'd watched maybe a dozen people die in St. Vincent's. My mini-tragedy and hospitalization was sort of a mocking imitation of the others. Do you call the parents or not? Who comes in to watch? Which lovers are you glad to see, which do you hope never to see you like this, even after it's all over?

Only the main difference, of course, was that I would be walking out of there the next day, and the others didn't.

"I'm sorry," I said. But it was too late. I had managed to make myself feel better, for the second time that evening, at the expense of someone else. I hadn't said anything that wasn't already out there, but still. "You don't have to stay. I'll be fine. I'll just see you at home tomorrow."

"Isak, I'm not going to let you lie here alone," he said. "It's drab."

I started getting drowsy and dizzy. So I closed my eyes. On

the red-white screen of my eyelids I saw my mother and father, dressed in leisure suits and staring down at me like everybody had been since I was picked up off the street. I heard them talking about me, and then when I opened my eyes, Stacey and Charlie were looking at me in the same way, referring to me in the third person.

Now Stacey looked like an angel too, both of them with their haloes. And they went on, having the kind of conversation that two people who have nothing in common (not even me) tend to have. When I closed my eyes again, my mother and father had the light haloes, like little Jewish angels, and they were speaking slowly about being worried, throwing some clothes on, and how difficult it is to get taxis in the East Village at this time of night.

I lay there, thankful that I wasn't needed for conversation. When I opened my eyes again, my parents were gone, and I barely recognized Stacey, who was now at my level and stroking my hand on the side with the IV.

"Isak, I'm so sorry this happened," she said. "If we didn't have words like that you would've been safe with me." It occurred to me that that was the funniest thing someone could say. And Stacey just said it. I looked for Charlie, who had his back turned to us.

Stacey stood and whispered something to Charlie, and in a moment of weakness, while everyone else's backs were turned, I felt what had to be the proverbial stab of loneliness in my chest. I'm sure it was only the broken ribs, but I know I felt something sharp, stinging, and, frankly, surprising. Maybe I missed my mother and father, even my brother. But I knew better. What I was missing wasn't really them at all, but rather something else that I was far too exhausted to figure out. But where else, then?

Stacey leaned back down toward me. "Isak, I'm so sorry this happened. I'm going home, but I'll be back tomorrow, okay?"

"You look like an angel," I said. But she wasn't the only one. There was a chorus of hospital angels everywhere. Every light—white, red, green, even the reflection off the metal bed and instruments—all of them twinkled with little haloes.

"She's been saying that all night," Charlie said. "It's supposed to be normal."

"The problem with normal is that it's very difficult to pin down in the first place," Stacey mused, very nervously. She slung her purse over her shoulder. "Thanks for letting me know, Charlie."

Stacey left, and the room was deliciously silent for a few moments. I went elsewhere.

"You don't even believe in angels," Charlie said quietly, mostly to himself. "I'll see you tomorrow." He put on his heavy coat and kissed me on the forehead. Even that hurt. Just a kiss from Charlie.

Los Angeles is the city of angels, I recalled. It's the cultural Mecca of the West. Perhaps, I thought, I would find whatever it was I was missing there.

6

TAYLOR

TAYLOR WALKED ALONG OCEAN AVENUE toward The Bluffs Restaurant and Bar. She thought about how skinny the palm trees looked. And slightly bent. Skinny, and bent toward the west.

It was sunny and seventy. It was always sunny and seventy in L.A. It was also so bright she should've been wearing sunglasses. Taylor thought this as she squinted at the star-specked Pacific and sensed the grumbling of a headache. She rarely got headaches. But she had lost her sunglasses somewhere in the car and didn't understand how they could've been lost. They had to be somewhere, between the seats or under them or something. It always happened like that. You dropped something in the car, then it fell out somewhere when you were getting out of the car, fishing around for quarters for the meter, or you were late and it was raining, and you didn't notice when whatever it was (you forget now) fell out in the first place.

Taylor crossed the street when she saw the restaurant. She wanted to pause and center herself, but right after she stepped onto the curb, a man on Rollerblades smacked into her, full speed. He blindsided her as she was looking up at the restaurant's sign. He grabbed her shoulders and then spun a clumsy circle around her before finally losing his balance and falling onto the concrete with a dull thud.

"Fuck, lady, could you watch out?"

"Oh my god, I'm so sorry, I was just–oh god, are you okay?"

She reached her big hand out in front of the man and nodded at him to take hold of it. He looked at her hand and then up her bare arm until his eyes stopped at her face. His mood changed at once, Taylor could see.

"No, no, no. It was all *my* fault," he said, slowly standing up and wiping the gravel from his tight Spandex shorts. "I should've been paying better attention to where I was going."

"You're cut," Taylor said, pointing down. There was dirt and sand ground into a small oval of crimson and tangled hair on his knee.

"Naw, it's just a little road rash, that's all. I'm fine," he said, finally looking down at his cut.

"God, I'm sorry, I was just heading over there to The Bluffs, and I, I don't know, I just spaced out. Can I get you some water or something?"

"No, but maybe I could buy you a drink," he suggested. Taylor shook her head *no,* but still smiled back. She thought he was kind of cute. "Okay, then another time?"

She laughed. "I have an interview. I'm actually late, I really gotta get going." Taylor started walking away. "You sure you're okay, though?"

"Yeah, I'm sure," he said, then started slowly skating behind Taylor. "You sure I can't talk you into coffee, dinner, a walk on the pier, bowling? No? You don't like bowling? You married? What, do I have some physical deformity I'm not aware of?"

Taylor kept walking and laughing. She went into The Bluffs, already warmed up for her next performance.

The restaurant was chic. Or that's what Taylor would call it. The walls were covered with stainless steel. The floor concrete, painted gray, but deliberately paint-splattered, like a pseudo-studio. Everything echoed. This is the kind of restaurant her mother would hate, Taylor thought. She'd say something ridiculous like, "I can't even hear myself think," over and over, nervously, and then expect Taylor to agree with her. "Can you hear yourself think in here, Taylor? *I* sure can't."

There were attractive young servers, bartenders, and busboys zig-zagging everywhere, prepping for lunch. They all wore crisp, blue button-down chambray shirts with colorful ties, khakis, and black boots or tennis shoes. Two women servers sat at the bar eating salads before their shift started.

"Do you ever go out to *eat* at restaurants at least?" the manager Bill asked Taylor, half joking. She had opened the interview with, "I have no experience."

"I manage to get out of the house once in a while," Taylor responded. Mocking self-deprecation.

"Okay, perfect. So you've watched waiters in action," he said. "You know basically what it is they do . . ."

The two women at the bar got up to clear their plates. Both gave Taylor the once-over as they passed by the booth. Taylor looked back at Bill, a balding-too-soon-for-his-age blond. He was good-looking though. Those girls were good-looking too. Everybody was good-looking there.

"Seriously, you ever work in the service industry at all?" he asked.

"My mom has a shop, and I worked there some. You know, doing inventory, stocking merchandise, helping customers– that kind of thing."

"What type of store?"

"Antiques and things. Baskets, furniture, folk art, jewelry. Frames, a lot of frames."

"Sounds nice. Where is it?" he asked.

"Oh, I also worked at a bed and breakfast for a couple of summers, and in the cafeteria back in college. I did dishes."

"Somehow I can't picture that. So where was your mom's store?"

"Rhode Island. But yeah, no, I did work in the cafeteria for a few semesters, so that would count as food service."

"You don't talk about home?"

Taylor was caught off guard. "No, it's just, well, that was there, and now I'm here, so, do I have the job?"

Bill looked surprised. And incredulous. A lot of people looked at Taylor that way.

"Well, seeing as you have, well, *no* experience in restaurants,"

83

he started, "I can start you off as hostess, then we'll see what we see. It's ten bucks an hour, plus you get tipped out by the servers, and then of course there're tips from customers."

"When do I start?"

"How about day after tomorrow? Night shift?"

"Great. What do I wear?"

"Oh yeah. We usually like the folks up front to get a little more dressed up than the servers you see running around. That okay? Like black. Something black, and tight. Tight's good."

Taylor put on a look of surprise. *Yes, I'm a country bumpkin fresh off the bus from the Midwest. A tight, black dress? My, but why would you want me to wear that?*

Taylor was getting better at juggling the monumental wishes and concerns of the over-important customers at The Bluffs restaurant. These ranged from needing to re-charge cell phones, to begging to be seated in a certain section because so-and-so was sitting there, and he had forgotten to consider someone for a job he needed to be reminded of, etcetera.

It was her third Friday night, and the bar was packed with people with reservations waiting for their tables. Forget coming in there if you didn't have a reservation. Taylor was wearing the same black dress she had worn to Kurt's wedding back in May. It seemed like a decade since that life.

Bill came up behind Taylor while she was updating table status at the hostess station. He put his lips close to her ear, and some of Taylor's hair fell onto his nose. She tucked it back safely behind her ear.

"You know who that is?" he whispered. The phone rang again, green lights flashing.

"Who?" Taylor inquired, glancing up at the mob of customers.

"Shh. By the door, tan jacket and tie."

"Should I?" Taylor asked, picking up the phone. "The Bluffs, can I help you? I'm sorry, could you please hold? What?" she asked Bill, slightly annoyed because he wasn't letting her do her job.

"Let's just say, you seat him as soon as possible. Table eight."
Bill counted out four menus, put on a plastic smile, and led
another party to their table.

Taylor finished the phone call and waded through some
customers on her way to this Mr. Big Stuff. He was just shy of
fifty, Taylor thought, stately (whatever that meant), and handsome in that older-guy way. Interesting. He looked like the
kind of guy who wasn't having sex on a regular basis, despite
the fact that he probably could've been. Taylor saw him reach
into his pocket and pull out a bill when he noticed Taylor was
approaching.

"Hi. There's five of us," he said, reaching his hand toward
hers.

Taylor ignored the offering and shook her head. "That's
okay. We'll have your table ready in a few minutes. Do you
mind if I ask you what your last name is, or what the reservation's under?"

He looked somewhat confused. "Are you new? That was a
tip."

"I know," Taylor said, staring at him. They both just stood
there looking at each other. Taylor separated out each of the
sounds that were swirling in the air between herself and this
new person standing in front of her: echoing dishes, dropped
knives, inane conversation, and scooting chairs. When overwhelmed she did that—meditated on all of the tiny the parts
that made up the whole of whatever environment she was in.

"Sykes," he said.

"What?" Taylor asked, tuning back in.

"You asked for my name. Robert Sykes," he whispered.

"Right. It's nice to meet you." With nothing else to do, Taylor
reached out her hand to shake Sykes's. "I'm Taylor."

He obliged, and they held hands that way for a few seconds,
in a slow, steady shake—kind of side to side rather than up and
down. Then there was another silence, with the two just
staring at each other and holding hands like they were trying to recognize each other through a mutual friend or lost
relative.

"Yo, Miss? I got a date I'm trying to impress here. Can you help me out with a table?" someone asked Taylor, with a heavy thud of a man's hand on her bare shoulder. She turned around to see it was the Rollerblading guy. Sykes looked at him.

"Hi. Oh, hey," Taylor said, although clearly distracted.

"Not such a good time, huh?" he asked, looking over her shoulder at the bar.

"There are better times," Taylor said, looking back at Sykes and smiling.

"Looks like you got the job. Okay if I come back some time?"

"No, yeah. I mean, sure. Earlier the better." Taylor was attempting the often-called-upon, medium-difficulty, subtle blow-off.

Rollerblading guy left with what must be his signature smile–produced for composite photographers, prospective agents, and at auditions for TV commercials hawking everything from mmm-good spaghetti sauce to guaranteed-to-work-overnight laxatives. It seemed like everyone was an actor around there. Or at least acted like one. Taylor turned back toward the door to speak to Sykes again. But he had disappeared. Maybe into the bar? She knew not to let him go; she could smell power like that, and she couldn't just let it go. So Taylor pushed through a few more parties who were vying for her attention to look for him. Sykes was last in the conga-train that was his dinner party, snaking its way through the bar and toward the dining room. Sykes broke from the other four when he saw Taylor. Bill held five big menus above his head and led the others off. It was so loud in there.

"So. Hi *again*," he said to Taylor, who was slightly out of breath. She didn't know why she was out of breath. It was a considerably short distance from the front door to the bar.

"Hi."

"When did you say you started at The Bluffs?" he asked. This Sykes guy seemed nervous. Taylor loved when people were nervous. It was like oxygen.

"I didn't say."

He smiled. "But you are new, because *I* haven't seen you."

"Well, if *you* haven't seen me–" Taylor flirted.

"Do you know who you're dealing with, Missy?" Sykes joked, poking her gently on the shoulder.

"No. You in the movies or something?" Taylor asked, channeling the country bumpkin. They both laughed for a while, then wound down into another bout of silence.

"What *do* you do?" Taylor asked finally. She didn't know exactly what he did, but she knew she should–that he wanted her to. She wanted him to think she didn't know or care what he did. Which is also the reason she asked Sykes for his name in the first place, despite Bill's warning.

"I'm a producer," he said softly. And it made Taylor appreciate him. The way he said it, so only she would hear. And like he was maybe a little proud. *Why shouldn't he be,* Taylor thought.

"That's great," Taylor said, deliberately tucking some hair behind her ear and looking into Sykes's eyes, right into them, without wavering. She could do this, as hard as it was. She pretended she was looking through a person, past them, like she could see right into their eye sockets and out the back of their skulls. Bill walked by and tapped Taylor on the shoulder as he passed.

"I should probably–" she started.

"You need to get back to work," Sykes cut her off.

"Great, yeah," she said. "Work, work, work."

For the rest of the evening, or until Sykes left with his party, Taylor went about her work as usual. But she was constantly aware of table eight. Like she was orbiting around it, sometimes closer, sometimes further, constantly going over that oval, around and around, like a fine-point pen drawing the same line over itself.

They locked eyes a few times. Sykes watched as another customer pressed a twenty-dollar bill into Taylor's big hand. And she took it while staring at Sykes over the back of the booth. She had never done it before, but Taylor slid her fingers

87

under her dress and tucked the bill into her bra. Sykes saw
that too.

Taylor and Sykes sat by the massive swimming pool behind
his home. It was well after midnight. His house was excessively equipped: tennis court, swimming pool, Jacuzzi, and
pool house. And that was just in the back. He poured Taylor
another glass of white wine.

An eerie bluish-green hum cut through the spaces between
things. The stuccoed wall of the enormous house, the white
statue of an angel pouring water from a shell into the pool, the
empty pool house that was the size of a regular house anywhere else but in Bel-Air. The waves of color and light
reflected everywhere–on the grass, the concrete, on Taylor
and Sykes's faces. There were few stars. Or if there were more,
they were sick of being on display.

"It's getting late. I gotta get home," Taylor said, sipping her
wine. When she put the glass down on the concrete it sounded
as though it would break. Like it got to the place right before
glass breaks, but then stopped.

"What's the rush? You don't work until, what, four tomorrow?" Sykes asked.

"No, I'm just totally blitzed. I might need a ride home."

"I'll have the driver take you," Sykes said. "You can come get
your car in the morning."

Taylor didn't say anything. She kicked her leg in the water,
submerging half of her calf. Then she finished off what was in
her wine glass.

"Or, why don't you just stay over?" Sykes suggested. She
had sort of wanted him to. "You can stay in a whole fucking
separate *wing* for all I care." He motioned up toward his
house.

They sat in the green glow for a few more minutes. Sykes
surveyed his property as though it was the first time seeing it
from this angle. Taylor splashed the water some more with
her legs, making oblong specks of water on the cement.

"You're into guys, right?" he asked suddenly.

"Robert—"

"What? I'm just wondering. Last week you said something about an ex-girlfriend, but when I came to pick you up tonight I heard you were going out with some actor guy you met on the street. That guy who came into the restaurant the first night we met."

"I went out on a couple of dates with him," Taylor said, "like it's any of your business."

Sykes didn't say anything.

"Who told you, anyway?" she asked.

"Sworn to secrecy."

"Tell me."

"Nope. Let's just say you have a lot of fans at that restaurant."

"What's that supposed to mean?" Taylor asked, but then she laughed it off, as though she didn't care about the answer. She dipped her hand into the pool and flicked some water on Sykes's face.

And then: "So, did you sleep with him?" Sykes was jealous. It first annoyed and then charged Taylor. She got that little rush in her chest, her heart surging for a second. It was familiar, jealousy as a form of caring—or control? So many cared for Taylor that way, starting with her mom, and most recently, Jules. It felt like something she might eschew, but then also a lot like the way things were supposed to be.

"Yeah, I slept with him. So?" Taylor looked at Sykes and tucked the hair behind her ear again, lingering with her middle finger over the cartilage. She could tell he liked that. He liked every move she made, and watching Sykes watch her, Taylor became exquisitely aware of her every move. "He's not the brightest guy this side of the Mississippi."

Sykes coughed out a laugh, a seemingly condescending one.

"What? When I was driving through St. Louis on the way out here," Taylor started, pursuing a drunken tangent, "I stopped at this diner where this waitress with a blond pageboy wig, she kept an extra pen between her breasts, but anyway, she was telling me about how she was sleeping with the stupid line cook back there flipping burgers—"

89

"That's an old line," Sykes blurted, probably seeking to cut Taylor's story short.

"What? I know. I just never said it before, and I thought it was really funny because, well, there we were on the Mississippi. So, like, which side was she talking about?"

"Mmm," Sykes pouted.

"So, can I trust you?" Taylor asked out of nowhere. She liked that she could ask for and then pretty much get anything she wanted from Sykes. This guy who made a multi-million-dollar movie every year or so.

"You can. I mean, I want you to."

"I know, but this sex stuff," Taylor said.

"Well, what is it that you want?" he asked. "That guy? A girl, what?"

Taylor pulled her legs out of the water. The sudden sound of splashing startled her, and out of habit she felt she should be more quiet.

"I'm just trying to figure you out," Sykes continued. "I mean, are you attracted to me in *that* way, or what are you attracted to, in general?"

"I just like people. I get drawn to people. Like you, I like you, but do I have to fuck you to prove it?" Taylor made a funny face—mostly to herself, like maybe the answer was yes. (It always had been.) "I don't have any self-imposed or artificial limits and boundaries in my life."

Sykes lifted his wine glass weakly. "Well, here's to no self-imposed, artificial limits and borders—"

"Boundaries," Taylor said, toweling off her calves.

"Boundaries."

"Hey, aren't *you* supposed to be the big old queen, anyway?" Taylor asked. "I mean, isn't that the word around town?"

"What, because I'm not married? Please. That's a good one," Sykes said, obviously rattled. "Just because work's always been primary for me? Who told you that?"

"Like you've never had any of those boys suck you off before. Give me a break. I may be new in town, but I didn't just fall off the fucking tomato cart."

"That's not how it goes."

"What?" Taylor threw her towel onto the chaise lounge but completely missed. She thought it might have been the lines of green light from the pool making her feel thick and dizzy, but standing up, Taylor realized she was just plain drunk. "So how the fuck *does* it go?"

"I don't know, but that's definitely not it, Miss This-Side-of-the-Mississippi." Sykes corrected Taylor the way Jules had. She didn't know whether it had always been others or herself who was constantly aware of her age.

"You're changing the subject," she said.

"What subject?"

"You having young hopefuls suck your dick to get in your movies."

"Feeling a little raunchy tonight, are we?" Sykes replied, putting his arm around Taylor. She tensed up at first. Her shoulders filled with what was like the precursor to rage. But the next thing Taylor knew, she felt Sykes's hands on her arms and they were warm and upright, and so Taylor just steered herself between them like two goalposts.

Taylor plopped down onto Sykes's bed, flapping her limbs and making a down snowman out of his fluffed-up comforter. She sighed into the pillow and smelled the wine on her breath like she'd just swallowed a tank of gasoline. Expensive gasoline. Robert sat down next to her. Taylor rolled over and looked at him. She had been spending so much time with him in the past month, but this was the first time in Robert's bedroom.

There was some famous art on the wall above his head, and in her own head, Taylor heard herself asking Sykes who it was by. So when there was no answer, Taylor was a little surprised.

"I don't even have to say it, do I?" Taylor asked, as soon as she forgot about the art.

"Of course not."

"Good. But I'm drunk. How's that for mixed messages?"

"Want me to sleep in the other room?"

"No, I want you here."

Taylor pulled the covers over her so that half the bed was bare. There were no covers left for Sykes, but he put his head next to Taylor's on a pillow and folded his arms across his chest, like a mummy preparing to go down in history. Taylor smiled and closed her eyes, inching closer and closer to him. She could feel Sykes watching her as she fell asleep. She believed he would watch her like that all night, and she liked the thought of it.

"Taylor?" Sykes whispered after a few minutes.

She didn't move.

"Taylor?" Louder.

"Mmm?" Taylor opened her eyes.

"Nothing." Sykes was looking blankly at another piece of art across from his bed. Taylor followed his gaze and saw that it, too, was humming with waves of green light coming off the pool outside. The whole room was. "Well, I, I just wanted to tell you something."

Taylor sat up, reached for the glass of water sitting next to the bed. She couldn't locate it, so Sykes handed it to her. Taylor dribbled some water on the comforter. She exhaled loudly, her eyes tightly squinting.

"What?" she asked drowsily.

"There's just, well, let's just say that a lot of things are hitting me differently these days. I know you're thinking it's my dick talking. I mean, what else does it look like here? But I can tell the way–"

"Robert–"

"You make me happy," he said. "No, listen. You do. Just being with you, looking at things. *Seeing* them."

Taylor slid down, straightening her knees under the covers.

"That was the first time I've been out at the pool. I paid two million dollars for this place, and that was the first time I used the pool."

"Yeah," Taylor managed.

"I know this is the last thing you want to hear now," Sykes went on. "But, I swear you are like some perfect creature coming in here–"

"It'll be different in the morning," Taylor said.

"No, I knew it the minute I saw you at The Bluffs. You felt it too, I know you did."

"I did."

"You could have anything."

Taylor threw her arm over Sykes's chest and it landed with a hollow thud. She knew Sykes would not sleep much that night. But she would.

In the morning Taylor crept out of bed, and her pupils ached when light hit them. Her head was still foggy inside; she imagined her hair was a fully-involved rat's nest. She pulled on her sandals and stood in front of a mirror that faced the bed. Over her shoulder she could see Sykes asleep with his right arm wrapped around his head. This mess was the million-dollar Hollywood mogul, she thought, and laughed.

Taylor looked at herself and confirmed that her head was, in fact, a rat's nest. She messed with her hair, running the tips of her thick fingers (which felt even thicker this morning) through it. She licked her fingers and tucked the hair behind both ears, smiled at herself, and then checked to make sure Sykes was still asleep.

She tip-toed out of the bedroom and passed through Sykes's den. It was filled with posters of his movies. There were so many of them. Taylor ran her finger along the first, an older film she'd remembered seeing posters for as a kid. She thought maybe her mother had seen it. Taylor put a finger over the name "Robert Sykes," rubbing it as she paused in front of the poster.

Taylor heard the rustle of sheets coming from Sykes's bedroom and hurried out, trying to keep quiet.

"'But I love you, Eric. I don't care if you impregnated somebody else while you thought you were impotent. I want to have your baby now. Slean clate,'" Taylor said. Then she corrected herself: "'Clean slate.' I'm sorry."

The casting assistant cleared his throat and crossed his legs.

"No, that's fine. Go on." He flipped through the pages on his clipboard.

"'I'm so sorry, Heather,'" the other reader said. He had beautiful blue eyes, and Taylor thought maybe she recognized him from a Diet Coke commercial. "'If Heath hadn't tampered with my potency results, I never would've left. I just wanted you to have everything you wanted–the house over the ocean, a beautiful child of our own–everything. But I thought I couldn't give it to you. I love you.'"

Taylor hugged the actor on cue. He smelled of chemicals, like he'd just dyed his hair for the audition. Chemicals concealed with a lemony smell. The one time Taylor dyed her hair, she had welts on her scalp that stung every time she showered for a month. She couldn't imagine having to do it every week for work.

"'Eric, I will never leave you again. I want to quit advertising and be a full-time mom,'" Taylor said. She sounded as though she were reading in middle English or something. Like every word had some form of punctuation after it. She continued, "'There is nothing wrong with that, is there? I always looked down upon my employees who took maternity leave, but no more. It is the mommy track for me from now on. Oh, I love you, Eric.'"

"Okay, okay. Why don't we stop right there," the casting guy said, standing up and stepping in between Taylor and the other actor. "Thanks a lot. So, yeah. I guess I'll be getting back to you both within the week?"

"I'm sorry, I just got a little tongue-twisted there for a minute with the 'clean slate,'" Taylor apologized again. "Slean clate, clean slate, ha, well." She couldn't remember, but she thought she had stayed pretty close to the script otherwise. The other actor picked up his bottled water and left the room, swigging from it as though he'd just run a marathon.

"No, not at all–a common mistake. That was great," the casting guy said, patting Taylor on the shoulder. "So you worked with Mr. Sykes before on a film? He said this was your first foray into TV."

"Yeah, no. Actually, I've never been in anything."

"Oh, well, I see," he said, looking back down at his clipboard. Taylor thought then: *This is a frustrated man.* There was a vein poking out of his neck that looked like a trail of purple sweat from his jawline to his collarbone. "Well, you're a, a real natural."

Taylor said, "Thanks," and left the room. *Maybe,* she thought, *Robert was right about this acting thing.*

Taylor decided to take Santa Monica Boulevard to the 405 to the 10 to get home. She hated the hassle of merging, but once she got into the center lanes of traffic, she didn't mind L.A.'s freeways. It was yet another beautiful day.

There were tons of billboards on Santa Monica. Calvin Klein underwear models with bigger penises than Taylor thought she'd ever seen. Or maybe they weren't so big, but it was just because they were larger than life, up there on the billboards. Then there was an ad for the new show premiering on Fox. Aaron Spelling's new brainchild. *Maybe that's what I just auditioned for,* Taylor thought.

"That's just how things work here," Taylor said all of a sudden. "You know someone who knows someone . . ." Then she realized she was talking to herself and slammed the dashboard to make the radio come on. She wouldn't have gotten in the door if it weren't for Robert. It was just a little push.

There was a billboard for the American Lung Association. The number of smoking deaths so far this year: *324,568.* Taylor thought about someone dying that second, as it changed to *324,569.* Someone in a paper-thin hospital gown with tubes and wires going in and coming out everywhere: dead and beeping.

Then she thought about the possibility of being on TV–how her mother would be forced to watch, and how her uncle might be watching already. When she was in college, Charlie would call her and they'd discuss the latest on *Beverly Hills, 90210* and *Melrose Place.* Sometimes soccer practice would go late and Taylor missed a show. She'd spend half an hour on the phone listening to Charlie's analysis of the drama. He liked most when anything gay would come up. And if it didn't, he'd make his own innuendoes and predictions–how all the boys just wanted to have butt-sex with each other instead of with the skinny, whiny girls.

Taylor pulled onto the on-ramp to the 405 freeway and craned her neck to see behind her. The cars came so fast. She swerved halfway onto the shoulder twice before someone let her into the next lane over. She banged the radio again, which had faded out while Taylor was occupied with changing lanes.

As she merged toward the 10 freeway west, Taylor saw her face, big, like that guy's dick in the Calvin Klein ad. Not exactly like his dick, but the size of it. She could see herself the way she saw herself in the mirror. She could alter parts of her to attain different effects: her smile crooked, her lips redder after she bit them for a while, her hair tangling with her eyebrows, fighting to free itself from behind her ears.

All that mattered was that they thought she was attractive. She didn't want to assume it. She liked being told. Robert told her all the time. She knew her edges were rough and Taylor wanted to be smoother, at least from far away, like on a billboard. She wanted that casting guy to be distracted from his work long enough to wonder what it would be like to wrap his hands around Taylor's waist and listen to her breathing change while he kissed her.

He was probably gay. And scared. Scared that Robert sent her to him in the first place, scared that he'd piss someone off for doing or not doing something right. What would he do with her, Taylor wondered. She knew he'd give her a part. He had to.

Taylor pulled out of the fast lane because a monstrous, green Range Rover was flashing its lights behind her, tailgating. She said aloud, "Slean clate," and thought: *I suck. I really do suck.*

ISAK

"NOW I'VE GOT TWO KIDS with thick, beautiful hair," my mother started, "and neither of them will let it grow."

My father hugged me awkwardly and picked up my bag, then hurled it in the way back of his truck, over the last seat.

"You can't open this back window," he said. "Just so you know, if you drive this car while you're in town. Don't try to open the back window or we'll never get it closed again."

"What happened to it?" I asked, climbing into the front seat, because my mother had already hopped into the back. I was wiped out from the plane ride. And if I suspected upon taking off at Newark that it was a complete and utter mistake to come to Los Angeles, the suspicion was now confirmed upon seeing the blank looks on my parents' faces.

"Oh, I don't know, you know these things always go out on the older cars," my father said. He lurched forward into the Absolutely-No-Stopping inner lane of airport traffic. He slammed on the brakes and then accelerated again, pinching the truck into traffic like a cab driver. I hated nothing more than the way my father drove: with both fucking feet, one on the brake and one on the accelerator. He slammed on the brakes and my chest wrapped around the seatbelt.

"Dad!" I yelled. "Can you give us a break?"

"What? This bastard won't let me in," he said, simultaneously accelerating and slamming on the brakes yet again.

"With both feet?"

"I have more control," he insisted. The guy in the car behind us was laying on his horn.

"They teach you to use *one* foot in driving school. Your right foot for both brake and accelerator," I said. It was the same argument we'd had for years.

"I don't care what they teach. That's for when all cars had clutches anyway." I shook my head and leaned up against the window.

"Your hair's so *short*," my mother said, reaching from behind me and scraping her fingers up above my ear. "Are you getting it *buzzed* these days, or what?"

"It's just like normal," I said, because there was nothing else to say.

"No. This is the shortest it's ever been. I swear, it's just like your brother's," she continued, rubbing the back of my head because I was tilting it down, letting her. "If we were going to have a short hair contest, I don't know who would win, you or Dan. And would you win if it was shorter or longer?"

"You say that every time you see me."

"I've never said anything about a short hair contest before," she insisted.

"Not exactly."

"Oh my god, what's this?" my mother shouted, retracting her hand from my skull. "Thea? What happened?"

"Oh, I just fell off my bike a couple of weeks ago," I lied. "It's nothing really."

"I didn't know you had a bike," she said.

"Well, I do."

"Honey, why didn't you tell us? Oh my god, it looks like you had a lot of stitches."

"Twenty-two."

"What?" my mother said. *"What?"*

"It took twenty-two stitches."

"Oh."

My father kept taking his eyes off the traffic to look at my head. He didn't say anything though. He swerved repeatedly.

"Honey, do you see this?" my mother asked him.

"I'm trying," he said, managing to avoid a pissed-off passer cutting in front of us.

"Well, jeez, Thea," my mother started, sitting back in her seat, "you'd think you'd tell your family something like this."

"Mom, it was nothing. Really," I tried reassuring her. "Really." She didn't seem assuaged. "And you guys, I know it's hard, but if you could remember to call me Isak. It's my name."

"It's just so new," my mother said.

"It's been ten years."

"Well, it's new for us," she countered. "Thea was such a pretty name. What am I saying? It still is. It still is a pretty name."

I wondered whether this was the curse of the geek that I'd inherited–chronically hoping things will have changed when they haven't. And never will. But no, it had to be worse. Perhaps L.A. was in fact a twisted version of purgatory.

We turned onto Sepulveda, then left onto Lincoln. We continued alongside the north runway as a jet's shadow dwarfed us and landed ahead. I pictured it skidding, spinning, and then crashing into the ocean at the end of the runway. But it was a fine landing. I'm sure the passengers were starting to unfasten their seatbelts as the plane made a final turn toward the terminal–way before the captain turned off the "Fasten Seatbelts" sign. I cleared my throat loudly. Otherwise we were silent.

There were new condominiums all along Lincoln, with big red and white banners: "Now Leasing, Condos for Sale, Pool, Jacuzzi, Two-Space Parking." All this new since I last visited L.A. Now with the new freeway, I supposed these stuccoed monoliths scarred with arched balconies and palm fronds climbing out of them were a good commuting distance from all the other freeways.

"Do you still celebrate Hanukkah, honey?" my mother asked, as though the previous conversation hadn't just happened.

"What do you mean?"

"I mean what I said: Do you and that man you live with celebrate Hanukkah?"

"Charlie? Ma, his name's Charlie, not *that man*." I tried to hold back. "I've lived with him for five years."

My father cleared his throat. I kept quiet, looking out the window at the new pink developments. Some had chintzy Christmas decorations wrapped around the redwood latticework on their balconies.

"Well then, does he celebrate Hanukkah?" my mother pressed.

"He's not Jewish, and he's an atheist. So no, we don't really celebrate anything," I said, hoping to put a cap on the conversation.

"Well, you'll stay through Hanukkah, right? *You're* not an atheist."

"Yeah, I think I will." I decided not to say, *"Actually, I don't really buy into the whole god thing."* Maybe it would be a conversation better suited to the telephone. Or never.

At their house, there were eight small gifts for me on a table in the living room, and eight for my brother. Like we were seven and twelve years old, not thirty and thirty-five. Like there weren't years of hard work at growing apart in the spaces between all that time.

My parents' home sported new off-white, wool rugs–not the most practical addition. But I suppose with the dogs dead, kids grown, and no grandchildren, it was a safe bet. There was also a lot of new southwestern-type art. Lots of horses.

I went upstairs to put my bag down and go to the bathroom. I entered the room I grew up in. At one point, well after I moved out of the house, the room was still plastered with '70s sports posters and movie stars. Charlie Brown and Snoopy sheets, threadbare, still stretched across the lumpy mattress. But this was no longer the case, as of the remodel a few years before. Now there was a lasso on the wall, a southwestern-patterned bedspread with buffalo on it, and matching pillows with leather fringe dangling off them. Outdated magazines fanned across the desk, and a two-cup coffee maker with sugar packets, spoons, and mugs sat on the dresser. The mugs were from Texas, with a cowboy and cowgirl on each. They both read, "Get along, little doggies" inside the lassoes.

"Thea–Oh! *Isak,* look: This is so great. You can have your coffee up here in the mornings. You still like coffee, right?" My mother had followed me upstairs. She opened the desk drawer to reveal shiny blue packets of Maxwell House coffee. "Doesn't it look great in here? We just had some friends in from Canada all last week. It's like a little hotel."

"Yeah, it is like a hotel," I said, still taking in the room. "You excuse me?"

"Sure." She was hurt.

"All right if I use the phone?"

"Of course. But honey–"

"Yeah?"

"This isn't really a hotel. This is your *home.*" She looked at me as though trying to convince herself of the very same thing.

I picked up the phone and listened to the dial tone. It sounded the way dial tones sound in different countries. I didn't know who I was going to call, so I put the headset back into its cradle.

I could check on Mary.

I picked up the phone again, dialed my home number. Charlie answered on the last ring before the answering machine usually picks up. "Hello?"

"Hey, Char. It's me." I sounded dead to myself in the receiver. "I'm here."

"Oh. So–"

"How's Mary?"

"He's fine."

"What are you doing? How are you?" I asked.

"Fine. We're both fine." He seemed miserable. "We're watching *90210.*"

"What's happening?"

"I don't know. It's a repeat again."

I could hear the TV in the background. There was no denying what I was doing to him anymore, on either of our parts.

"Hey, Char, listen. I–" But then the connection was broken by erratic beeping, and I realized my father had picked up the phone downstairs and started making a call without bothering to listen for a dial tone. He always did that.

"Hey, Pops!" I yelled downstairs, but he kept punching in the numbers. "Fuck," I muttered, half in and half out of the receiver.

"Oh, sorry," my father finally said, obliviously, over the phone to me and Charlie. I could hear him start to say something to my mother as he hung up noisily.

"See what I have to put up with?" I said.

"What? You're at home. What did you expect?"

I looked around the room and pulled a finger across the tabletop. There was a thin dusting of what salty air leaves behind. "So, you want to play Age and Occupation?" I asked.

No answer from Charlie, so I continued: "When I got off the plane, I was probably thirty-five and a tour guide on those red double-decker buses that take off from Times Square. And now I'd say I'm about seventy-five and still hustling, but with dentures."

"Huh," Charlie managed. He didn't seem too interested in the little game we always played.

"What about you?" I asked. "Age and occupation?"

"Isak, not now."

"Oh, okay," I said. Then the realization that I'd possibly just made a huge mistake reared up, but as though he could see it too, Charlie graciously changed the subject.

"Will you call my niece while you're out there?" he asked in that way that really means: *"You've let me down in every other way, but do you think you could stop being a self-centered bastard long enough to manage doing this one tiny thing for me?"*

"Okay. Yeah," I said, but all I wanted to do was go back five years and lie down next to him and Mary and have Charlie explain the asinine television show to me: When Donna almost lost her virginity to David on a trip to New Orleans; how Dylan had to travel to Mexico to retrieve his family for-

102

tune; squeaky-clean Brandon's illicit affair with a college pro-
fessor; the lesbian who fell in love with Kelly after the two
almost perished in a house fire together, and so on.

We used to laugh for hours at that show. Charlie could recite
lines before the characters did, and I pretended to hate it, but
that was part of the fun. It was one of the best things to sit
together like that. Especially after Charlie's diagnosis, when
he didn't leave the house for months. I kept being overwhelmed with longing for a time when things were better–
with my folks, with Charlie, everything. But I couldn't
remember a time when I didn't wish things were different
than they were.

"Want her number?" Charlie asked, breaking a silence and
interrupting my thwarted nostalgia.

"Whose?"

"Taylor, my niece? Remember?"

"Oh yeah. Give it to me," I said, trying to sound interested.
This girl was about the last person I wanted to see or spend
time with. I remembered meeting her when she came into
town to stay with us for a weekend. She was wild without
actually seeming so. She ended up with about five or six
phone numbers from men and women alike over those two
days, and without even trying to get them. When we all went
to lunch one day, you could see it, people literally throwing
themselves in her path. She only toyed with people though,
never following through. The waiter comped half of our check
just because she struck up a conversation with him about the
merits of Diet Coke versus Pepsi. I don't know how, but that
conversation was infused with sex.

"I think she lives not too far from your parents. They're in
Santa Monica, right?" Charlie asked, and then gave me the
number. It seemed as though he was particularly invested in
my seeing Taylor. "Maybe you can meet for a cup of coffee or
something."

"Yeah. Maybe. We'll see what her schedule's like," I said,
wondering why he was so insistent. I knew it wasn't a set-up
of any kind, since Charlie had threatened me with my life if I

laid a finger on Taylor. (Not that I ever would.) Maybe it was a big-brother type of dynamic he was arranging–for when he was gone.

"Isak, don't blow it off, okay?" Charlie said. "Mary's fine. Don't worry. I'll take him to the dog run in the morning."

"Thanks, Charlie," I said, honestly. "Are you okay?"

"Yep, we're fine," he replied. And I knew he wasn't, because he used the collective *we*. "We're gonna watch the show and get some sleep."

"Okay, well."

"Bye. Thanks for finding the time to call." A zinger. He hung up.

So I hung the phone up as well. The house was oddly silent. I looked over at the bed and wanted to get into it. It was early for New York time to sleep, but really early for L.A. time. My somewhat healed cracked ribs–hell, my whole chest–throbbed dully.

Just as I was pulling the bed's comforter down, exposing the crisp, clean sheets underneath, my mother called up: "Honey, want to come down and visit?"

I went to the door to call back to her, but she had already come upstairs to see me. It sort of surprised me that she had come so close.

"I think I'm going to take a quick nap, if you don't mind," I said.

She put her hand on my forehead, and then on the back of my neck. "Are you okay? You feel hot."

"I'm okay. I'm just really tired."

"Maybe you're jetlagged," she said, sliding her hand off the back of my neck and onto my shoulder. She patted it awkwardly. "Okay, go get some rest, and then your brother's going to try to stop by later for dinner."

When I got into bed, the sheets were cool and damp. I didn't feel comfortable enough to take all of my clothes off, although I wanted to. I left on a tank top and jeans, in case someone came in to wake me up later.

I couldn't sleep even though exhaustion tugged at my eye-

104

lids. My breathing was shallow, and no matter how deeply I inhaled, it never seemed enough to fill my lungs. I turned on the TV and noticed that my parents had deluxe cable with all of the channels listed on a sticker on the back of the remote control, just like a hotel. I flipped to the Learning Channel, my favorite.

They were in the middle of part two of a two-part series on the construction of New York's bridges. These guys bundled in thick clothing just hung there over the Hudson River, halfway done with the George Washington Bridge. Their faces were so swollen, tipped I'm sure with red, although the images were black and white so you couldn't tell for sure. When they took a break, their legs dangled over the river, seeming to blow with the wind. Their thermoses were all lined up on a wooden platform. They were so thick and dented all around; one worker clutched his thermos with both hands and guzzled its contents as though it were oxygen.

I fell asleep then.

"Where are you going?" my mother asked. "You fell asleep so we didn't even get to see you last night, and now you're spending the entire first day away?"

"Ma, I'm thirty."

"What? I was inquiring about your age?" She rubbed her thin eyebrows as though I was giving her a headache. "When will you be back? I made reservations at the Steak Haus, and your brother might come with a new girlfriend. He was really upset he missed you when he stopped by last night."

"I don't eat steak."

"Well, they have plenty of other things there, and everybody else likes it," she said. "You can have a nice, big salad and a baked potato."

"Fine. I'll be back by five or so. Want me to meet you at the restaurant, or do you need your car before that?"

"Take it, no. My daughter comes home, I want her to have everything she wants." My mother was treating me like my brother. The way mothers treat sons, it's different. It's almost flirty, an accommodating intimacy under a guise of freedom. It wasn't always this way with me.

"See you there, then," I said, reaching to hug my mother. She seemed surprised.

"Well, the reservations are at seven-thirty. I don't care what you do besides that," my mother conceded. The skin on her face was greasy and tan, the lines like little arroyos all leading to her mouth, which was scrunched into a questioning oval on its side.

It took me about forty-five minutes in traffic to get out to Pasadena. I went there every time I was in town. I almost had to. The old Colorado Street Bridge appeared to me as gothic as it always had—dark and sagging. It was closed for earthquake retrofitting. The design always made me think of the dripping objects and structures in Dalí paintings. The bridge seemed like it could be one of the oldest things California had to offer. Now I stood beneath it, the way I had over a decade before—after my high school soccer coach jumped off.

He was wearing his dark blue windbreaker when he jumped. It had been a cold and windy day like this one. On the day after the funeral, I hiked down the side of the ravine and stood where he had landed just a few days before; the dirt was still caked with blood. This time, I estimated the point of impact, based on that first time I was there. But I could find no traces. I searched under the bridge as though I actually expected to find remnants of something that occurred twelve years earlier.

I piled some rocks and pebbles into a messy pyramid that kept toppling onto itself. The eucalyptus trees shimmered, and a woman trotted by on a shiny, brown horse. I stood when they approached, then went back to stacking the stones as they passed. When I was satisfied with my makeshift monument, I stood up again, but too quickly, and I became a bit dizzy. The cattails hummed in the breeze and water trickled through them, probably remembering a time when a concrete bed wasn't there to guide it through the ravine. "Randy's a Dick" was spray painted in black on the aqueduct.

Another older couple rode up on horses, one brown, the other speckled gray. They looked as though they'd been riding this ravine together for dozens of years. The man paid more attention to me than his wife, who was struggling to get the spook out of her horse.

"You like it?" he asked me. It was an odd question. But I had been staring up at the bridge. "They call it Suicide Bridge." I thought for sure he was some sort of a modern-day, mounted shaman.

When I didn't respond, he asked, "You know why?" I shook my head *no*. "Daredevil pilots used to try to fly under it during the war," he explained, looking up at the arch in front of us. The hair follicles on his neck were raised and red, seemingly from shaving. "Only one or two ever made it."

His wife said, "Okay," and the man tipped his hat at me and turned his horse around. I couldn't manage a good-bye.

I decided to go up top. Despite signs telling me otherwise, I parked in the Norton Simon museum parking lot and walked down Colorado Street and onto the approach to the bridge. I could see the Rose Bowl up the canyon, and the steep hills rising above it. And to the side, the newer, wider, more modern bridge that carries cars on the 134 freeway more efficiently from Ventura to Pasadena. More efficiently than the two-lane Colorado Street Bridge had for so many years.

107

They'd made it hard to get onto the bridge during the retrofitting. There were no workers around because it was the weekend. Reverse spikes pointed out like the few palm trees poking their heads up around the ravine. I started climbing the fence that was blocking the entrance to the bridge. My palms and fingers burned with cold and rust.

"Hey, sir!" I heard a woman's voice behind me. "You shouldn't be doing that."

I turned around. "What?"

"Oh, sorry." She was attractive, L.A.-style. She became visibly confused, and thus uncomfortable. "I, I just saw you from behind."

I jumped down, wiped the rust off my hands and onto my jeans.

"It happens all the time," I said.

"What are you doing?" she asked, as though I was her responsibility.

"My friend jumped off."

She looked at me, then out toward the middle of the bridge. She appeared even more concerned, waiting for me to confirm that she had just saved me from ending up yet another holiday statistic.

"I mean, years ago. I come back sometimes when I'm in town," I added, looking back at the bridge. Traffic buzzed by on the freeway, and just then I realized how loud it was.

All she said was, "Why?"

I opened my mouth but didn't have anything to say. We stood there in silence, a small gust of cold wind flipping her blond hair up and over her forehead.

"Why he did it, or why do I come back?" I finally asked.

"Either. Both." She was making me a little nervous. The way attractive people make you nervous.

I didn't answer.

"So, you're not from here?" she asked after another long silence.

"No, I mean, yeah, I'm from here. But I live in New York. I grew up here. Santa Monica." I crossed my arms, staring at this woman. She was just starting to poke her head into my consciousness. I usually tried to ignore things that were going to be gone so soon.

"Oh, well, I grew up in Connecticut, outside Hartford." Self-deprecating. But it was textbook how to distract someone from doing something terrible. Share a little of yourself.

People were always leaving places like Hartford, Connecticut. I pictured her mother there, strong and bony, pulling a small, shriveled turkey out of the oven and thinking, *Maybe next year she'll come for Christmas.*

We had mastered the art of awkward silences. And in such a short time too. Clearly she wasn't leaving until she was convinced I wasn't following my friend over the edge.

"I think he was gay," I said all of a sudden. "But he was engaged to this woman, and he had just traveled through Tibet and Nepal without her. He was really brilliant and complicated and beautiful."

"Those are all good things."

"What?" I asked.

"All of it," she said while moving closer to me. I think I was crying, but I couldn't see myself from the outside. I must've been, because she put her hand on my shoulder. A perfectly L.A., supposedly shallow stranger squeezed my shoulder through my jacket. And I could feel it.

"I was pretty attached to him," I said finally. "For obvious reasons."

"Not so obvious," she said. Then: "Do you want me to stay here?"

"No–I mean, thanks. But no, I'm fine," I insisted. She didn't look convinced. "You've been great though. Sorry I unloaded on you."

"You didn't unload at all," she said, patting me on the shoulder again, like she was about to leave, but hesitantly. "Okay then." She turned to go.

"So why are *you* here?" I yelled after her, before she was too far away.

"Joint custody," she yelled back, holding up both arms. "Drop-off and pick-up here–it's halfway."

"Oh," I said, and waved, nodding my head like it made all the sense in the world.

It was cold enough that she headed to her minivan to wait for the kids. It was a long way off. She must've really thought I was going to jump to have come all the way over to me. I watched her until she slammed the door, but I heard it after my eyes said I should've. I turned around and started climbing again, hanging practically upside down and parallel to the ground by the time I reached the top. Like those workers on the GW Bridge on TV the night before. My hands and pants were stained with blood-colored rust when I landed–too hard—on the other side of the fence. My knees rattled. The traffic seemed farther away now, almost silent, muffled.

About one-quarter of the way across the bridge, I realized I had left New York. I wasn't just visiting—a terrible prospect, something I never thought I'd do. Or had I even left? Was leaving Charlie leaving New York? I didn't want to go back, but then again, I didn't want to stay in L.A. either. An asshole was still an asshole, even three thousand miles away. My telephone conversation, or non-conversation, with Charlie confirmed that. Getting my ass kicked had something to do with coming here. It had made perfect sense in the hospital. My head started to ache again, just a hint of how it felt that night.

Then I realized suddenly that I was in the middle of the bridge, looking down from where Scott had jumped off. I looked back and saw the tiny minivan with the strange and beautiful woman in it. I couldn't tell whether she was watching me. I must've looked like a tiny cartoon character out there clutching the tiny toothpick of a railing. But I was anything but invincible. If I jumped, there would be no harmless *Poof!* at the bottom. There would be real blood, and splinters of bone and tissue, and my skin and scalp: all saturating the earth like Scott did.

At the funeral for Scott all those years before, another strange but less beautiful woman came and spoke at the service. There, in a Catholic church in Pasadena, in front of dozens of Scott's friends, family, and students. There she was, a perfect stranger, but the closest thing he had to a friend or family in the seconds before he died.

"I almost got to him," she started, and then began crying for what seemed like five full minutes. We all stared. "I ran out to him as soon as I figured out what was going on. I swear I ran as fast as I could, and it was so cold and windy and loud, I don't think he could hear me yelling." She kept crying. We sat there—teachers, students, athletes, friends, family—all of us silent. I wanted her both to go on and to stop right there.

"He was in a blue jacket, just standing there on the railing and holding onto the bridge, looking down so concentrated." She cried and mumbled so that she was almost inaudible. I cupped my ear with a palm, hoping to pick up every detail she was offering. "I had just gotten to him, and I think that's when he finally heard me. Then he just looked at me with the most peaceful smile on his face and let go. I swear I tried—seeing you all here, I swear I tried. I wanted to get there in time, but he wouldn't wait, he didn't want to wait. I couldn't believe it— he did it in front of me and God and the mountains and every- thing. I'm so sorry . . ."

I looked back at the beautiful strange woman, who was by then outside her minivan, corralling two bundled little kids through the side door. She looked at me too, I think, and I could see her ex-husband or whoever he was leaning against his car, watching her and the kids. I raised my hand in a half-wave, but it could've been a stretch. I think the mother waved back after sliding the door shut with the kids inside. But it was windy, and she could've been fixing the flip of her hair.

111

Downtown looked blunt and clear through the color yellow. I pulled off the 10 freeway somewhere west of downtown and dropped a quarter into a pay phone next to a tire store with torn, flapping silver flags overhead. I pulled out Charlie's cousin's number and dialed it. When an answering machine came on, I was somewhat relieved Taylor wasn't there, but then someone picked up, and the greeting stopped with a loud click.

"Is Taylor there?" I asked.

"No. Who's this?"

"I'm actually calling for her uncle, and I'm in town for—can you just tell her Isak called? I can leave a number."

"Taylor hasn't lived here for a while. You want her number?"

"Sure."

"Hold on."

After she gave me the number, I found another quarter in my pocket and dialed it.

"Hello? Robert Sykes's."

"Taylor?"

"Yes, who's calling?"

"This is Isak, Charlie's—"

"Right, Isak. How *are* you?" Taylor sounded excessively nice. Perhaps I'd been in New York too long, but it made me nervous when someone tried to sound that nice.

"Did Charlie tell you I was in town?" I asked.

"Yes. Yeah, I'd *love* to go out or get a drink or something." Painfully positive.

"Well, yeah, I didn't know if I'd have the time, but I had some now, so I thought I'd call," I said. "But it sounds like you're at work, and I'm sure you're busy. So I'm sorry I didn't give you more of a heads-up."

"No, no," she reassured me, her voice rising. *Shit.* "I'm actually pretty free right now. My boss is pretty flexible. Let's do it now. You're in Santa Monica, right? Want to meet around there for coffee?"

"I don't want to interrupt anything—"

"No, this is great, I'm feeling really open right now. It'd be great to share it with someone." I supposed it was either L.A. bullshit-talk or she was actually like that. I was hoping it was the former. "You know that place, the Living Room, off Main Street?" she suggested.

"I think so."

"Okay, how about I meet you there in, like, an hour? How does that sound?"

"Uh, okay. That'd be great. I'm actually meeting my family for dinner a little later on, so yeah, we can sit down for a bit, and then I can—I'll just go after that."

"Yeah, I guess that's what you would do." She sounded like she was talking while making the crazy sign next to her ear—little circles with an index finger.

I don't know why this girl made me nervous. I hadn't even wanted to call her in the first place, but I figured I'd get it over with as soon as possible. And now I had to deal with her "feeling open," and coffee and chit-chat and everything. Why

112

was she telling *me* what we're doing? I couldn't communicate like a normal person. I was used to giving orders. I decided I wouldn't let her take charge at coffee. I had no interest in any real depth–not in this city, and certainly not with her. I would honor my promise to Charlie and that would be it.

"I'm just really enjoying this space I'm in," was her reason for quitting her job as a hostess and trying "the acting thing." I tried my best to look cynical while stirring sugar into my coffee at the same time.

"Why are you so cynical?" she asked.

"I'm not, it's just–" I started. She looked at me seriously, a little hurt. "No, I mean, how many people go to L.A. to make it in show biz?" She was not entertained. This was the first time we'd had to have a conversation when Charlie wasn't around, and it was clear the senses of humor weren't jiving.

"So? I met someone who knows people, and he said I should give it a try," she continued, slowing down as though realizing how ridiculous it all sounded. "I don't care if nothing happens. I have nothing to lose."

We sat down in a bright booth with our frothy drinks. The sun slanted in through the blinds and dust floated aimlessly in the strips of light.

"So, do you *want* it?" I asked. "I mean, in your heart, have you always wanted to be an actor?"

Taylor thought a moment. "Not really, no. Should I?"

I looked at her squarely.

She went on: "I guess, it's just 'cause of my looks or something. I mean, what else can I do?"

She did not just say that, I told myself. I shifted in my seat uncomfortably.

"That sounded bad," she added. "Listen. People out here have said I have 'the look'–whatever that is–so I thought I'd see what it was about before just shunning it."

She was, I had to admit–*anyone* would admit–very beautiful. And even more so when she was flustered and a little

113

nervous. I was treating her like my brother used to treat me–patronizing, and like nothing I did had weight. It used to drive me crazy, but I couldn't help it; Taylor was threatening to me. It was written all over her body that she probably got everything she wanted. And assumed everybody else could too.

"I think it's great you're going to be on a TV show," I said finally, trying to sound sincere. I couldn't remember the last time I cared about sounding sincere.

"Well, it's not just any TV show," she said. "It's *Beverly Hills, 90210*."

"No way!" I said. "No fucking way. Charlie's going to pass out. Have you told him?"

"He knows."

"That is such a trip." I could actually see Taylor on that show. "So, do you get to swap spit with anyone, or what?"

"Shut up," she said. "No wonder you and Charlie get along so well."

"What?"

"He's such a bitchy queen, and you, you probably fit him like a sock."

114

"A glove?" I asked. She began to laugh a little. I could tell she was as uncomfortable as I was. I could also tell she didn't know anything about Charlie and me, what was going on.

We sat in silence for some time, watching the customers come in with nothing and then go out with something warm that seemed to make them relax–if only for a few seconds. A middle-aged man in tight sweatpants with stripes down the legs poured soy milk from the box into his coffee. He wore big brown sheepskin boots as though it were fifteen degrees out, as opposed to fifty. His tiny cell phone swung from a cord around his neck. He checked Taylor out, and she smiled at him until he had no choice but to smile back. I guess that's what you do to get along out here: You just keep giving them what they want. Every time, without fail.

"So, I guess this means you're through with the soccer thing," I said, hoping to start something–anything to get off the topic of acting. "I remember the last time you were in New

York you were talking about training with the national team or some such?"

"Yeah, that's over. I didn't want to play for that team. I trained for a year, but I just thought it was too much, you know what I mean?" She said this as though everybody had the opportunity to play for a national sports team.

She sat there, looking right into my eyes, and I looked away and then back again a few times. She was treating me like she probably treated everyone else—like the guy in the frou-frou sheepskin boots, for god's sake. Waiting until she knew she had me interested enough to hold her gaze.

"Damn, I didn't even make it all the way through college playing soccer, and I was at a Division-Two school," I said. "I bet it was intense in D-One."

"It wasn't so bad." She cocked her head and looked at me even more intensely than before, tucked the little bit of hair behind her right ear. I looked at her hands and could see them spanning a soccer ball—all scraped and chafed, fitting right into the seams between the black and white geometry. Her hands looked big enough to palm a ball. And they looked entirely different from the rest of her pretty much perfect body.

"Wait, you played soccer in college too?" she asked.

"Yep. Nothing major," I said. "Did you ever play anything but goalie?"

"If we were really kicking ass, they pulled me out and put me at fullback."

"I never played anything but fullback," I said, remembering how bad my old dirt-caked cleats smelled.

"Oh, so basically I spent my whole soccer career looking at the asses of players the likes of you." She laughed, letting herself go.

"Yeah, I guess you did," I said. Then I laughed too. And it felt kind of good. I wanted to dislike her. I wanted to write her off with each new detail she offered. But something kept me thinking that underneath it all, she wasn't as phony as she looked.

* * *

115

On the way to Taylor's car, we crossed the park on Fourth Street, climbing to the top of the hill. I felt like we were the only people out on the streets, and it was in the middle of the fucking afternoon, in the middle of Santa Monica. In fact, I think people were staring at us. I always felt like a space alien walking the streets of L.A. because nobody walked anywhere in the whole city, not even downtown.

The brownish lawns seemed to glow in the low sunlight. It was that time in the afternoon when even the air between your fingers is charged—particles everywhere, visible and otherwise, spinning and vibrating with energy. We sat on some swings in the sandpit, and I looked over the one-story houses and webs of wires across the street, chopping up the distant view of the ocean. I could tell Taylor was looking at me.

"What's going on with Charlie?" she asked.

"What?" Although I knew exactly what she meant.

"Cut the bait, Isak."

"What?" I started laughing. Was that supposed to be, *"Fish or cut bait,"* or, *"Cut the crap"?* Who could tell what she meant? Who cared when she looked that earnest saying it? Taylor tried to stay serious, but she finally laughed with me. At her.

After a while of swinging in silence, I stood up and balanced myself in the middle of the see-saw. Taylor followed me.

"I know he's HIV positive, though not because anyone told me," she started. "I mean, Charlie intimated as much, but I figure until someone lets me in on it, there's nothing I can do."

"You didn't hear it from me," I said, almost falling off the center of the steel bar.

"Do you know why he doesn't want me to know?"

"I didn't know that you didn't know," I said. I wanted to hear what she had to say before offering anything of import. I couldn't believe, though, that her family, such as it is, would keep something like this from her.

"My mom's acting weird. Or weirder than normal." She put a foot on the see-saw, which threw me off balance, so I jumped from the bar.

"Made you fall," Taylor said, with a hint of a smile.

I looked at her, and she looked back at me, practically right through me. I thought: *This beautiful person is flirting with you. But she is the kind of person who does that only when you have something she wants.* What could she possibly think I had to offer her? It was hard not to think about what she would look like underneath me if we had sex. It was just a flash.

She was waiting for me to give her something she deserved, something her mother wouldn't give her, and all I could do was think about banging her. I thought that about almost everyone who made me nervous.

"So?" she prompted. "How long?"

"What?"

"How long has he had it?"

I shook myself back into the topic at hand with the memory of the day Charlie told me. It was raining, and I had run into him on the corner of First Avenue and Sixth. I was in a rush to get somewhere. That was when I used to rush places. I remembered his dry cleaning was slung over his shoulder, and it was sopping wet underneath the thin plastic.

"Maybe five, six years?" I said to Taylor, almost like a question, as though it was all the information I had. There. That's what she wanted. Taylor didn't look like she was buying it though. She knew I lived with this, that I knew all of it. She looked back over the houses toward the ocean. The sun was sinking into the haze over the coastline. I thought I could see all of those agitated particles in the air between us and the sun. Things looked like they were made up of billions of little, multi-colored dots.

"Well, since AIDS is supposed to be over, I guess we have nothing to worry about," I continued, thinking if I shifted into sarcastic political mode we could avoid getting into something serious.

"Listen, Isak. I know you–" She stopped. Taylor didn't know what she wanted to say, but I appreciated the sentiment. "What's this about him moving to Providence with my mom?"

117

she continued. I guess she knew more than I'd thought. "Is he sick?"

"Not like you're thinking."

"What about you two?"

And with that question, Taylor proved herself more knowing and intuitive about the nature of my and Charlie's complicated relationship than either of us. What *about* us?

Taylor remained silent, letting the question hover for a moment before eventually punching me lightly, playfully, on the shoulder. I tensed up immediately, becoming highly aware of the skin underneath my clothes where she had touched me. She sighed loudly, and I mimicked her. This went on for a couple of rounds, and then I said, "Come on," and pulled my hat down further over the tips of my ears.

"My car's right here," Taylor said. It was a fancy new car, a BMW. I hadn't thought Taylor had much money, but apparently she wasn't doing too badly in L.A. with this job of hers. "Need me to drop you somewhere?"

"No, thanks. I'm just going to walk." I nodded in the direction I was heading. "You should call Charlie. I'm sure he needs you more than he lets on." Everyone does.

"Isak," she said like an afterthought. I turned around to look at her. Taylor's eyes seemed acorn-sized. She didn't need to point out the obvious. So she just said, "Thanks."

Which made me feel even worse.

That night in my parents' hotel-suite bed, I saw Scott, and he was the same age as when he jumped off the bridge in Pasadena. We were sitting in the bleachers of some high school–part the one I attended, and part every-high-school. There was the soccer field below us, damp. The newly drawn, white chalk lines were thick and batterlike, so white they were almost blue, like skim milk. The field was empty except for one player, who was running agility drills back and forth in front of the mouth of the goal, a ball in her big, gloved hands. She was wearing a goalie's jersey: bright orange with black stripes and thick elbow pads on the sleeves. It was windy and cold and wet, and also very gray, and Scott was wearing his blue jacket zipped up around his neck. He still had patches of acne around his jaw line–more than most thirty-year-olds have. But he was so handsome. He nudged my shoulder the way he used to, the way that said it all in the middle of a game without his having to call a play. I was me now, but it must've also been me back then, because I couldn't express anything as well as I wanted. I couldn't decide whether I wanted to be with him, or just *be* him. He knew, though. I asked, "What? What do you mean?" and he said, "You are down by two and it's the second half. It's not worth risking another. Don't forget to use the backdoor. She's got good hands."

When I ran into the faculty lounge the day one of my team-mates found Scott's obituary in the *Los Angeles Times,* they told us to keep it quiet until the emergency assembly after second period. They would break it to the school community then. The young science teacher who was friends with Scott grabbed me by both shoulders and shook me gently. I must've been crying. I remember feeling big between her hands, that my shoulders were strong and big and that I could kiss her. She looked at me like she knew. I didn't go to the assembly where they introduced the grievance counselors who were there to help us, but afterwards I watched the kids and teachers and some parents file out of the gymnasium, and I caught the science teacher by the shoulder and pulled her behind the lockers where I'd been smoking and drinking Coke for the hour it took everyone to learn about Scott and how we could mourn as a community.

"He died instantly," she told to me. "Actually, some people contend that something in the body triggers death before impact when people jump to their deaths, like a self-preserving mechanism that shuts off before life ends." She said: "If you land feet first, compression fractures shoot the bones in the legs up into the chest cavity and everything gets shredded up and ripped apart instantly."

I know she said the first two, but the last part I might have imagined from something else she didn't even have to say.

8

CHARLIE

"HOW SOON CAN YOU GET OUT of your lease?" Arlene asked me on the phone.

"Nothing you need to concern yourself with," I said. "And don't get your panties all in a bunch until–"

"Oh, Charlie, do you have to be so nasty?"

"No, I'm just saying nothing's settled yet. Plus there's this other matter we have to discuss."

"Oh?"

"I might be bringing a dog up with me. You know, Isak's and my–Isak's dog."

"Oh. Well."

"His name's Mary."

"He has a girl's name?"

"It's the same dog we've had for years. You met him."

"What about your friend? Is she coming? Is it your dog now?" she asked, not pausing in between questions for an answer.

I could tell these things were orbiting outside Arlene's atmosphere. I heard her ferreting through paperwork in the background. I thought I'd give her a moment to digest. Arlene was like our mother that way.

"It's our dog, but I think ultimately he'll stay with Isak. She'll probably come up and get him after a while."

"Oh."

"Would you be okay with that?"

"Well, what does it do all day?" she asked after a few seconds of churning.

"Eats, shits, pisses, sleeps, plays the stock market. What the hell do you think he does?"

"I don't know. I just, I don't know what we'll do with a dog around here. There's the yard out back. And I suppose a lot of people in Providence have them. Does it go inside?"

"You mean to the bathroom?"

"Well, anything."

"He's completely housetrained, and he's an indoor dog. He usually sleeps in bed with Isak. Or I guess me." This was a lot for my sister to absorb. Dogs in beds.

Arlene let out a quiet "Oh."

"Listen, think on it for a bit," I added calmly, "and we'll talk tomorrow." I know she just needed a bit of time with every new piece of information. All these new things for Arlene, each of them further out of her control. "I'm calling the rental place later, so I'll know when I can get a truck to move all this stuff and then come up."

"Do you have help?" she asked.

"Sure," I said, but I was lying, because there was nobody to ask anymore. "Taylor's good, I hear."

"Oh? Did you talk to her?"

"She had coffee with Isak out in L.A.," I said. "Sounds like she's doing well though."

"Your guess is as good as mine," Arlene said. "Her show's on tonight. She called to say last week. Didn't she tell you?"

"Oh, yeah, shit, I forgot. I can't believe I almost forgot. I've been so crazy with the move."

"What's the show called again? I wrote it down, but I don't remember."

"*Beverly Hills, 90210.*"

"Right, tonight at eight."

"Aren't you excited to see her on TV? I can't believe it. It's so fabulous."

"Well, I guess it will be interesting to see her on the TV."

"I'll videotape it for you."

Silence. Then Arlene exhaled loudly. I heard the crisp snipping of scissors as she worked in her store. Then she said, "I want this, Charlie. I know you don't think I know what I'm doing. But I do."

I told my therapist that I had decided to leave town, to move to Providence with Arlene. She noted that it was a somewhat sudden decision. Finally, a genuine emotion from the other side of the room: surprise. I bet she never thought I'd actually get up off my ass and go somewhere. It was much easier to complain and do nothing. I joked: "I'm crawling up there to die like a poisoned rat."

But she didn't get the joke, instead saying, "You're not dying. Why would you say something like that?"

I finally 'fessed up about Isak's abandoning me and how it did in fact hurt, but suddenly I grew very tired of processing the fact that Isak would no longer be in my life. I'd been sitting with it since Isak came through the door on the morning after she got beat. She was so pale, and I could see the faint brown stain that the cleansing solution left across her temple and cheek. She hadn't waited for me to come pick her up from the hospital with a car service. She just walked the whole way home.

I asked my therapist if it would be okay if we were to shift the topic to my friend Bryan, whom I would be taking to the museum after his next seizure; I was at once apprehensive and ecstatic about it, but this we did not address. She instead asked why I was asking permission to change topics. I alluded to feeling as though I always had to finish a thought out before she was satisfied enough to drop a subject. As though there had always been these rules we'd proceeded by. Then the discussion grew further complicated—"Why do you feel like there have been rules? Did they come from you, or do you think they originated with me?"—and I expressed frustration with not being able to talk about what I wanted to talk about when I wanted to talk about it. It was as though my declaration about leaving for Providence freed us up in some way. Like it was with Jack and me—those brutal truths—the week before he left me for the last time.

And like a cocky teenager packing up to leave home, I could see the wide open road ahead of me, and I was ultimately terrified that I wouldn't be able to make it on my own. It was obvious that the era of therapy–and my dependence on it–was over. Ten years and something like fifty-thousand dollars later, I'm still completely alone. I just have a few more "tools" at my disposal for coping with it. Come to think of it, I was beginning to resent the hell out of the entire notion of therapeutic honesty, and looked forward to spending time in the la-la land that is Arlene's world, where I wouldn't have to talk about anything except the weather for weeks on end, if I so pleased.

"So, why is it that you haven't called?" I asked Isak when she finally did call again, almost two weeks after the first time. I had needed to ask her something about the apartment, but I had lost her parents' phone number in all of the packing. So I waited around for her to feel guilty enough to call again.

"I'm sorry. I've been really busy dealing with my folks. And kind of out of it, to tell you the truth," Isak said. "I did end up seeing your niece. She's doing fine."

Isak sounded more compassionate than the last time we spoke. Still, she was probably only checking up on the dog again. She felt lost to me.

"I know you saw each other. Taylor called."

"Oh, well, it was fun. We talked a little," she said, trailing off.

"Thanks for seeing her. In some cockamamie way it makes me feel better that you did," I said, but I didn't really understand why. "Well, anyway, I'm getting ready to move, and we need to talk about some things."

"When? I thought it wouldn't be for a while." She sounded genuinely surprised.

I couldn't help being angry with her. She didn't say when she was coming back. She just left, a couple of weeks after she got out of the hospital–not a word of explanation. And I wasn't going to let her have the corner on the leaving market.

"Well, at first I didn't think I'd leave until the spring. But when you figure out what you want to do with the rest of your life, you kind of want to get the rest of your life started as soon as possible. You know what I mean?"

"Yeah. I guess."

"Things simplify," I added. "The years—well, *people* school you, you know what I mean?"

"Yeah."

"So what do you want to do with Mary?" I asked. "I can take him up with me until you get back and settled somewhere."

"What do you mean?" she asked. I could tell she was getting upset.

"Well, I don't remember your telling me when you were coming back."

"I didn't say."

"Exactly."

"I don't know," she said. "I don't know when I'm coming back."

"Do you want me to send him?"

"What, in the mail?"

"No, on an airplane," I said. I didn't feel like joking. All this hurt.

"No. I would never do that to him."

"Listen, it's not like torture for him to be with me," I said. "I'll take him up to Providence, and you can come get him when you get back East, if you want."

"Okay," Isak said softly.

"You are coming back East, right?" I asked.

"Yeah."

"Then just come up and get him when you do. He'll be fine until then."

"Charlie?"

"What?"

"Nothing."

"What?"

"Well, what about the apartment and everything?"

"I'm putting some of my things into storage and giving the rest away," I said matter-of-factly. "Do you want me to put your stuff in storage too?"

"I don't have much," she said, as though considering this for the very first time.

"Well?"

"What about the apartment?"

"A friend of a friend is coming to look at it and maybe sub-let it. I told him you might still be living here with him. But you haven't been in contact, so I didn't know what to tell him. You'll have to work out the rent together. It'll obviously go up from what you're paying now."

"I'm not really paying anything now."

"Oh, well, then. There it is." It was probably the first time Isak admitted this little detail in the open.

"Charlie," Isak said. My name sounded like a request. A final request. I didn't want to hear it. This stuff was too hard, and I wasn't going to make it any harder by indulging in it further.

"You left, Isak. This is what happens when people go their separate ways. The pack breaks up and they go their separate ways. That's the definition of 'separate ways.'"

126 Half of Bryan was slack. He waved with his left hand when I pulled up in front of his building in the back of a taxi.

"The last seizure was yesterday," he said, like it was a good thing. He seemed to speak faster in person, but I think this was because I could look at him while he spoke, whereas on the phone, there was nothing else. He struggled so much– there wasn't one word, even, that didn't give him trouble.

I realized then how good it made me feel to see someone who was dying faster than I was. Then I felt bad for feeling good.

"I look like shit, really bad, right?" he asked. He was wearing a wool ski-hat, but I could tell he had no hair underneath it–or the kind of hair that tries to grow back after dropping out from chemotherapy. And then there he was in the cab, and we were accelerating, and that was that. We turned up Sixth Avenue, threading through pedestrians who had the right of way in the crosswalk.

I supported Bryan up the stairs in front of the Met. It was

CHARLIE: How They Are

crowded. People took pictures of other people at odd angles, aiming up at the colorful banners hanging off the museum's facade. A square-chinned Italian guy asked me to take a picture of him and his wife. "Columns in the forefront, also, please." You'd think there were better and older columns in Italy, but anyway. I snapped his picture. It was bitterly cold out.

"Are you warm enough?" I asked Bryan, because I could tell it would take us quite some time to scale the steps.

"I can't feel half of me anyway," he said. I didn't get that it was a joke until I saw the left side of his lips curl into a semi-smile.

The lobby was humming, and utterly overwhelming. I started to panic again, afraid I would lose Bryan in the throbbing crowd. It reminded me of the first time I took care of a baby by myself: I was about eighteen or nineteen and Taylor was almost two. Arlene and Ken were going out of town—a last-ditch effort to save the marriage by way of a remote island in the Bahamas. Arlene asked me to come up and look after Taylor for the weekend. She hadn't wanted to tell Mom about the surprise trip because she knew Mom would instantly divine the motivations behind it.

When I got there, I was sure I would squeeze Taylor too hard, hold her the wrong way, or drop something that would end up lodged in her throat. It was worse when I went outside with her. Even in that quiet town, I was sure someone would steal her from me. Or a car would hit us and send our skeletons splintering all over the sidewalks.

Needless to say, Taylor survived, which is more than I would say for myself. I came out to Arlene right after that stay (like she didn't already know), and then Ken forbade Arlene from letting me see—much less take care of—Taylor ever again. Or at least until the divorce, after which Ken didn't care what happened to Taylor anymore.

This was how it felt with Bryan—like something would happen to him and it would be due to my failure or inattention. He kept pulling in the wrong direction, like a car with a misaligned front-end–always to the right. I corrected him by tugging lightly at his elbow, but then I realized he probably couldn't feel me. So I moved around to his left side and did the same thing. We made it to the ticket-booth line. Bryan breathed heavily. His breath was stale.

"You ever use, or think about needing, or using–" I started. He was looking up at the admission board, still catching his breath from the journey.

He looked back down at me slowly. His pupils were huge–dilating in the dark. They looked green, and I imagined I could see my distorted head in them. And so there I was.

"A wheelchair?" I blurted. "You know, a wheelchair."

He paused. Perhaps gathering his thoughts like he told me he did. Or maybe he was offended. I couldn't tell; it wasn't exactly him anymore. We moved up in line.

"I never did think of that. No," he said finally, excruciatingly.

"Two, please," I said, and pushed our old company identification cards across the counter. "We get complimentary admission with these still, right?" The woman behind the counter looked at me as though I were stealing something from her.

I unwrapped the wool scarf from around Bryan's neck, clipped the green metal tag to his shirt collar. I reached up to take off his hat, but he ducked. I saw my fingers shaking. The more I did for him, the more they shook. By now he was probably used to having people do things for him. I wondered if the hands of friends still felt different from those of nurses, doctors. Or was it all the same?

"I don't want to go in," he said.

"Oh. Well, we're here. I thought this was what you wanted."

"No."

"Okay. What, then?"

"Maybe something less eventful, like a shoeshine. But where?" He looked down at his black boots, wiggled the toe of the left one, but slowly. Someone bumped into us because we were half in line and half out of line. "And maybe fries."

"Okay, I know where to go," I said, as though I were the

128

most flexible person in the world. "Bottom of Rockefeller Center. It's the best place."

After an interminable stumble back down the steps of the Met and a bitter fight for a taxicab, we ended up in front of a McDonald's on Sixth Avenue. We went in to order two extra-large fries to go. I paid, then grabbed a handful of ketchup packets on the way out. We made our way cautiously toward the Time-Life building–the place of our past employment–each step more potentially perilous than the last. Soon we slipped underground.

I helped Bryan up onto the shoeshine platform and sat him down; he handled the placement of his left leg onto the pedestal as deftly as the next person, but I had to handle the right. I put the bag of fries on his lap and then rolled up his pant legs a couple of times. They were too long, as though he'd shrunk. I sat in the seat next to him as the shoeshiner went to work silently. His T-shirt was stained with an earthy collage of shoe polish shades.

"You want one too?" Another shoeshiner approached me.

"No, that's fine. Okay if I sit?"

"Get it done, Charlie," Bryan said. Both shiners looked up at him when they heard the way he spoke. "My treat."

"Okay. Yeah, thanks." I reached into Bryan's lap and pulled out a handful of fries.

Coupled off, we four were silent for some time. I could hear Bryan's breathing evening out. It felt good to be touched through the leather uppers of my shoes. Familiar. I watched Bryan's shoeshiner, but I concentrated on how mine felt. There was just a suggestion of sensation beneath the shoes, under the socks, finally on my skin–the persistence of another body. I looked up at Bryan a few times; once he was looking at the top of the shoeshiner's head, and the other two times his eyes were closed–though not tightly–in some form of bliss. It must've been nice to be touched out of luxury for once, and not out of necessity.

His right leg fell off the pedestal and his shiner looked up at me, panicked. I recognized his look as exhibiting the same emotion I'd felt earlier in the taxi, when I first ascertained what we were dealing with in Bryan. I nodded to him that it was okay, and he gently placed Bryan's leg back onto the pedestal. He held it there from that point on. Bryan hardly noticed any of this.

Bryan reached into the bag of fries as though he'd forgotten they were there. He probably had.

"Ketchup?" I asked. He moved his head slowly, up, down, and around. I couldn't tell if it was a yes or no.

Bryan ate three handfuls of fries (which took a considerable amount of time), and then a deep breath.

"Do you see her?" he asked. I knew who he was talking about. The woman he had been in love with when he had the first seizure that tipped the docs off to the brain tumors.

"No. Why would I see her?"

"The band's getting big. She got an interview in *Rolling Stone* last month. Did you see?"

"No, I didn't." I wanted more than anything not to talk about this woman who abandoned him, or her subsequent musical success. He didn't seem to want to drop it though.

"You know what I was thinking? Even when things were really good for me and really bad for her." His shiner snapped a dirty rag loudly. Seemed to snap the thought right out of Bryan's riddled brain. And then finally, resigned: "I don't know what I was thinking."

I sat and waited. Bryan didn't say anything else. He'd given up on her again. Or at least until the next time the memory of her forced its way back in. My shoeshine was over, but Bryan's continued, perhaps because his guy was taking extra care with the unpredictable right leg.

When he leaned forward in his seat, I reached into Bryan's back pocket and pulled out his wallet. I paid and tipped the shoeshiners before helping Bryan off the platform. His lips curved into that question mark of a half-smile, and I thought: *There is nothing more solitary than this.* I could still feel the faint symphony of fingers pressing into my feet as we shuffled back upstairs, into the cacophony of the city.

When I dropped him off at his apartment, his aide was waiting. Bryan was too tired to say good-bye, instead making a beeline for his bed and falling into it. The aide looked at me apologetically, knowingly, like, *You know how they are, the sick.*

When I exited his building, I was assaulted with a blast of frigid northerly air. I pulled my hat down over my ears and the back of my neck, and said, "Bye."

Jack looked as good as ever. Better. He was beautiful in that way that makes you wonder if you'll ever be allowed to have something as beautiful again. Or whether you get one shot, and one shot only.

His hair was clipped close. A few gray hairs on the temples. Very sexy. The grays had come in since we'd broken up. His boyfriend looked twenty-five, and Jack himself looked younger than he should've–thirty, tops. He fit into jeans better than anyone I knew.

Jack and his boy strolled toward me on Seventh Avenue. They were heading uptown as I walked down from the clinic. There was no avoiding a direct hit. Bull's eye.

"Charlie?" He let go of the boy's hand. Clearly there were a lot of muscles underneath all those clothes, because the boy's arm didn't rest along his side like normal, spindly people's do. Both arms just stuck out like a robot's. I wondered whether they had penetrative sex. And what kind.

"Hi, Jack," I managed.

"This is Edward. Edward, Charlie." My name was so loaded–with what I didn't know. But there were no further explanations necessary. It had been six years or something.

Edward reached out his hand and I took it. He squeezed harder than one should be allowed to squeeze when it is cold out. We three pinched up our faces and waited as a fire engine went by, sirens screaming. *What does he know about me, this Edward,* I wondered.

"So, how are you? You look *good,*" Jack said. I didn't recognize anything on him. Not a single article of clothing, an earring, his messenger bag. Nothing.

"Oh. Please. You. You look great," I said. I was overcome with an urge to feel the flushed red circles on his cheeks with the back of my hand.

"How are you *feeling?*" he asked. And I knew what this meant.

"Oh, you know. Same ol'."

"*Good.*" Jack stepped back. His tennis shoes were neon orange. They matched his bag. "Yeah, well, me too."

I nodded my head at him, looked at the boy. Jack might've looked good for Jack, but this boy was next to perfect. He was straight out of a porn video.

"So, you still at, uh–" he asked.

"No. I'm on disability."

"Mmm. Great. That, uh, covers–"

"Yeah. Well, not everything, but most."

"Great. That's *great,*" Jack said, bobbing his head.

I'd had just about enough of our walkie-talkie conversation. Besides, I could tell that porn-star muscle boy's attention span was seemingly the equivalent of a five-year-old's.

132

I tried to swallow but couldn't. There was phlegm in my throat. I worried that my glands were sticking out. But I knew they weren't. They hadn't ever been. I would not tell him about Providence. He could find out after the fact. After Isak's and my apartment was packed up, the dust bunnies spinning in the corners on the empty, cracked floor.

"You don't think we should have lunch or anything," Jack asked, leaning in, "do you?"

"No, no. I don't." I looked down: Gym-boy's shoes were the same color as Jack's. In fact, they must've been on their way to the gym. A tandem workout. How sweet. I looked such the fool. I'm sure passers-by could read the situation on sight: *Boy loses boy. Boy turns into sick, old fag. Other boy doesn't age, gets young buck with big dick, big pecs.*

"Because if you think we *should,* or I don't know–"

"Should, what's should?" I asked. And then: "I'm leaving. Town, of course. I'm moving."

"What? Where?" Jack seemed genuinely surprised.

"Providence. You know, Arlene's there."

"What about Isak?" he asked.

"I don't know."

Jack cocked his head at me. Then that elusive declaration from therapy returned: *I'm going up there to die like a rat.* Only it hovered over this entire block of Seventh Avenue, instead of just over my therapist's couch. And this time it wasn't as funny. Seeing it up there made me realize a dying rat was less apt than something like, say, a poisoned cockroach returning with his poisoned exoskeleton for the rest of the nest to feed on. I tended to be a champion of the dramatic. My levels were low, really low. I wondered where Jack's were. Who was healthier. Because I was pretty damn healthy. That's what they had just told me at the clinic.

And then I forgot where I was. Sometimes I did that. I grew dizzy as another siren shrieked by–an ambulance on its way to St. Vincent's. Jack put a hand to my shoulder as if to steady me. But that's all he could muster. His boy was emptying noisy plastic wrappers and wadded up paper from his messenger bag into a trash receptacle. Gum wrappers were tumbling out of the diamond-shaped spaces in the can and blowing onto the curb. He was stainding there littering.

"You sure you're okay? Do you need to *talk?*" Jack asked, patting me roughly on the shoulder. Then, "Hey, Edward!"

The two walked away. Shameless, and still not entirely certain of my whereabouts, I watched until they crossed the avenue. Jack still had the better ass–even though he probably had a good ten years on the kid. I'm sure if I looked long enough, I'd find matching tattoos on the two of them. Somewhere, two scorpions, or something equally regrettable.

So for the third time in as many days, I said good-bye and went on my way.

9

ARLENE

MRS. WILLIAMSON CAME INTO THE STORE while I was trying to get some old invoices paid. She'd been coming in a lot more frequently those days, and I wondered whether it was because she was lonely, or because she thought I was.

"You heard about Jill Smithers?" she asked inadvertently, and ringing a hand-painted antique cow-bell.

"No, what?"

"Well, Elaine came back from school yesterday and said she came out to her students. Came out as a *lesbian.* Did you know she was a *lesbian?*"

"I guess I hadn't really thought about it," I lied. I was getting awful good at lying. Just about the last thing I wanted to talk about with Mrs. Williamson was that Jill.

"Well. Didn't Taylor play soccer for Coach Smithers? I don't know whether I'll let Elaine play now, she's all upset about it. I mean, I think it's fine if she wants to be a *lesbian,* but I don't think she should be advertising it to the *children.*"

Mrs. Williamson picked up a steel bud vase with a test tube in the middle where the flower goes. She examined it at eye level. The glass clinked against the steel when she put it back down on the wrong shelf. Mrs. Williamson was a caricature of herself. The trapezoid-shaped designer purse slung around her elbow, the dyed auburn, close-cropped hair framing her salon-tanned face, the skin pulled taut from eye to ear. In this way she was almost a caricature of me too. I could have just as easily been her as I was me. She could've been fretting over

past-due bills and wondering how to cover them, while I care-
lessly nosed through knick-knacks in her charming little
store, figuring how much of my husband's money things were
worth.

She was looking to engage me about Taylor and Jill. There
had been rumors.

"I don't know, dear," I started. "I don't keep up much with
what's going on at that school anymore."

Another customer came in, ringing the bell hanging off the
doorknob. "Hello," I said. "Let me know if I can help you with
anything."

Mrs. Williamson leaned in closer to me, where I was kneeling to dust a low display case. "Didn't Taylor leave before
graduating?"

"I moved her to a boarding school for eleventh and twelfth
grades, yes," I said. "The sports program was stronger."

"Oh, the sports program." Mrs. Williamson wanted to crack
me open. The other customer made eye contact with me
again, so I said, "How are you doing today?" I wanted an
answer, but the girl just smiled. She looked like a Brown
student.

"What's Taylor up to these days?" Mrs. Williamson asked.

"Well, to tell you the truth, I don't know. She's in L.A., and
she seems to like it a great deal," I said. Which was technically true, according to the brief accounts I got from Taylor on
the phone every couple of weeks. We didn't talk anywhere
near as much as we used to.

"She made it on a TV show," I continued, remembering
again. "Well, just an episode of a TV show. But it's supposed to
be on tonight."

"Really? Which one?" Mrs. Williamson seemed genuinely
impressed. "She was always so beautiful, that Taylor. Really.
The boys just went crazy over that one."

"Yes, well," I sighed, and locked the back of the glass case.
The Brown student left. She had picked up a picture frame
and looked at the price on the back before putting it back
down on the shelf. At least she smiled before pulling the door

closed behind her. I added, "It's one of the shows the kids watch. *Beverly Hills*–"

"*90210*. Oh, Elaine *loves* that show. She's been watching it for years. I've got to tell her. Tonight?"

"That's what Taylor said." I looked at the clocks on the wall. Most of them said it was coming up on six. The show was on at eight. "Well, I'm going to close up."

"I'd be so proud. Are you having a party to watch the show?" Mrs. Williamson asked, but then stopped herself because she was probably doing what I did as she said it: wondering who I would possibly invite to such a party. She realized the mistake and pulled her purse close to her side. "Well, thanks for the chat, Arlene. I hope you're well. I'll watch for Taylor tonight."

I locked the door and pulled down the shade after Mrs. Williamson trotted out. Finally alone. I looked around the store. There was still so much to do for the Christmas display. Then I remembered I had nothing in the house for dinner. I felt like something bland, involving rice. Some of the clocks were ticking at me. The cuckoo came out, and I flipped the sign from "Open" to "Closed."

137

At the market I picked up a small shopping basket on the way in. I needed only a few items, and then I had to be back by eight for Taylor's show. I didn't need to be pushing a big cart around and getting loaded down with things I didn't need.

The broccoli looked like rubber. It felt a little less so, but that was all they had. The fresh shipment was probably due in tomorrow. Just my timing. At least it was only a dollar a bunch.

I picked up some rice. Coffee. I could get some extra fruit for the rest of the week. And English muffins. I decided to stroll by the coffee shelf to see if they had any of the hazelnut-flavored beans. I loved those. Then there was all the dog food across the aisle. So many brands, I'd never noticed. All the dogs on the packages looked so healthy. One was a long-haired blonde, with a perfectly groomed coat, flowing as the dog strode toward its loving family and a heaping bowl of food. A boy in a striped shirt knelt down with his arms outstretched to receive the dog. The dad had his arm around the mom. The layers of color were off though, and I could barely make out their blurred faces. There was a big tear in the corner of the red bag, and some multi-colored kibble scattered onto the linoleum floor. What a mess.

Why would they name that dog Mary if it was a boy? I supposed it didn't really matter either way to him. I wondered what kind of food it ate.

Then I looked at the toys, leashes, the knotted bones. How many times did it go out a day? Did it bark, or bite? Taylor had wanted a dog when she was in grammar school. I told her we couldn't afford it. Which was simply not true. Kenny was giving us enough at the time. I was afraid of dogs. Always had been.

I was cornered by one when I was in high school, walking back to our house. Too old to be frightened of anything so much. At least that's what I thought at the time. Charlie happened to be outside, and when he heard me screaming, gently coaxed the dog away from me and into his arms. He was kneeling at the dog's level, as I recalled, just little Charlie with this big vicious dog. This dog that had seconds before been peeling its lips over teeth at me wiggled in front of Charlie as he rubbed its thick neck. They can just smell the fear in some people.

There were so many commercials. I never realized, or even cared, until I was waiting to see my own daughter on the television. It was almost surreal. Taylor on TV. Leave it to Taylor to go to L.A. and then end up on TV in six month's time.

I sat on the couch with my broccoli and rice in front of the TV. And a glass of white wine. The bottle of wine had been in the refrigerator for weeks. In fact, it tasted like the inside of a refrigerator. And the broccoli didn't quite smell right either.

More commercials. The opening sequence. I hadn't ever seen this show, except for one time, by accident. Charlie had filled me in; it seemed as though he watched it religiously. A grown man watching this show about teenagers. I didn't understand it. I knew that the kids had all been to high school together, then college, and now they were working in Los Angeles, still living together and becoming involved with each other, and making adult decisions in their young lives. Some of these kids looked to be in their thirties though. Charlie said that his favorite character left the show. He claimed she was too bitchy in real life and got kicked off the set. I don't know how Charlie would have known this, but I figured I could take him on his word in this realm. I wondered whether Taylor was "bitchy."

The opening scenes were at an outdoor coffee shop. It was so sunny and bright. I looked everywhere for Taylor, so I didn't even hear what the characters were saying. No Taylor. Something about a stolen baby. Or an abandoned baby. Something about a baby and a clinic. The sweet-faced, pretty blond girl was upset about a baby.

I stabbed at the broccoli. Though it was less limp than when raw, there was something off about it. It just didn't taste right.

Still more commercials. Then someone in trouble at Beverly Hills City Hall for drunk driving. It was a Jeep, all in what must've been flashbacks because it was in black-and-white and looked like MTV. The character in question was a spoiled boy with a husky voice who got arrested for a hit-and-run while intoxicated. His hair stood up on end, although I gathered it was supposed to be that way, and wasn't because he was frightened. At the next break, I got up to put my dishes in the sink and get some Windex and a paper towel. The coffee table was filthy.

Then the handsome boy was walking with his friends outside the courthouse, and Taylor walked up to him from behind. She asked, "Are you Mr. Noah Hunter?" He answered, "Yes," and then she said, "This is for you," and handed him an envelope. His jaw hung open as Taylor smiled as though there was nothing she could do about it, and then he watched her walk away. I realized as he was opening the envelope in front

139

of his friends that I had no idea what Taylor had just looked like. What she was wearing even. That was it. Charlie said he would tape it, so I could see it again. But that was it. It was as though she hadn't even been there—she was gone as soon as I saw her.

I did, however, feel her presence. That is, the distinctive look she gave Noah after serving him with those legal documents—I'd been the recipient of that look a thousand times. And it registered that she must've looked good—great, beautiful. But I couldn't picture her after that. I looked to the soccer-team photo framed on the mantle. Taylor was dead center, in her bright red goalie's jersey. She stuck out. She always stuck out.

Oh my gosh. She's gone.

I could feel my chest becoming a knot. I called Charlie. I concentrated on breathing evenly. We were back to the blond girl who wanted to keep the abandoned little baby. She wasn't ready for it, I could tell.

Charlie didn't pick up the phone. The answering machine came on. It was his roommate's voice. She sounded like one of the boys on the TV show. I left a message on the machine.

At the clinic, a homely social worker came to take the baby from the baby-faced blond girl back to his rightful owners—the parents who had abandoned him at the doors of the clinic. They had changed their minds. Then it was back to the boy, worrying over a lawsuit, and cut to commercials. No more Taylor. The phone rang.

"Didn't she look great?" was all Charlie said when I picked up. "Wasn't she fabulous?"

"Yes. It was . . . great."

"Her hair, my god. It was fabulous. I mean, honey, I knew she was beautiful, but she just looked fabulous. And healthy. And her *eyes.*" Charlie went on. Charlie always tended to go on about Taylor's looks anyway. And he said "fabulous" more than anyone I knew. In fact, I noticed that a lot of people from New York said "fabulous."

She's gone, she's gone. My breathing hollowed. There wasn't air. This was what I saw, these words, floating out from me, but I didn't say anything to Charlie. I kept the phone to my ear and rifled through the kitchen cabinet for my prescription while he rattled on about the television show.

The calm came. My muscles felt doughy, my skeleton still somewhere in there, trying to stay rigid. But times like these made me wonder where my bones went. I sat on the couch. There was a pile of twisted hairs on the arm rest. I hadn't even noticed picking them out. I must've been doing it while I was on the phone with Charlie. Or during the show. I brushed them into my palm and emptied them into the trash can.

Charlie called back. I didn't remember having hung up. The phone rang several times before I could pick up.

"You okay, hon?" he asked.

"Yes. I'm fine."

"You had me worried. You stopped talking in the middle of a sentence. What happened?"

"Nothing, dear. I'm fine."

"Arlene–"

"No, really, I'm fine. It just gets a little hard sometimes."

"Taylor?"

"No," I said. Charlie didn't say anything. The dog barked in the background. "Yes. Taylor."

"Oh, honey. What?"

I didn't want to tell Charlie the same thing Mom told him. That I didn't know what Taylor was anymore. Implying she'd turned into some sort of monster or something. A creature that may have come out of me but turned into something entirely different. Not part of the original plan.

But Taylor wasn't so bad. She just wasn't there. I missed her hands. She always put them on me at times like these. When it felt like I had lost something I couldn't identify. When my chest tightened and my skeleton seemed to dissolve. Her hands were so strong.

"Arlene?" Charlie prodded me. I hadn't been speaking for a while.

"Oh. I was actually just wondering what kind of beverages you like to have around the house."

"What? Why?"

"Well, I wanted to start keeping an eye out for things. Maybe I'll catch a sale in bulk or something."

"Arlene, come on. You don't need to start worrying about that. Or anything."

"Why not?" I asked. "You're going to be here sooner than you think."

"Listen, honey. We'll figure this stuff out once I get up there," Charlie said. "Are you okay? Are we okay here?"

"Oh fine, yes, by all means." My muscles were coming back. I could get in bed and read for a spell. "Charlie?"

"Yeah?"

"You're excited, right?"

"What? About Taylor?"

"No, Providence."

"Honey, yes. I really am. It's a good idea," he said, sounding somewhat annoyed.

I had no idea what it might've been like to be him. I wanted to know, before I lost the chance, like I wanted to know about Taylor, with whom I'd already lost the chance.

"Charlie? One more thing–"

"What?"

"Well, I thought–do you know what kind of dog food that dog takes? They have a ton of it at the store, and I thought I could pick up a bag or something in case he ends up coming up with you."

The book I was reading wasn't putting me to sleep. The pill hadn't, and then I kept noticing over the top edge of my book that the armoire was completely in the wrong place. All these years in the exact same place–the same place Ken and I decided to put it after an hour of heated discussion, if I remember correctly. I got up and put my robe on, pulling the sash tight around my waist.

I closed the doors to the armoire and locked them with the

tarnished, old key, and went around the left side. I pushed with all my body's weight, and it budged; I could certainly manage it on my own. How couldn't I have noticed all those years? *It was simply on the wrong wall.* The dresser should've been where the armoire was, the armoire where the mirror was. The mirror on the back of the closet door, or not in the bedroom at all. I never looked at myself anyway.

I pushed the armoire into the middle of the room. It had old wooden wheels, so it rolled, but in fits and starts. I knew I could do it alone though. Then I took out some drawers from the dresser and put them onto the bed. I unhooked the mirror from its place on the wall. Behind everything I moved there was filth. I went downstairs into the kitchen to get the dustpan and broom.

After cleaning, it felt like nothing was clean enough. But I wanted to see the new configuration, so I decided I could still do more cleaning later. I felt a pain in my lower back as I was giving the armoire one last push into place. It was a burning, pulling sensation, which I assume meant something was wrong, but it didn't hurt.

143

I sat back on the bed, looking at the furniture. I was out of breath, worried for some reason that I'd made too much noise. But there wasn't anyone else in the house. There hadn't really been anyone for years.

There were some scratches in the wood where I'd dragged the legs of the dresser across the floor. I didn't care. It looked so much better in there. The room was completely trans-formed. More air, almost. And I could finally breathe. I tossed my robe over the rocking chair and crawled back under the covers. I picked the book back up, but I had lost my place.

While searching for the last line I remembered reading, I kept looking up at the new configuration. *Much better. Much, much better,* I chanted in my head. But still there was some-thing wrong. I set the book down and went to put my robe back on. This time I left it open and didn't tie the sash. It flew open on either side of me as I went back downstairs to the kitchen. I could feel the house's cool air between my legs. I found the tape measure after fishing through the utility drawer for a while and went back up to Taylor's old room and stood inside.

I'd never measured anything in this house. I never knew how long or wide things were. I started with Taylor's room. It was hard to get the end of the tape to stay put, so I put one of Taylor's old cleats over the hook to hold it in place.

Taylor's room was 11' x 12'. The guest room, a little smaller: approximately 10' x 12'. The master bedroom, Kenny's and my old room–*my* room: 14' x 14'. The biggest. I wrote them all down on a pad of paper and posted it on the refrigerator with a magnet the shape of Cape Cod. (Taylor had brought it back for me from one of her trips.)

Back in bed, I decided this would no longer be my bedroom. It would be Charlie's. I could take Taylor's old room. She wouldn't need it. I didn't know how we'd manage the bathrooms because I couldn't see giving up my master bathroom for the guest bath. Or maybe it would be just fine. Charlie might want more space in that kind of a room anyway. Who knows what he was going to need, but if it's like anything I've seen on TV, he could be spending a lot of time in the bathroom.

The furniture could wait until the next day; I'd move it all in the morning and go into the store a little late. The dresser, the armoire, the bed. I didn't think anything else would fit, so I'd play it by ear after that. But not me. I couldn't wait to start sleeping in my new bedroom. So that's what I did. I picked up my orthopedic pillow, my reading glasses, and that damn paperback, and I peeled back the tightly tucked bedding from Taylor's bed and slipped inside.

10

TAYLOR

TAYLOR'S CELL PHONE VIBRATED on the glass table in front of her. She looked at the display and saw it was Sykes. She answered, "Yep?"

"Hi, hon. Listen, where's that one o'clock? You said Spago, but they have no reservation, and I don't see our guy anywhere."

Taylor had fucked up Sykes's appointment. She forgot to call for a reservation after settling on a time and place. "Oh my god, Robert. I forgot to book it. I can—"

"No, it's okay. They're gonna open something up for me. But it was Spago though, right?" Sykes sounded peeved, but not angry. Never angry. "I guess he's late."

Taylor didn't say anything.

"Tay?" Sykes asked. He sounded farther and farther away to Taylor. And there was a surge of echoing voices in the background. "Taylor, you there?"

She had placed the phone in her lap and looked toward the sun above Sykes's pool house, which Taylor called home. Taylor lived in a mansion in Beverly Hills, and when the weather was nice, her office was its backyard. It didn't add up: She was the worst actor in Hollywood, and yet after she moved in with Sykes and became his personal assistant, Taylor was the worst actor with the most potential work.

"Taylor?" Sykes was yelling into the phone, and Taylor could hear it coming out on her end. She couldn't respond though. She kept looking into the sky. She had also lived in

The Sun, the Moon, and the Stars B&B once. She had lived where she worked. If you could call it work. It was sunny there too. She did her "work" outside in the courtyard, in the summers between college. If she couldn't run a bed and breakfast, couldn't wait tables, and she couldn't act, then she must be able to run a guy's life. It was just one moderately important guy's life.

"Tay? If you don't answer, I'm canceling this lunch and coming over there," Sykes shouted into the phone. It might've been Jules's voice coming at her on the other end of the call, threatening to come and take care of Taylor. "Hello? Taylor? Can you hear me?"

"Taylor, baby? What's wrong?" Sykes asked as he pulled Taylor toward him. She hadn't moved since the phone call. Her arms felt sunburned. "Honey? Tay? You okay, Taylor? Are you sick?"

She looked at him, dry-eyed, the cell phone still on her lap. "I fucked up, Robert. I'm sorry. I fucked everything up."

146   "No, no you didn't, baby. It was just a mistake. A little mistake." He pulled Taylor to her feet, and having no choice, she stood to let herself be guided inside to Sykes's cool bedroom, which opened onto the pool. "We rescheduled for next week. It's all going to work out just fine."

He sat her down on the bed, the bed they'd shared the night before, and so many before that. Taylor insisted upon keeping her own place in the pool house, but most nights she slept in Sykes's bed.

"Here, sit down. I'll get you some water," he said.

"I don't want any water."

"Okay. No water."

The room was damper and significantly cooler than it was outside in the sun, yet Taylor felt her face burning hot.

"I think I confused today's lunch with tomorrow's dinner, so we don't have reservations tomorrow night with those guys from Fox, either," Taylor said, very slowly.

Sykes sighed. A heavy sigh, as though dinners and lunches were where the world both began and ended.

"I just can't keep it all straight," Taylor added. "I don't know if this is working out. You should hire your old assistant back; she was much better at this than I am."

"Honey, it'll be okay," Sykes said, putting his arm around her. "Why don't we just get you an assistant?"

Taylor looked up at him, pushed her hair out of her face and neatly behind her ears. She watched him watching her hands, her hair. Usually this charged her, his attention to her. She could at least see herself in him—what he saw in her. But the heaviness put out the charge. "An assistant to the assistant?" she asked.

"Yeah. Maybe it's too much work for one person," Sykes said. "I need to hire an assistant for my assistant."

Sykes laughed a little, and then the next thing she knew, Taylor was climbing on top of Sykes, kissing his neck, and, once she unbuttoned his shirt, his chest and stomach. Sykes moaned the groans of a happy man and lay back in bed to let Taylor go to work.

Taylor kissed Sykes's dick and held his balls in her hand, even explored his ass gently with a finger. He was in good shape for fifty-one, she reminded herself, coming back up to his stomach. She would get him just to the place before coming, and then she would sit on top of him and let him fuck her that way. With her hands on his hairy chest, Taylor rolled her hips and arched her back. She looked at the art on the wall above the bed and then back down at Sykes, who always kept his eyes closed except for when he came.

Taylor felt like she was going to come too, but squeezed it off to wait for Sykes. "I can feel that," Sykes whined, and so she squeezed some more.

She liked coming when he did, liked the complete and utter control she had over this man, even though on the outside it probably looked the opposite. It wasn't necessarily the money, although that was part of it. It wasn't the fame either, but that was part of it as well. When he came, and finally looked at her with such utter disbelief, devotion (love, even?), that's what made Taylor come too. That someone could feel something

147

that intense for her, could offer her anything, despite every-thing.

It was something Taylor not only couldn't relate to, but she couldn't understand. Why her? And it made her sadder than anything else. Which is why she cried sometimes when she came. It got to where she thought Sykes wanted her to cry more than he wanted himself to get off, so he could hold her after, quieting her and telling her he was going to take care of her, and that everything was going to be okay.

"Stay home for the rest of the day," Taylor said, once she stopped crying. And so he did.

Taylor was the best-looking woman at the gym. She knew it too, but sometimes she could convince herself otherwise, and then she'd do another twenty minutes on the Stairmaster and surreptitiously take stock of who was cruising her as they strutted by the endless rows of cardiovascular machines. It was mostly men—the straight ones at least—and then some women who looked at her, but you could never tell who was a lesbian in L.A. like you could in the northeast. Whether women were looking because they were threatened by her, or because they were *looking*-looking.

Taylor glanced down at the digital display on the machine. A bead of salty sweat dripped off the tip of her nose and onto the shiny plastic. She had three minutes to go, and her wrists ached from holding onto the rails so tightly. When Taylor got off the machine, a guy with a thin build stepped right on behind her.

"Don't you want me to wipe that down for you?" she asked, reaching for a rag and a squirt bottle. He looked down at her, and there was a glimmer of recognition.

Taylor had worked with the guy at the end of the summer, when she was on the TV show. He was Noah, the guy she served with legal papers. They had talked a lot on the set. She couldn't remember his real name though.

"Hey. Taylor, right?" he said, punching beeping numbers into the machine to begin his workout. "Paul?"

"Paul! Right, *hey*," she responded, too enthusiastically, and throwing her towel around her neck. Paul looked like he never sweat. And his hair was perfect—just like he wore it in the show. She had thought nobody in the real world actually wore their hair like they did on TV. His face was so handsome that the rest of his body looked awkward, unable to compete.

"What are you doing now?" he asked, quickly working up to a steady pace on the machine. Taylor saw that he was slightly pigeon-toed as he stepped.

"Nothing much," she said.

"C'mon, you've got to be working."

"I actually kind of gave up the acting thing," Taylor admitted.

"Oh? Why?"

"It's not where I want to be right now," she said. "And I don't think I was so good at it."

"No one's *good* at it," he said, smiling slightly. The way he might give a wry smile on cue for the camera. And then he went on: "You think I *like* playing a rich, drunk kid half my age on that show? Fuck no. But what the hell else am I going to do?" He was talking as if on a panel. It made no difference whether Taylor was listening or not. But she tried to listen. He did have a point about being entirely unequipped to do anything else.

"Listen, with that face, you're bound to get some more work thrown your way. If I'd have given up every time someone said I had a pretty face but couldn't act for shit, I'd still be washing cars right now at the Nu-Look down on La Cienega."

Taylor shook her head. She thought of a car wash's spinning buffers. Then she thought about going for a swim in Sykes's pool when she got home. And she prayed Sykes wouldn't be there.

"I used to work at Nu-Look, I swear. It's in every article they've ever written about me, you can go see for yourself. It's even in *People*."

"Oh, I believe you," Taylor said. Mostly because, what do you say to something like that?

Paul just kept climbing, up and up and up. To nowhere,

149

Taylor realized, as she stood watching him. They were silent for a few moments. A huge crash came from the center of the weight room, where a guy threw down his barbells, bouncing on the rubber mat.

"You know it's the last season for the show?" he asked.

"No, I didn't know that."

"I've got a few projects lined up," Paul began, "so I'm not too worried. But what *are* you doing now?" he asked, as though he couldn't possibly fathom that there was anything else to do but be in the business.

"I'm a personal assistant."

"A personal assistant?" he echoed. "Well, at least it's not waiting tables. Anyone I know?"

"No, I don't know," Taylor said.

"Who?" he pried.

"Robert Sykes," she whispered.

Paul cocked back his head and choked a laugh.

"What?" Taylor asked.

"I used to know someone who was Robert Sykes's 'personal assistant,'" he said, making quotation marks with his fingers. "Only she's now perusing more scripts than she can handle, and I'm not supposed to say anything more about it."

"It's not like that," Taylor protested, suddenly feeling very unsafe with this guy's having the knowledge she had just imparted to him. Stupid. She felt stupid.

"You live in the pool house?" he asked.

Taylor just looked at him. The anger was coming now. Calm and clear, but right under the shell, it bubbled up. She said, "It's been nice seeing you, Paul. I hope we run into each other like this again soon." And she turned and walked toward the women's locker room to get cleaned up and changed.

At the juice bar outside the gym, Taylor put on a pair of sunglasses and perched herself upon a plastic barstool. She ordered a carrot and wheat-grass juice, with garlic and ginseng for an extra boost. She wanted to re-center herself. She had never been centered in the first place.

She started to think, *This is all so ridiculous.* But was it any more so than, say, keeping hundreds of soccer balls out of a big net behind you, or wearing skimpy bathing suits and serving drinks to rich, middle-aged dykes on Cape Cod?

There was never anything more vapid than Los Angeles. But she wanted to believe in it more than anything else. *Where else in the country would I be sitting outside sipping fresh juice after a great workout in the middle of winter?* she asked herself, because that's what you're supposed to say about the place. But then Taylor couldn't even smell the garlic in her drink because of the exhaust from all the sparkling cars speeding by every which way. Several convertibles had their tops down, the owners in sunglasses and jackets. *This is supposed to be Christmastime?*

Taylor missed her old Corolla. Sykes had bought her a BMW to do errands and get around town. He said she didn't have to keep it if she didn't want to—he knew how "independent" she was. She missed how the stick shift poked her in the ribs when she leaned over to roll the passenger side window up or down in her old car. The BMW was a color called British Racing Green, with fully automatic seat adjustments, sunroof, moonroof, mirrors, door locks, and, of course, windows. She hadn't even known there was such a color as British Racing Green.

There was nowhere else to go.

Taylor couldn't go back to Sykes's pool house. Anywhere but there. She had very few friends. She had no friends. There was her mother in Providence. Her uncle Charlie.

The alarm in her British Racing Green BMW chirped a five-beep warning when someone in the neighboring parking space slammed a door shut. She didn't want to get back into that car. Not now. Not ever. Somebody else's car alarm went off, right next to the juice bar where Taylor was sitting, and the piercing sound sliced into her head until she thought it truly wielded the power to drive her crazy. She got up to walk to the curb, gym bag in one hand and car keys in the other. She didn't know where she was headed. Traffic on Santa

Monica Boulevard whizzed by, kicking up windy gusts and bits of street dirt. She had to keep tucking the hair behind her ears every time it blew into her eyes.

She thought of Paul step-stepping away in there, and then of Sykes, who disappeared as soon as he appeared on the screen of Taylor's brain. Then she remembered Marlene, who wrote Taylor a check for a thousand dollars just like that in Provincetown. How some people can just buy you like that. Or buy her.

Taylor cocked her arm and hurled her car keys into the street, hoping a car would run over them or something. Anything to happen. But they landed safely and uneventfully on the median, in some bushes. Robert would be getting home in a couple of hours, and then he and Taylor were supposed to go have sushi with some director and his wife.

There were no buses, no subways, no taxis. If there were, where would they take you? There was a pay phone at the gas station down the block, but Taylor had no money to call anyone. She had no credit card number, no back-up plan. Just a dead battery in her cellular phone, which she could never remember to re-charge. Nothing. There was the beach. She always went to the beach to think. But then she'd have to get into the car and drive to it. There wasn't anyone to call. *Here I am in the corner again,* she thought, over and over, and laughed at herself. Stuck somewhere again, with someone again.

People *wanted* her. There wasn't anyone who wouldn't want her once given the chance. Taylor wove in and out of traffic until she reached the median where her keys were. Suddenly it was the most important thing in the world to find them. It was something to do. She got down on her knees and pushed aside branches of the bushes. There were Kentucky Fried Chicken cups, Coke bottles, and empty, shredded plastic shopping bags. She looked everywhere.

From behind her she heard steps and then a felt hand on her back. It was Paul, finished with his workout, and—as Taylor had suspected—not a drop of sweat on him, his hair still perfect.

"What are you doing?"

"I lost my keys."

"Here? How?" he asked, almost disgusted.

"Are you gonna help me or not?" she said, moving trash aside to scan under the bushes.

"I'm going to help you, but not like this," he replied, pulling out his wallet. "Here's my agent's card. I never give it out. Never. But I think she'd be really good for you."

Taylor looked up at him, having finally located her keys behind a faded pink Diet Coke can.

"My number's on the back if you want to get some coffee or something sometime. But let me know how it goes with her. Okay? Call her. She's a gem."

"Thanks," Taylor said, and then thought for a moment. "Wait, do you have a quarter?"

He fished around in his gym bag. "Yeah." He looked puzzled. "Here."

Taylor took the quarter and put it in her pocket. Paul still held out the card for her. She took it and then watched him turn and carefully cross the street. He walked pigeon-toed, too, didn't just climb that way. She flipped over the card and looked at what he wrote. It was scribbled in child's writing: "Paul Rodgers–home (private please!!)," and then the phone number. Taylor folded it up and flicked it into the rest of the trash beneath the bushes.

153

Taylor found Isak's phone number on a piece of paper in her car. She pulled the quarter out of her pocket and went to the pay phone next to the gym. She didn't know what she was going to say if she got Isak on the phone. She was hoping she wouldn't have to say anything.

The phone rang several times before Isak's mother picked up. "Yes?"

"Is Isak there?" she asked.

"Who's calling?"

"Tell her, well, Taylor."

"Okay, dear. Hold on. Thea!"

Taylor waited and wondered who Thea was. Isak must not have been Isak's original name. When did she get the name Isak, Taylor wondered. It took a long time for Isak to come to the phone, and when she did, Taylor thought she was going to begin crying uncontrollably right there. But she inhaled sharply and held it in.

"Taylor?" Isak asked, surprised.

"Hi. I hope it's okay I'm calling," Taylor said.

Isak didn't respond.

"Is it okay I'm calling?" Taylor asked again.

"Sure," Isak said, but it didn't sound very sincere. "Are you okay? What happened?"

"Nothing. I just, I don't know. I was wondering whether you'd meet me for coffee again."

"Uh, well. Okay. I guess I can. How about this weekend?" Isak asked.

"I was actually thinking more in terms of, well, now," Taylor said.

"Now? Well, okay. I guess I can do that. Are you sure everything's okay?"

"Oh, yeah. I just thought it'd be nice to talk, is all. I'm sort of in a rough place, and I don't want to go home right now," Taylor said, which for her was revealing enough. "Meet at the same coffee shop as before? I'll be there in about twenty minutes."

Taylor sat down at the same table where she and Isak had sat the first time they met for coffee, a couple of weeks before. Isak was late. Taylor was barely holding it together. She felt anxious about summoning Isak, and she didn't want to talk about anything. Rather, she just wanted to sit there with this new person, practically a stranger, who came when Taylor called.

When she saw Isak making her way to the door of the coffee shop, Taylor closed her eyes, took a huge breath in, and then exhaled heavily. She felt instantly better now that Isak was there. That was all it took sometimes, just some interest on another person's part. And a new person's interest went miles for Taylor, much more than somebody who was always there. It told her she still meant something, that she could still drop it all and start anew, if need be.

She rose when Isak came to the table, Taylor expecting a hug or something more intimate than the cool nod and "Hi" Isak offered. They went to buy their drinks in silence.

"So how long are you going to stay in town?" Taylor asked once they sat back down at the table with their drinks. Isak drained the last drops of hot water from her tea strainer and set it on the saucer. She hadn't taken off her hat or jacket.

"I don't know," Isak answered.

"When's your return ticket for?"

"I don't have one."

Taylor thought about how much wasn't being said, on both sides of the table. *No return ticket,* she thought to herself. *That's something.* It was much more fun to focus on other people's situations than on her own.

Taylor watched Isak stir some more sugar into her dark tea. For once, Taylor thought, it might be real. There was so much to talk about honestly, she knew. If she only could. Thing was, Taylor never quite figured out honest conversations. In her heart she wanted to have them, but they never ended up that way. It seemed as though everyone already knew what they wanted out of her before she even opened her mouth, so by the time she did, she had no choice but to say what other people wanted to hear.

She thought she was doing it with Isak, but Isak didn't seem to have everything scripted the way everyone else did. Still, Taylor couldn't stop herself. *Here goes,* she thought.

"So you don't know when you're going back," Taylor said, looking around the coffee shop. She didn't know what else to say. This was supposed to have been easier, Isak's coming to her rescue. "It's nice enough in L.A. if you stay."

Isak didn't respond. She seemed to be in a bad mood that might or might not have been related to Taylor—it was hard to tell.

"Well, you grew up here," Taylor babbled on. She couldn't

155

make herself say anything of substance. "So your perspective might be a little different . . ."

"From what?" Isak asked.

"Oh, from mine, you know, someone who came with stars in her eyes," Taylor said, shifting easily into her ditzy mode.

"Did that guy hurt you?" Isak asked suddenly.

"Who? Robert? Oh no, please. No, he's not like that at all," Taylor insisted. "Why?"

"You said you didn't want to go home."

"No, no. I'm fine."

"Why did you ask me to meet you then?"

Taylor was somewhat rattled by the question, but she could just play her game. "I asked you to coffee because that's what I do. That's what I've always done, throughout my life. I ask people out to coffee or drinks or lunch when I want to get to know them. Then I sort of flirt with them mild to moderately, determine whether they are attracted to me, and then see where it goes from there."

Taylor and Isak stared at each other. Which one would back down first was rather unclear. Also unclear was whether there was anything to back down from. Because Taylor usually won these kinds of stand-offs, and because she was so familiar with them, she just assumed that's what she was doing with Isak, and that Isak would fall in step like everyone else.

Then Isak said, "Well, this is as far as this is going, for your information. No offense, but you're too young, and I'm not interested in becoming involved with anyone right now, much less ever. Not to mention you're Charlie's niece."

"I assumed you'd be like that."

"Like what?" Isak asked.

"Don't get me wrong," Taylor continued. "This isn't about sex. I don't want to sleep with you. There are other kinds of attraction."

Suddenly things brightened for Taylor, and she figured out what it was that she wanted out of the encounter. She had a new project in Isak. She was so handsome, Taylor thought, like a little kid. But then there was something else there that attracted Taylor to Isak. Or at least made Taylor feel like Isak could need her one day. Isak was in need, Taylor could tell, even though she seemed to do everything in her power not to look it. Why else would Isak be staying indefinitely with her parents in L.A. when her life was in New York?

Taylor had no patience. She didn't want to wait to get this thing started. Isak wasn't going to bite readily though. And Taylor knew she needed to consider taking a new tack as she watched Isak walk out the coffee shop door and into the late afternoon haze. For once in a long time, there was nothing Taylor could do to stop a boy from walking out the door. Not, perhaps, since her father? Taylor wondered, and then took comfort in the fact that since then, she'd made damn sure to be the one doing all the leaving.

After three unreturned phone calls to Isak's parents' house, Taylor decided to give it one more final try.

"Ah, hello?" It was Isak's mother.

"Yes, this is Isak's friend Taylor again? Remember me?"

"Yes, honey."

"Well, as you know, I've been trying to get Isak to return my calls for the last couple of days or so, and I just wondered, I guess, is there anything *wrong* with her?"

"Well, dear. Isn't there a little something *wrong* with all of us?" she asked, entirely pleased with herself. "You're in luck though; she's just come in. Honey?"

Taylor waited for a seemingly endless amount of time before she heard a door slam shut, and then Isak: "What, Taylor?"

"Hi, Isak." Taylor tried to make herself sound like sugar.

"What do you want?" she asked. "I've locked myself in the bathroom, so I'm all yours . . . Isn't that what you want? Let's get it all out right now. What is it, Taylor?"

"I don't want anything, I just want to talk to you," Taylor said sweetly.

"Listen, I don't know what game you're playing," Isak started in an angry whisper, "but I'm not living on movie-star time, and I have no interest in getting manipulated into your drama. I have a lot of shit I need to figure out–on my own."

"You know what I think? I think you're afraid of opening yourself up to me. I think you're afraid of being vulnerable and finding out that you could like me."

"Were you actually on *General Hospital,* or do you just write the scripts?"

"You're so mean," Taylor said. She couldn't think of anything else to say. People often resorted to being mean like this, putting Taylor down, as soon as Taylor stopped giving them what they wanted. Usually, Taylor never intended for things to go so far, to the point where someone would be mean like that, but it happened.

All she could hear was Isak's breathing into the phone. It sounded like she was squatting down in an empty bathtub. That's how Taylor pictured Isak: her tough skin contacting the cool porcelain at various places on her body, her elbows, the bottom of her feet, the tips of her shoulder blades.

158

"Why did you call me all freaked out the other day, and then you pretended nothing was wrong when I dropped everything and came to meet you?" Isak asked. "Did you have nowhere else to turn? Are you sick of your sugar daddy? Or just want a new one? 'Cause I'm not it."

They sat on the phone in silence for another minute or so. Taylor thought of hanging up, but didn't. She realized that Isak wasn't the kind of person who would come running after her. A hang-up would mean never speaking to Isak again, except perhaps some time way down the road, at Charlie's funeral or something. The instant she thought it, she wanted to take it back. She wondered whether Isak had conjured a similar image.

And then, finally: "I'm sorry. That was out of line. I apologize," Isak said softly, and Taylor's heart double-pumped against her ribs. The winds had just changed, and Taylor reminded herself to let them. It would come. Isak would come around.

"You know what I think?" Isak said suddenly, loudly. Taylor thought Isak was going to cuss her out. "I think you need to play some air hockey. You ever played air hockey on the pier?"

"No, but I–"

"Well, I didn't imagine you would have. It's not the kind of place your boyfriend would frequent," Isak interrupted.

"Easy now," Taylor warned.

"So, you up for it?" Isak asked.

"It's actually one of the best ideas I've heard since I've been in this hellhole," Taylor said, panicking briefly about what she was going to tell Robert. "I'll come pick you up at your parents' place?"

"No, meet me at the coffee place."

"What time?" Taylor asked.

"Seven."

Taylor hung up the phone and immediately called Sykes at his office. "Robert, it's me."

"Hi baby, what's up?"

"Listen, I need to go out, so I'm going to be off for the rest of the night. Are you gonna be covered? Is there anything else you need me to do?"

He didn't answer.

"Robert? Did you hear me?"

"I heard you. Where are you going?"

"Just to see a friend," Taylor said, but she knew it wouldn't float. So she added, "Remember my uncle's friend? She's still in town and I wanted to see her before she leaves."

"What time will you be back?" he asked. "You know we have that dinner at eight. I told you how important it is, right?"

"Yeah, I know," Taylor said. "But Robert, I think I need a break from it all tonight, okay?"

"What's 'it all'?"

"You know, just everything," Taylor said.

"But Don and Jessica love you. They were looking forward to seeing you. And I miss you. I feel like I haven't seen you in days."

"I know. I'm sorry," Taylor said. "I just need to spend some time with different people right now. I hope you're not upset."

Taylor thought Sykes would keep pushing, making her feel bad and provoking her to put up a fight. But much to Taylor's surprise, and probably because somewhere Robert knew that he had just entered phase one in the process of losing her, he simply said, "Okay. I'll see you at home."

After four intense bouts, Isak and Taylor were split, two and two. Isak told Taylor to hold their place at the table while she went to get some more quarters. While Isak was waiting in line, Taylor took a deep breath and exhaled slowly. There was more at stake here than an air-hockey title. But Taylor couldn't figure out exactly what. She just knew that she wanted to win more than anything else at that moment.

"You and your boyfriend don't fuck around with the air hockey, huh?" a guy asked Taylor. Strangers were always talking to Taylor.

"Oh, he's not my boy—" Taylor started. "He's not my boyfriend. But yeah, we're serious."

"Well, we got next," the guy said, and his girlfriend sidled up next to him, dressed way too scantily for such a cold night.

"Okay," Taylor said. "We just have one game to go. The tie-breaker."

Isak returned to the table, jingling change in her pocket as she strode up. "Is there a problem?" she asked, leaning down to put the quarters in the side of the big machine.

"Nope," Taylor said, noticing for the first time how cold it was in the arcade, which was open to the north, looking out over the Pacific coast.

It was such a cold game too, Taylor thought, what with the shiny silver surface and all the icy air blowing up through the holes. Even the sides of the table were cold, where Taylor rested her hand when she had to reach for a tight shot. Not your typical sunny California pastime.

Isak pulled the puck out of the dispenser and slid it gently toward Taylor. The guy and his girlfriend stepped back to watch the game, and when Taylor saw Isak look suspiciously at him, she reassured Isak with a simple nod that he was cool, and there was nothing to worry about. Isak seemed like she had a lot to worry about.

After a few slower exchanges, Taylor hit the puck at Isak's goal, and Isak returned the shot much harder, banking it twice off opposite sides before it slipped, noisily, into Taylor's goal.

"Shit, fella, you ever heard of letting the girl win?" the guy said, laughing.

Isak didn't say anything; she just waited for Taylor's next shot. Taylor didn't know how she could've let that shot go. She had let her mind wander, when she should've been focusing on the game. It was hard to take any sport less seriously than she used to take soccer. Taylor told herself that she would need to stop thinking and just start playing if she was going to win this one.

She banked a shot that almost caught the right corner of Isak's goal, but Isak blocked the shot by slapping the puck hard against the silver surface and one of the walls. The slap echoed loudly. People in the arcade looked over at their table.

Isak made the next goal, but Taylor answered with three in a row, and it looked grim for Isak from that point out. The spectator guy was laughing into his jacket, which Taylor knew wasn't making things any easier for Isak. A heckler in the crowd could sometimes blow an entire game if he got to you at the right moment.

They traded goals like this, Taylor just one ahead each time, until finally, she nailed another shot with three touches on opposite walls. And then the table blinked, sucked up the plastic puck for good, and the fizz of air blowing up through the table ceased.

Taylor looked at Isak hesitantly, and instead of a sad loser, she saw a satisfied, flushed face on the other side of the table. This had been serious business, but now they could relax a little into the evening, Taylor hoped. Still, she was pumped that she beat Isak in hand-to-hand anything.

"I forgot the whole goalie thing," Isak said, picking up her jacket from the floor and putting it back on. "Hand-eye coordination, that helps."

"Yeah. But I swear I never played air hockey before."

"Oh, that makes it better," Isak said, brushing her hands off. "I'll have you know, I was the reigning champion here for a few years, back in high school."

"Wait, what about another game?" the spectator guy asked, as the two started to walk away from the table. He was lining up his quarters along the side of it.

"Oh, no," Taylor said.

"Come on, guys against girls," his girlfriend added.

"Nope, I think we've had enough competition for the night," Isak said, and she put her arm awkwardly behind Taylor and guided her out of the arcade.

When they got back outside and onto the pier, Isak immediately dropped her arm from Taylor's back, and Taylor wondered why.

"They thought you were my boyfriend," Taylor said.

162

"I know," Isak responded, expanding the distance between them. "Want to get some popcorn and sit at the end of the pier?"

"Okay. But you're buying, because I won."

"Fair enough," Isak nodded.

When they got to the end of the pier, there were a few benches free. After a bit of confusion over which to sit at, ultimately they ended up at the one Taylor thought was summoning them, which faced west, looking at nothing but water.

Isak looked out at the horizon and Taylor followed her gaze. The purple-black sky was barely distinguishable from the ocean. A twinkling tanker floated very far out on the horizon, but Taylor couldn't tell which way it was headed, north or south. Or maybe straight out to sea, toward Japan or something.

Taylor peeked at Isak's handsome face, and then at her whole head, which had an oddly delicate and beautiful shape to it. She noticed a pretty large and fairly new-looking scar on the side of Isak's head, underneath the short, stubbly hair. Taylor didn't know how she could've missed it before. As she wondered whether she should say anything about it, Taylor remembered that Isak had left her hat on the previous two times they met. Taylor decided to leave it, for now.

"I feel like I've known you for a longer time than I have," Taylor said. "But I don't really know anything, like what you do, how old you are, what the deal is with you and Charlie, stuff like that."

Isak looked pained by Taylor's words. "What do you want to know?"

"Well, what do you want to tell me?" It was hard not to slip into her regular flirtatious mode. Taylor had to play this differently. She had to stop and try to think about why she wanted this, whereas she rarely gave things like this a second thought. She just did things, went along, took what people would give her, and yet she knew so well how to make them give her things they didn't even know they wanted to give.

Isak watched Taylor with a strange look on her face. Taylor grew immediately insecure that she didn't know how to handle Isak, and so she just sat there silently. A rarity for Taylor, usually so in control of conversation.

"So who's this guy you live with?" Isak asked.

"Robert? I don't really live with him. I work for him."

"But you go out with him too, right?"

"Yeah."

"He's rich and famous, huh?"

"Yeah, I guess he is," Taylor said.

"Are you happy?"

"Not really. No," Taylor admitted, although she couldn't believe she heard herself saying it. "I mean, I'm happy. I just need to make a change."

"Like what?"

"Like I think I'm going to go back East. Maybe New York some day," Taylor started. "But probably Providence to start out."

"You want to live in New York? Why?"

"I don't know, I've always thought I'd like it there," Taylor said.

"What do you want to do there?"

"I don't know," Taylor admitted. "I don't think I'm really qualified to do anything." And she stopped there, which was honesty enough. What she really could've said was: *"I've never done anything, barring soccer, that hasn't been given to me by someone else. I could've owned part of a bed and breakfast, been a no-talent actor, or just continued to be a terrible excuse for a glorified personal assistant."*

"You don't need to know what you want to do," Isak said suddenly. "I didn't. I still don't."

"What is it you do?" Taylor asked.

"Ah, that's a complicated question." Isak sighed loudly and stuffed a handful of popcorn into her mouth. A few pieces fell onto her lap, and it took some time to chew.

"Why?" Taylor asked.

"It just is. Do you really want to hear all of this? It's kind of boring."

"No, it isn't," Taylor said, and she meant it.

Isak slid down on the bench and kicked her heels up onto the railing in front of them. She brushed the popcorn away, moving almost like a pouty, adolescent boy.

"Well, I cashed in on my middle-class privilege and went to college, and when I came out I was optimistic enough to get into corporate publishing, where I slaved away as an assistant for a few years before giving it up to become a professional temp and part-time street artist."

Taylor watched Isak.

"Better known as 'graffiti.'"

"Oh," Taylor said.

"So basically I've been doing that, being an activist around New York—mostly AIDS-related issues, but other things too—and then most recently I was a member of a freak show, and a sometime accidental hustler."

Taylor didn't know what to say. But she could relate. She hoped Isak could see she could relate. Taylor hadn't paid her

164

own rent but for maybe three months of the last five years. And it wasn't because she was independently wealthy.

"So what are you doing here?" Taylor asked.

"I don't know," Isak said, looking sad. "I fucked up with Charlie."

"It's not too late. It never is, right?" Taylor wanted to put her hand on Isak's head, but she knew she shouldn't. It was so heavy and damp, the salty breeze, and even though she was shaking, she wasn't cold. Taylor imagined that all she ever needed could be sitting here at the end of the pier, but how she would go about getting it was an entirely different story.

"No, I'm afraid it is too late," Isak said then. She stood up and gripped the railing of the pier, and she seemed to be transported elsewhere in that moment, so Taylor let her go. It was just as easy to let something be as it was to make something happen. Maybe even easier.

"Do you want to go?" Isak turned and asked Taylor suddenly.

"Not really, but if you do, that's fine with me," Taylor said. Isak sat back down on the bench, facing Taylor.

"There's something I always think I'm going to get the answer to when I come back here," Isak started, cryptically. "And I never do. It's all I can think about when I'm in this town—that split second before you let go, and everything stops until you land in the dirt under a bridge, a puddle. Somewhere in that second of silence is where I get lost, and I keep thinking I'll figure it out, but then I never do."

Taylor watched Isak. She thrived on intense moments of connection like these; they were so few and far between. She had no idea on what basis they were connecting, but with five air hockey games won and lost, a cold, wet breeze leaving a salty film on every surface, and lights flashing erratically on the outside of the carousel in the distance behind them, Taylor knew it was one of those rare moments. And so she tried to remember every detail at least, even if she didn't know what it was Isak was getting at. Again, she wanted to touch Isak, or for Isak to touch her, but knew it wouldn't be right.

"I guess I just get to the place where I figure out that the answer is that there is no answer," she said. "And you let it go and do the best you can, try not to make the same mistakes over and over again. And that's all you can do."

Taylor nodded her head.

"I'm so sorry," Isak said. "I am being so rude; you didn't ask for any of this. I guess I just got a little caught up listening to myself natter on."

"No, not at all," Taylor insisted. They sat in silence for a long while. Gulls fought over some fish remains on the other side of the pier, their high-pitched calls piercing the dull, thick air.

"I'm going to drive cross-country," Taylor said. "Do you want to come back with me?"

Isak looked up at Taylor.

"I think it'll be pretty soon," Taylor added, "and you said you didn't have a return ticket, so I thought maybe . . ."

"That would be great," Isak said. "Yeah. That might work out. Thanks for offering."

"I mean, we'd have to take that fancy car I have, but it's all I got since I sold my old one when my boss bought me this one for work. At least we know it won't break down." Taylor felt self-conscious of what she was saying, as though it was having less and less relevance with every word.

The two of them walked slowly back toward land, where Taylor had parked the aforementioned car. As she unlocked the door for Isak, Taylor asked, "What happened to your head?" before she could think better of it.

"Ah, well, another long and complicated story," Isak said. "Perhaps if we end up driving cross-country, you'll see for yourself."

Isak directed Taylor to her parents' home. Otherwise, it was a silent ride. When they got there, Taylor pulled up hard on the emergency brake and said: "I was thinking, well, I'm not really doing anything for New Year's Eve, and I was wondering, do you think you'd want to hang out on New Year's together?"

Isak smiled, and Taylor thought something to the effect that this had the workings of a beautiful friendship, or however that saying went.

166

But then Isak said, "No. Thank you, though," and she got out of the car. "Call me when you know better when you might want to leave town," she added, leaning into the car with one hand on the hood and one on the door. Taylor was still slightly shocked from Isak's flat-out refusal to the New Year's proposition.

"I think it'll be sooner rather than later," Taylor managed, but she didn't remember forming the words in her head before saying them.

"You're a pro at air hockey," Isak said. "Don't give that up." She closed the door gently and turned to walk up the brick path to her parents' home. Just before she got to the door, she turned to wave at Taylor, who then put the car in gear and drove back home to deal with Sykes.

11

ISAK

"DO YOU WANT TO HELP ME with this?" my mother asked, holding up another piece of the puzzle. "I'm almost at the tippy-top, and the best part's always the end."

"Aw, leave her alone, Suz," my father said. "She doesn't want to sit around every day making puzzles."

"Sure, Ma," I said, slipping my legs under the coffee table and sitting on the floor next to her. I didn't have much else to do, and it was the only time my mother actually sat still, so I took advantage of the opportunity. And puzzles were easy. It either fit or it didn't.

"Let's see what we have here," I said, hovering over the remaining pieces, feigning interest.

My father poured himself another drink and turned on the TV set. "It looks like some sort of a tire iron is sliding around in the back of this truck here," a news anchor was reporting. My father turned up the volume. "Yeah, that's what I think it is there," the commentator continued, "and a small, shovel-type of instrument. And so, every time this driver makes a sharp turn, what's happening is, these items are *slamming* against the side of the truck bed."

"Oh, hey, Suz, Thea," my father called above the TV, "there's a slow-speed car chase, look here." I crawled a few steps and looked around the corner at the TV set. A red pick-up truck was in fact making its way through the streets, beside a free-way. The camera in the helicopter shook wildly as it was trained on the big truck, followed by four cop cars with their lights flashing. The helicopter's chopping punctuated the news anchor's comments. My father said, "What does this guy think he's gonna do? What a trip."

My mother ignored him and put a large section of the upper Empire State Building into its place. She was much better than I was at both making puzzles and humoring my father. She rested her hand on mine. I had just managed to fit my first piece. I looked down at her hands: there were liver spots all over.

"Did you know it took them only fourteen months to build this thing?" I asked loudly, so my father could hear.

"No, I didn't. That's an interesting little tidbit," my mother said.

"They can't even get the on-ramp to a freeway built in fourteen months," my father yelled over the TV. "Oh, look you two, he's gonna get onto the 10 Freeway, heading west. Right toward us!"

My mother looked at me. She slipped another small section of the base of the building into place. The commentator continued: "Well, I don't know whether you can tell from the pictures, but this truck is what's sometimes called a 'deully,' which has two sets of tires in the rear—that's six tires in all—and it looks like one of the four rear tires is blown out—Whoa! That certainly was a narrow miss in that, uh, intersection there . . ."

"Who's this girl you've been spending so much time with?" my mother asked suddenly. She seemed to be trying to ignore the noise from the television.

"Oh, no one," I said. "Just Charlie's niece. I guess she's still pretty new out here in L.A., so I thought I'd, you know, drop in and see how she's doing for Charlie."

"Oh. That's nice. Is she a, uh–"

"No, no," I said, although I didn't want to be having this conversation. "No, she's seeing some famous director-type guy; she works for him or something."

"Oh, well," she replied. We continued building the Empire State, but my mother was doing all of the work. "Would I know him?"

"Who?"

"The director."

"Oh. I don't know. I can't remember his name. Sykes? Something."

"*Robert* Sykes, the producer?" my mother asked, genuinely impressed. "Wow. Well, he's quite a bit older than she is then, isn't he?"

"Can we talk about something else?" I asked.

"Oh. Okay." I could see my mother's mind spinning. "I'm sorry if I made you uncomfortable."

"You didn't make me uncomfortable. I'm just not that interested in all of that."

"Why, what do you mean?" my mother asked, seemingly hurt.

"Nothing, can we–" I was getting annoyed. "What's your New Year's resolution?"

My mother didn't say anything. She looked toward my father, maybe to see whether he was listening to our conversation. We could hear the helicopter sputtering on the TV and the commentators babbling on, but it seemed as though my father had turned down the volume at some point. My mother looked back down and concentrated hard on the puzzle, fitting a large part of the sky into place.

"Look at this guy!" my father yelled. "They're gonna get him now."

My mother continued to ponder the puzzle as though it were quantum theory. "Your father's been a little depressed lately," she whispered quietly. Previous conversation forgotten. Erased. Next topic.

"It's nothing to worry about," she continued. "I wasn't going to mention anything to you, but since you're here for a while– you're here for a while, right? Well, anyway, I just thought I'd let you know so you could, I don't know, just so you'd know."

"What's going on?" I asked.

"He still has dreams about Hitler, you know. Almost every night," she whispered, looking toward my father to make sure he couldn't hear her. "And personally, I think he's drinking a little too much, but he wouldn't admit it. And he doesn't have a hobby like I do—I've got my tennis—and he doesn't even like playing golf anymore. He doesn't seem to want to spend any time with anyone but me and your brother. And of course you—now that you're here."

"Of course."

I leaned back against the couch. It smelled freshly cleaned. The glass table under the puzzle was streaked with liquid stains. As though she could read my mind, my mother got up to go into the kitchen, and when she came back, wiped up the streaks with some Windex and a towel. *Ah yes, my brother . . .* In the couple of weeks I'd been in town, I'd seen Dan maybe two times, and only in passing at that. We hadn't even had a conversation. If my mother was bad, my brother *really* never sat still.

"When's Dan getting here?" I asked.

"He'll be over soon, after he finishes up with his last client," she said.

"I'll believe that when I see it," I said. My brother wasn't the most reliable sort.

"Oh, give him a break," she said. "He works so hard. And he was out of town for the first week you were here. Anyway, I thought we could all go out for Italian. How does that sound?"

"Fine."

I excused myself and stepped out on the porch. The sun was just going down, and a warm hush settled over the trees and narrow street. A white Volkswagen van parked across the way reflected orange back from the sun. I noticed my stomach muscles were completely tensed, making me curl forward a bit. It felt like I might've been cold, but I wasn't.

A big black truck pulled up behind the van, and my brother jumped out, his dog Bella following behind. He slammed the heavy door behind them, and I watched as he opened the back door to unload a huge laundry bag and sling it over his shoulder. Dan's shoulders looked bigger than I'd ever noticed, harder. It seemed like I hadn't seen him in years. His hairline had crept up his forehead a bit, but he still looked handsome, just more his age. He didn't check in either direction before crossing the street. It occurred to me then that I wanted him to miss me. But I knew he didn't.

Dan didn't notice me watching him from the porch. He spit on the sidewalk before the top of his head disappeared beneath me. He waited as Bella peed on the sidewalk. I went back inside.

"Hey, dude, what's up?" Dan said when he came in. He dropped the laundry bag on the floor. We hugged stiffly: a grab and double-slap on the back, followed by a quick release. I tried to pet Bella, but she went right into the kitchen, as though she lived there.

"Oh, wait, let me get a picture of you two," my father said, coming in from the TV room with a camera. "This is the first time I've gotten you two together since Thea's been in town." He slowly removed the camera lens, while my brother and I waited in an uncomfortable pose for the camera. "Wait, just one more," he said, stepping back without looking. He bumped into a table and some envelopes fell onto the floor. "Put your arms around each other."

173

"That's so sweet," my mother chimed in.

"So, what's up?" I asked as the flash caught Dan in the midst of pulling his arm away from me. "I can't believe I haven't seen you this whole time."

"Nothin', nothin'," he said. "What have you been up to?"

"Nothin'," I said, because it was true. "How's work?"

"It's been good."

"Good?" my father yelled. "Good? You call having more clients than you can handle 'good'?"

"Yeah, I had to hire a couple of other trainers to take some of my clients," Dan said. "Business is good."

"Wow, that's great," I said, looking at the mass of him. His body was huge, his muscles seemingly too big for his frame. It was a miracle we were related.

"I want to see if they've caught this guy," my father said, heading back into the TV room.

My brother looked at me. "Slow-speed chase," I said.

"Shit, what happened to your head?" Dan asked, reaching up and almost touching the scar. I could tell my mother was uncomfortable with the question.

"Oh, I just fell off my bike and hit my head on a curb," I said, pulling away from his hand. Dan had been a lifeguard before he became a personal trainer.

"That looks bad. Must've been some fall. Did you have a concussion? How many stitches?"

Before I could answer, my mother broke in: "Anyone hungry? I'm starved. Let's get some dinner."

We sat in a squeaking, plastic booth at the Italian restaurant, the one on Main Street that had changed names five times since I was a kid. When it was called Sal's, there were bottles of wine in straw hanging from the walls, red booths and red and white-checkered table tops. Now the decor was less gaudy, save for the Christmas decorations draped all over the windows and walls.

I never forgot a time we went there when I was about ten. This young guy had an epileptic seizure at the table next to us. My father tried to catch the carafe of wine that the seizures sent off the table, but he didn't get there in time, and the red wine splattered all over my father's sweatshirt and jeans. He wiped himself off with a shredded napkin as the kid's tongue was rolling out of his mouth and his eyes froze beneath twitching lids, pleading for peace. My mother held my head against her breasts, but I struggled to look through her arms and managed to witness the instant before his muscles relented, returning him to the table–to the present, all sweaty and exhausted. He panted, lungs whistling. I remember thinking that must be the best feeling in the world, knowing that it's over.

I looked at the table where the kid had his seizure. It wasn't a booth anymore, but a table set for six. My father had asked for a different table when we were pointed toward that one. He glanced at me to see if I remembered, but I offered no flicker of recognition.

Dan's pager beeped madly after we ordered. My father

jumped as though it were for him. "Oh, I just have to make a quick call to this client about our session tomorrow morning," Dan said, getting up and tossing his napkin on the table. "She's a big-time model. Be back in a minute."

My father watched him walk toward the front of the restaurant, banging his hand along the top of each booth as he passed. Dan walked around like he owned the world. It must've felt like he did, taking up so much space. I poured three glasses of wine, clinking the carafe against the rim of the last glass. The noise seemed to break my father's gaze.

"I'm glad you're staying in town for so long," he said awkwardly. It was his first attempt at serious conversation since I'd been there. He reached for the glass of wine I poured him. "Your brother's happy to see you too."

"Yeah, it's nice to be with you guys," I agreed, nodding an especially kind *thank you* to the busboy who dropped off four waters.

"You're just looking different these days," he said, sipping his wine.

"I don't work out as much as I used to, the last time I was in town. I mean, compared to Dan–"

"No, that's not it."

"Maybe it's your haircut, it's so *short–*" my mother offered, rearranging the Parmesan cheese and hot-pepper shakers into the center of the table.

"No, that isn't it either," my father interrupted. "I don't know." He stared at me, and then Dan came back to the table.

"Are you seeing anyone, Dan?" I asked immediately upon his return. We weren't going to discuss the topic of me. At least if I had anything to say about it.

"Not really," he said. "A few different girls though."

I nodded. My mother caught my eyes, shook her head in mock disapprobation. Like she could be disappointed with him.

"What? No grandkids in sight?" I asked.

"Well, this last girl with all the credit card debt, she had a couple of kids," my mother said. "But yeah, it'd be fun to have our own some day–"

175

"He's working on it, Suz," my father broke in. "You want another glass of wine?"

"Honey, is that the way they're wearing it in New York these days?" my mother asked after a few seconds. I realized she was back to the hair. "It's almost like a buzz cut or something."

"Yeah, I guess it is."

"Oh, we should have that short hair contest I was talking about the other day," my mother said.

"That's okay, Mom," I said, looking at my brother. "Maybe we can do it later, when we're not at a restaurant."

After dinner, I waited for them outside, leaning against a newspaper rack as shiny cars sped by, reflecting the streetlights. I didn't realize I was shivering until my mother came out with my sweater. I had left it at the table. I felt thirty and ten again at the same time.

When we got back to the house, Dan went into the garage to fold up his laundry and pack up some of his camping equipment. My mother went into the kitchen and unloaded the dishwasher. I sat down in front of the TV with my father.

"I wonder if they caught that guy in the truck," he said.

"They always do," I replied.

"Not always." My father flipped through the channels. "Is this light bugging you?"

"No, why?"

"I don't know, it's just reflecting off the glass or something." He squinted, lifting up his glasses. "It's fucking up the TV."

"I don't see it," I said, picking up a section of the *L.A. Times.*

"I'm gonna–Suz?" he yelled. "Do we have any sixty-watt bulbs?"

My mother came into the TV room, unwrapping a new bulb. My father took it from her and stepped onto the bottom shelf so he could unscrew the old one. My mother went back into the kitchen.

"Ouch, that's hot!" he said, holding the base of the old bulb and stepping back down. "Oh, it's a 120–that's way too much. Who put this in here?"

"Dad, let me do that," I offered, but it was useless. He stepped back up, completely off balance, to screw in the sixty-watt bulb. But he couldn't get it threaded the first few tries.

He stretched so a ribbon of white skin appeared above his sweatpants, bulging on either side over his hips. There was hair there, where I'd forgotten some men get it. Still reaching, my father let his head hang down and grimaced as he twisted the bulb. Thin, wispy hair hovered over his head like a silver halo against the white wall. I chuckled to myself, recalling all the angel talk I was muttering on about in the hospital. I remembered it vaguely, not the specifics, just that twinkles of light were everywhere . . . It looked like heaven in a B-movie or something. It was all my eyes could register through the concussion.

My father finally screwed the bulb in tightly, and went over to flip the switch. "There. That's so much better," he said, a little out of breath. He sat back down in the brown leather recliner. "Don't you think?"

"I can't really tell the difference," I said, looking for another section of the paper.

"What? It's worlds apart from how it was. It's so much better now, can't you see?"

"Dad, I can't tell the difference, okay?" I got up and tossed the paper back into its pile, more upset at the fact that I was annoyed with him in the first place. "If you think it looks better, then it's better." I left the room.

"Suz?" I heard him yelling.

I stood by the kitchen as my mother passed me on the way to my father, clicking her fingernails. She gave me an I-told-you-so look. "What, honey?" she asked.

"Doesn't this look better now with the lower-wattage bulb in there? I changed that one."

"Yes, it looks much better. You can see the shadows in the sculpture *much* better."

"No, that's not it," he said. "Look at the TV. No glare."

"Oh, I see, you're right. It's much better."

"Thea couldn't see the difference."

"Maybe she's tired, honey. Or maybe she just couldn't see the glare from where she was sitting."

"Maybe."

It was strange to hear about myself in the third person again, like they were discussing the odd C on my latest report card. I went into the garage and sat on the hood of my mother's car, watching Dan fiddling with flint, propane, and collapsible fishing rods, among other musty things.

"Where you going?" I asked.

"I'm taking this girl camping up near Tahoe for New Year's."

"Won't it be cold?"

"We're getting a cabin."

"What if the power goes out–you know, big millennium bug?"

"That's a crock of shit," he said.

"So, who is she?"

"Just some girl. I met her at work."

"Ooh, dating a client," I teased. "Sounds torrid."

"She's not my client. She's my friend's client."

"What's her story? You serious about her?"

"I don't think you should sit on the car," Dan said. "You could dent the hood."

"It's a *car*, Dan."

He shrugged. Neither of us said anything for a while. The only sound was my brother's banging around the equipment. Bella slowly plodded into the garage to see where the noise was coming from. Dan rubbed her on the chest and pushed her nose out of the closet. She shook before she turned around and went back into the house.

"So you leave Bella here with them a lot?" I asked.

"Yeah, sometimes when I go out of town. And also when I have long days at the gym. It's just nicer here with the yard. And the beach is so close by."

"And free laundry service too. Not such a bad deal," I said, laughing. But Dan didn't seem to think it was very funny. "Why aren't you taking Bella up to Tahoe with you?"

"This girl's allergic to dogs."

"Oh," I said. "I have a dog."

"I know. I know you have a dog. How is she?"

"Fine, I guess." And then I asked, "Dan, do you think Dad's okay?"

"Yeah, why?"

"Doesn't he seem a little agitated or something?"

"I haven't really noticed. He seems fine to me."

"Are you kidding?" I asked.

Dan held out both of his arms, palms up. He stared at me for a moment. "Thea, you're the one who seems agitated." He turned back to the closet and stuck his nose into a sleeping bag to check the smell.

My mother came into my room as I was pulling on boxer briefs and balancing on one foot. It was the day before the last day of the year, the last year of the millennium. It certainly felt like something was over, though I wasn't quite sure what.

"Ooh, sorry, honey," she said, ducking back out and pulling the door toward her.

"No, it's fine, Mom. Come in."

"Oh, I don't want to rush you, I'll come back," she said from behind the door.

"No, Ma. I said it's fine." I found a shirt and turned my back to her while I pulled it over my head.

"Your shirt's on inside-out."

I looked down. "I know."

"Oh, well. Are you okay?" she asked.

"Yeah, I'm fine."

"You sure?"

"Yep."

"Oh, well, I just came up to tell you that your father wanted to take Bella for a walk down at the beach. I thought it'd be nice for you to go with him. Breakfast will be ready when you get back."

"Did he want me to come?"

"Yes, he's out in the car waiting for you."

"Don't you need some help with breakfast?"

"No, go ahead, honey."

I pulled a sweatshirt over my T-shirt and found some of my father's sweatpants in the old chest of drawers. I rubbed my head but couldn't get the stubbly hairs in the back to lay flat. I rubbed my fingers over the scar and it felt numb. I pulled a ski hat over my head.

In the car my father offered me a no-spill cup of coffee that my mother must've made because it had just the right amount of sugar. Bella jumped from side to side in the back seat, and we headed west.

I wished I had on another layer of clothing. It was windy and cold on the beach, though fall-like in New York terms. The hint of warmth on the breeze from the day before was gone. White caps flickered over the brownish swells. Bella waded in up to her chest, then turned her head to see if we would follow.

"Watch out for the shit," my father said, pointing at the sand. He sounded farther away than a few feet, because the wind drummed relentlessly in my ears.

I laughed, making a production of checking my shoes for any damage already done. I picked up a small piece of driftwood and enticed Bella out of the water. She got sick of my teasing and took off after a gaggle of agitated little sandpipers.

My father and I walked along the high-tide line in silence, which basically just served to make me anxious. I tried to think of something to talk about.

"You warm enough?" he asked, finally.

"Yeah, I'm okay."

He glanced at me and swung his arms behind his back, clasping his hands. He looked out over the waves, toward the peninsula, squinting his eyes at the wind. Then he reached into his jacket pocket and pulled out a small camera. "Call Bella. I want to take a picture of you and her on the beach."

"Do you dog-sit a lot?" I asked.

"Yeah," he said, "we don't mind having her around at all."

"Bella!" I yelled. "Bella, come!" She came after a few seconds.

"Okay, kneel down there–Bella, sit! Good girl," he directed

us. "I hate this dinky thing, but your mother's right–I shouldn't bring my nice equipment out on the beach."

My father kept turning the camera horizontally then vertically, then back again. And then he knelt, stood up again, crouched down low.

"Dad–just take the fucking thing, okay?"

"Just one more second . . . I can't get it to look quite right–there," he said finally, standing up and sliding the lens cover closed. "I don't know why you're being such a pill. Mom will love it." I knew he was right. That was exactly the kind of thing that would make my mother happiest: a picture of me and Bella stuck to the refrigerator with the Big Apple magnet I sent one year in lieu of myself for the holidays.

And then my father said: "You're not really happy, are you?" He didn't look at me after he spoke.

"What?"

"I said, this life–this life you claim to have in New York, it doesn't really make you happy, does it?"

"I'm happy."

"I'm your father, don't you think you can tell me?"

"There's nothing to tell."

"What? What is it, what happens every day in that little apartment of yours? What are you doing back here after all this time?"

"Dad–"

"Don't think we don't like having you here, because we do," he started, holding up his hand to silence me. "But you got to give us a little something. Tell us what's going on with you."

I didn't say anything.

"Are you here for good, or what?" he asked after a while. Still, I didn't respond.

"Is it money?" he asked. "Because if that's it, then just say the word."

I looked down at the wet sand and stomped a footprint into it.

"All right, you don't want to talk to your father. Fine."

"What is this? We *never* talk," I finally said.

"Well, we can talk now, I'm here, I'm asking now, so talk to me."

We both stopped. I watched Bella, who was chewing on a stump of driftwood. It looked like the tanned elbow of a deer or something.

"I've actually–I've been the one worrying about *you*," I started. I could never get through any discussion with him without that rush through my system that kills my appetite and makes me a little nauseated. And it hit then, so I stopped what I was saying and knelt down, planting my knuckles in the cool, wet sand.

My father came over and put his hand on my shoulder–as though he hadn't touched anything like me before. "You okay?" he asked, patting my back awkwardly.

"I'm fine," I said adamantly.

He just stood there staring at me. I don't think he knew whether to bend down and wrap himself around me, or to haul off and kick me. I don't know which I'd have preferred. Probably the latter.

I finally stood up and looked right at him. He waited for me to say something–anything–but I wouldn't. He shook his head at me the way he always did at my mother. I rolled my eyes and bent again to pick up a flat rock from the sand.

I wound up and hurled the rock over the foam. After I released it, when it was too late to change, I realized that I had wanted to skim the rock along the surface of the water. But it sank without a bounce.

My father shifted his weight, clearing his throat in that way I hate because sometimes I catch myself doing the same thing. I stepped closer to the water line, drenching the tips of my tennis shoes. The water was cold. I saw a bigger rock, picked it up, and threw it as far as I could. No bounces. We used to skim flat rocks for hours like this when I was a kid.

Then I threw another, and another. They got bigger and bigger each time, none of them skipping like they are supposed to. Or at least supposed to if you are playing the rock-skipping game. My father watched me until I winced when a ligament in my shoulder popped over a bone. Maybe he heard it. I think I heard it. I turned to head back to the car, and I could see out of the corner of my eye my father's hand hovering over the space where my shoulder had been a second before.

When I was a kid, I was the only girl in the peewee football league. Most of the kids didn't know I was a girl, and the rest didn't really care, because I was such a good wide receiver. I remembered when the biggest bully in the league, Jake Wilder, cracked my collar bone during a game we played against his team, the Mini-Steelers. I was so humiliated that I was the one who got hurt, that I ended up cracked and broken when I was just trying to stay under their radar. But really, it was an unfair hit. Jake got ejected from the game.

I remember sitting in the back seat of the car with my father while he supported the weight of that same shoulder all the way to the emergency room. My mother drove us there—with one foot on the accelerator and one on the brake. It was probably the last time my father actually thought he could hold me together.

183

My father didn't speak much to me after we returned from the beach, but when we got back to the house, he immediately went to the bedroom and came back with over seven hundred dollars in cash in his hand, and gave it to me without saying a word.

I hadn't taken money from them since college, and the last thing I wanted to do was start ten years later, but I just took it. I started to say, "Thank you," but he shushed me and walked away.

Breathing was hardest for me on the last day of the year. It was like I couldn't fill my lungs. Taylor had called to say that she wanted to leave a week or so after the first, and I told her I would definitely drive cross-country with her. I couldn't wait to get out of there.

My mother and father were getting ready for a New Year's Eve party. "Honey, I'm sure you have big plans for tonight," my mother said. "We're going to a party at the Silvermans's, but we'll be home right after midnight."

I pictured a bunch of older married couples–the women in layers of fabric swathed around them like sarongs, the men in spruced-up leisure suits–sipping champagne and discussing technological stocks.

"Of course, you're welcome to come with us," my mother added unconvincingly. Then I pictured myself standing in the middle of the Silvermans's living room–with all of them staring at me like I was an auto wreck. All I could think of was maybe escorting one of the single or widowed older ladies, and making a few bucks on the evening. But somehow I didn't think my folks would approve.

"You two go along and have fun," I said to my mother. My father shuffled into the room holding up two shirts, one after the other, like an offering at an altar. My mother pointed twice at the one in my father's left hand–a beige button-down with two chest pockets. "I'll be fine. Mind if I take one of the cars tonight?"

184

"No, not at all," my mother said. "Where are you going?"

"Remember how crazy it is around here on New Year's," my father interrupted, his comb-over not quite settled on his scalp. "The crazies are out. You be careful, Thea."

"Isak."

"What, like New York doesn't have its share of crazies?" my mother asked. "Go finish getting dressed; we're late. Isak, have fun, but be careful. Happy New Year."

She kissed me on the cheek and sort of winced, as though in pain. Maybe I smelled different to her, or the skin on my cheek was a different texture than she remembered. My mother's perfume assaulted me too; it made the inside of my nose twitch and sting. I felt a sneeze coming on.

"Oh, I wanted to let you know I figured out when I was leaving," I said, just as they were about to walk out the door. My father looked at me knowingly, while my mother seemed surprised.

"Why? I mean, when?" she asked.

"Probably in a week," I said. "Taylor, that niece of Charlie's, she's driving cross-country, so I'm going to hitch a ride with her."

"Oh, well," my mother said. "No rush. I mean, it's been a pleasure having you."

"I know, thanks," I said. My father jingled the keys. "It's just time to get back, is all. You know."

"Where's she going?" my mother asked.

"Who?"

"The girl, is she leaving that man?"

"I don't really know," I said, utterly confounded by my mother's interest in Taylor.

"Oh, well, okay," my mother conceded. Then it was on to the next thing, and she leaned over to plant another kiss on my cheek. Again, her perfume overwhelmed me. "Have fun tonight. Be safe. Love you."

They closed the heavy door behind them. I peeked through the curtain and watched my father pull my mother's car out of the garage, my mother getting in once he was in the street. Their front bumper scraped the curb. I could hear it from inside the house.

185

After sitting around and watching TV in my parents' empty house, I decided to get in the car and take a drive. The streets were relatively empty. I found myself driving through Westwood, past the Mormon temple, which was bathed in gold light. I pulled up in front of the American Lung Association's billboard over Santa Monica Boulevard. It displayed the number of smoking-related deaths so far that year: *430,688*. Seemed feasible. But how did they know they were smoking-related, and how did the ALA get the statistics so quickly? Or was it an estimate, based on the number of deaths from last year?

I parked where I still had a good view of the sign, got out of the truck, and climbed onto the hood. I reclined on the windshield and looked up at the sign. I'd driven by it so many times, watched the numbers climb. Usually by four or five in the time it took me to drive through the neighborhood. I'd always wanted to spend a New Year's Eve in front of it. Real exciting stuff. None of my friends (or those people I used to spend time with in high school) ever wanted to do it with me. Never even wanted to drive by it on the way to somewhere else.

So there I was, finally. Twenty-one minutes until midnight. *430,690. 430,691.* I decided I needed a drink, so I ran over to the 7-Eleven across the street and bought a Schlitz malt liquor. It seemed like the thing to do. Plus, it was on sale.

It was at *430,694* when I got back up on the truck's hood. *430,695. 430,696.* Nine minutes until midnight. I was nursing the brown-bagged, wide-neck bottle. The shit tasted like shit, but drinking it felt warmly reminiscent of something. Of what, I didn't know.

430,697. Of course. People were croaking all the time. From everything. Why not cigarettes? *430,699.* The street was eerily empty. A cold, blue haze seemed to wet everything down. *430,700.* One minute left until three A.M., according to my watch, my time zone, which I had never switched over to Pacific Standard Time.

430,701. A few gunshots went off to the south. *They're jumping the gun,* I thought, cracking myself up. I couldn't resist. *430,702.* I looked up at the yellow glow that was the sky and wondered briefly whether I should get underneath something. There was that tourist from Florida who died when a falling bullet lodged in her head one New Year's Eve in New York. What were the odds of that?

A few more gunshots. I wondered if this was what my father meant by "the crazies." The gunslingers. Or maybe me. *430,703.*

Then it cleared to all zeroes. But I couldn't remember what number it had been before it turned. Just like that—infinitely quicker than an old car's odometer turns. But less satisfying. And so I sat there waiting for the first smoking-related death of the year. Of the millennium. I took another sip from my bag, listening to the crinkling of the cold paper. The street remained eerily silent for a few more seconds before horns started honking and more gunfire peppered the wet, muffled hum of the streets. I waited still, but it was all zeroes. No one had died yet. Or maybe the bug had struck.

I remembered that many people here in L.A. base their New Year's Eve midnight time on New York's—or at least on when that stupid ball falls in Times Square. It seems ridiculous to base something like the passing of another year on something that happened three hours before, not to mention three thousand miles away. But I always watched that show, thinking that was where I wanted to be more than anywhere else. In New York, where I could stay a few steps ahead of everyone else because things happened there first. But when I got to New York, I never even considered coming within fifty blocks of Times Square on New Year's Eve. And I can't say I ever figured out whether it's an apple or a ball that drops.

I slid off the hood of my father's truck, which was slick with a dirty layer of mist. My butt left two distinct paths through the misty film. I looked back up at the sign: still zeroes. A few more delinquent gunshots went off. I got into the car, dropped the malt liquor bottle on the gravel underneath the truck, and closed the door behind me.

When I looked up again through the tinted strip in the top of the windshield, the sign had changed. The first death of the year. And I had missed it because I was littering. Our civilization was supposed to collapse because of 1's and 0's, and yet this dinky, morbid sign had gotten it right.

Then there were two deaths, and three, and so on, in that seemingly deliberate, quasi-random, and semi-believable pattern. The tint in the windshield made the numbers look green. Like time on a digital clock. Keeping some fucked up, mechanical time, clicking in the same place over and over again.

And constantly resetting itself.

187

12

ARLENE

CHARLIE'S MOVING VAN was a bright yellow color. It looked unnecessarily loud in the otherwise tasteful neighborhood. He pulled up in front of the house, waving out the window with his left arm. The dog jumped from the dashboard to the open passenger window, and then back again.

"Hi, honey," he said, as soon as he got out of the car. Charlie immediately went around to the other side of the truck, clipping a leash to the dog's collar and then letting it jump out onto the street. It pulled hard on the leash; Charlie had to lean backwards to hold the dog back.

"Arlene, this is Mary." I just stood there, but then it felt like I was expected to do something, like pet the dog. But it was so hyper.

"Hi, Mary," I said, and Charlie laughed. I didn't know whether he was laughing at me or the dog.

"He's a little excited after being cooped up for four hours in the truck," Charlie said. "Plus, the move's kind of freaking him out. Isn't it, boy?" The dog jumped up on him. I'd never seen Charlie act like a parent, never thought I would. But here he was, as much of a caretaker as I'd ever been. Never mind the species.

I looked at the yellow moving truck with all of Charlie's belongings in it, then back at Charlie and the dog. Charlie was letting it pee on a tree pushing up through the brick sidewalk. I wondered if there was room for second thoughts.

"Well," I said. But I didn't have anything to say. "Are you tired? Do you want to come inside?"

"Sure."

We walked up the stairs to the house, and I wondered what Charlie was going to do with the dog. It was silverish, like no color I'd ever seen on an animal. And Charlie didn't look sick at all. A little thin, but no, not sick.

"Do you want to put Mary in the yard?" I asked.

"Uh, well, he's kind of nervous," Charlie started. "I think it'd be better if he stayed with me, got used to you a little, you know, smelled the house."

"Oh, okay."

Charlie unhooked the leash and Mary immediately started sniffing everywhere, frantically, with his nose down and tail up. Charlie went into the kitchen, and I followed him.

"Do you have a Tupperware container or something to give him a little water?" he asked. "His bowls are packed away somewhere in the truck."

"Sure, sure," I said. I didn't know what I had that I would want a dog's mouth touching, but then I found an empty plastic margarine tub and handed it to Charlie.

He filled it up with cold water and placed it on the floor next to the refrigerator. "Mary? Mary, come!" he yelled.

The dog came running into the kitchen, the tags on its collar jingling loudly. It looked up at me on the way in, before heading to the water and lapping up the entire contents of the bowl. There were splashes of water everywhere, on the wall, the floor, the side of the refrigerator.

"I guess he was thirsty," Charlie said.

"Would you like something to drink?" I asked, surveying the splashes everywhere.

"No. I'm fine for now," he replied, noticing me notice the mess. Charlie found the paper towels under the sink and wiped up the water. Then he filled the bowl with water again, and the dog repeated the same scene as before.

"So, the store's open right now?" Charlie asked. "I mean, you didn't close it on my account?"

"Oh, no. No, I have a girl watching it for me, Elizabeth. She's great. She's a Brown student who just wants to pick up some extra money on the weekends. She's the first person I've found who I can actually trust to be alone there for a few hours."

"You should get back. I mean, if you need to, don't worry about us."

"She's fine for now. I'll go back in a couple of hours," I said. "Do you want to sit down, or do you want me to help you unload some of your things?"

"I don't have much stuff," Charlie said. "And a lot of it can go straight to the basement."

"Sure."

"Are you okay, Arlene?"

"What do you mean? I'm fine."

"You just seem anxious or something. Is this too much?"

"No. No, not at all," I said. "Come upstairs and I'll show you what I've done with the rooms." Just then I realized Charlie and I hadn't touched once since he arrived.

We left the kitchen, and quite by accident, I made eye contact with the dog. It came running at me from across the living room, and I knew it was going to jump on me. All the terror involved in inviting an unknown quantity into my house like that, all of it came rushing at me in slow motion as the dog approached. Its ears flapped, tongue wagging with teeth flashing underneath. Vicious. I shielded my midsection with my arms. I didn't care what happened to my arms, I just didn't want the dog penetrating my center. I tensed up and prepared for the worst, but then Charlie yelled "Off!" very loudly, and the dog stopped short right in front of me.

"You should pet him," Charlie said. "He probably senses you don't like him."

Catching my breath, I patted the dog on the head, and much to my surprise, it just sat there and let me.

Upstairs, Charlie looked into every room and said the same thing: "Fabulous. It looks really great in here."

I showed him my old room. "And I thought this is where you could stay."

He looked at me, puzzled. "Wasn't this your room? I can't stay in here."

"I want you to," I said. "It was Ken's and my room. It's time to move on, don't you think?"

Charlie didn't answer, just looked at me.

"I'm staying in Taylor's room," I added. "I think it'll be comfortable for you in here."

"Arlene."

"What? I've already been out of there for a few weeks now. It feels great."

"It just seems odd," Charlie said.

"Well, there's the guest room too."

Charlie seemed to think for a moment. Mary came up the stairs and entered the room in front of us. It looked bare in there, with all of my things removed. This was the first time I'd been in since moving out and scrubbing it wall-to-wall. The room looked smaller than I usually thought of it, with the dog standing there in the middle of the tattered throw rug. He looked up at us expectantly.

"I think I'll just stay in the guestroom, if you don't mind," Charlie said.

"Suit yourself, but it's just going to sit here empty."

"I have to take a leak," he blurted. Charlie could be crass that way.

And then there we were, just me and the dog, who stared at me and then at the bathroom door where Charlie was, then back again at me, and so on.

I went downstairs and the dog followed me. I felt an overwhelming urge to feed it something, but I didn't know what that would possibly be. I went to the back door and opened it, but the dog wouldn't go outside. He kept looking in the direction of upstairs, where Charlie was.

"Go on," I whispered, but it just looked at me, picking up its front paws, one after the other. "Go on, you can go out there. It's for you."

Charlie came down the stairs. "I'll take him on a walk. Do you want to come?"

192

"Oh. Okay," I said. "I was just seeing if he liked the back-yard."

"He'll warm up to it," Charlie said, hooking the leash to Mary's collar again. The dog spun around in front of us. "Do you have a bag?"

"What kind?"

"You know, like a poop bag, a plastic shopping bag?"

"Oh, yes, in the kitchen," I said, heading to get some.

When I came back with several, Charlie smiled. "One's fine."

It was a naked, gray winter day. I saw Eva Boorman across the street, rolling a garbage can down her driveway and onto the curb. She waved, so I thought it would be rude not to cross over and visit.

"What a nice dog," she said as we approached, but she was looking at Charlie.

"Eva, this is my brother, Charlie. Charlie, Eva Boorman."

"Nice to meet you," Charlie said.

"Likewise." I could tell Eva was curious. She rubbed her nose with the back of her work glove. Her cheeks were red from the cold. Broken blood vessels crisscrossed the surfaces where the sharp features protruded from her face.

"Charlie's staying with me for a while," I offered.

"Oh, that's nice. What brings you to Providence? Work?" she asked Charlie.

"Yes, you could say that," he said.

"Arlene, who knew you'd have such a young and handsome brother," Eva started. "Have you been holding out on us? You're probably not even forty yet."

"Oh, Eva," I said. "I'm forty and then some. This is my *baby* brother."

Charlie stood there with a small obligatory smile on his face.

"Well, that's a very pretty dog you have there," Eva said to him again. I prayed she wouldn't ask what its name was. "What's his name?"

"Mary," Charlie said.

"Oh, she's a *girl*." Eva looked back at her house, toward the garage. "Well, since George is out of town, I'm the one who has to get this recycling out for tomorrow. Nice meeting you, Charlie. Welcome to Providence."

"Thanks. Nice meeting you too."

"Good-bye, Arlene. Thanks for visiting."

When we got to the park, Charlie asked, "What's her story?"

"Eva? Oh, she's nice enough. George is a pilot. Her third husband. She's a loyal customer, comes into the store all the time."

"She's kind of nosy, then," Charlie said.

"No, not any more than anyone else. She was just being nice."

A couple of hours later, I left Charlie to unpack some of his things. He refused my help, so I figured I'd be more useful back at the store. I wondered about dinner too, but Charlie seemed uninterested. He had a look on his face that was sort of stunned, but calm. His skin was so soft-looking, like a little boy's. I wanted to touch it.

194

When I got into my car and closed the door, something popped inside of my chest, and I simply couldn't catch my breath. I sat there with my hands on the steering wheel for a few moments, but then Charlie came out and unloaded a few more bags from the back of the big yellow truck. Mary shadowed his every step. Charlie looked over at me and waved, so I mustered enough energy to wave back and start the engine. I didn't want him to think anything was wrong. It wasn't.

When I got to the bottom of College Hill, I started shaking. I hadn't known I was shaking until I looked down at my hands on the steering wheel and saw that the fingers were blurry through my wet eyes. I pulled the car over just after crossing the river, and I cried.

I cried without stop until I noticed it was dusk.

I pictured the blood in Charlie's veins, and I told myself it was bad blood. That though I wasn't sick with anything, I had it too.

You spend your whole life getting hurt, and out of it you hope for some grace somewhere in all that hurt. But Charlie just got more hurt. A death sentence not too far off from his life sentence. Or maybe it was all the same. I didn't know, because nobody told me anything.

Our father used to hit Charlie with a candlestick, and there was nothing I could do to stop it. Invariably, he used one of a pair of candlesticks that our mother kept on the dining room table, though they were never used for their original purpose of holding candles. I would always be on my way out of the house, and I would hear Dad on the couch berating Charlie for the way he walked, talked, or sat. Or the way Charlie wouldn't make eye contact with you when he spoke. *If Mom would only take those candlesticks off the table,* I remember thinking.

I didn't know what I was going to do with this Charlie either. Didn't know how to save him. I simply got up in the mornings and went to the store, made phone calls, opened boxes, dusted, paid bills, talked to customers, and then drove home at the end of the day. This was the extent of my existence. But I had a sense that all of this was going to change.

195

I wiped my eyes, blew my nose, and then went to close up the store. Charlie would be waiting for me at home.

New Year's Eve: Charlie and I sat on the couch and ate some dinner. He cooked some tofu-rice-vegetable type of a dish, which was actually, to my surprise, quite delicious. And healthy, he claimed. I had always thought tofu was bland and tasteless, but I'd had it only once.

We flipped on the TV to watch Dick Clark just about an hour before midnight. Charlie went to get the sparkling cider from the kitchen. Mary was curled up next to me on the couch, and he was surprisingly warm and soft.

"Cheers," he yelled, when the cork popped out.

"Cheers," I echoed. "To the next millennium."

"Actually, it doesn't really start until next year," Charlie said. He poured the cider carefully.

"I don't get that," I admitted, but I didn't want him to explain. Charlie must've understood, because he just passed me a glass of cider and then clinked his against mine. We drank from the fancy crystal champagne glasses Ken and I got at our wedding. A gift from Ken's parents.

Besides the TV set, it was dark in the room. I watched Charlie as I sipped. His face appeared eerily gaunt in the blue glow from the TV. He looked at me when he sensed my stare.

"Did you ever go to Times Square to watch the ball drop in person?" I asked.

He paused for a moment, perhaps considering why I was staring, what I was thinking. He still looked sickly, the dark shadows collecting in the hollow spaces of his beautiful face.

"No. I've never been," he started, slowly. Charlie took another sip of his cider. "I don't think anyone from New York City actually goes to that thing."

"I always wanted to go," I said.

196

"Mind if I get some light in here?" Charlie asked. I shook my head.

As soon as he turned on the light, Charlie immediately returned to the living, cheeks rosy, eyes bright. His hair was longer than he used to wear it, and he looked particularly young, handsome.

I stopped staring at Charlie, but now he was staring at me. The phone rang and I was glad to hear it. I picked up. "Happy New Year?"

"Mom, hi." It was Taylor.

"Hello," I said. "How are you? Where are you?"

"I'm at home, getting dressed."

"What are you doing tonight?" I asked.

"Going out to some industry party. My boss is taking me. It's nothing special, just a schmoozing type of a thing." She spent a great deal of time with this boss of hers. She even lived in his home, or in the guest house of his home. She didn't say much about him.

"How are you doing?" Taylor asked. She sounded particularly sweet. "What are you doing?"

"Well, Charlie and I are sitting here watching Mr. Dick Clark on the TV," I said, remembering that before Taylor moved out of the house, we watched Dick Clark on every New Year's Eve, religiously. I wondered whether she was remembering the same thing. "We just finished dinner and now we're having some pseudo-champagne."

"Sounds fun," Taylor said, with a hint of melancholy in her voice. "Is everything okay, Mom?"

"Sure, we're okay, honey. Are you?"

"Yeah, I am." She didn't sound very okay. But then, I suppose, neither did I.

"Well, what a surprise to hear from you. What a pleasant surprise."

"Yeah. Well, I just thought I'd call and wish you a happy New Year," she said. "Listen, I can't talk much right now, but would it be okay if I came back home for a while?"

"Of course. Of course it would," I said. I wondered what in the world could be going on, but I knew she wouldn't tell me. "Is everything all right? Why can't you talk about it?"

"Oh, it's nothing. I just haven't told my boss completely yet, and I don't want to say anything until I know for sure that I'm leaving. Can I say hi to Charlie?"

"Sure. Sure," I said. "But Taylor, there's one more thing. I'm staying in your room now. I hope that's okay."

There was silence on the other end of the line.

"Tay, did you hear me? I'm in your room now, Charlie's in the guest room, so I hope it's okay you'll be in my old room."

"Okay, whatever," Taylor said. Maybe she would understand once she got here.

"How are you getting here? When are you coming?"

She didn't respond. Her boss must've been in the room because she just said, "Okay, I will."

"Can you call and tell me the details at a more convenient time?" I asked.

"Sure. You bet."

197

"Okay, well, here's Charlie." I passed him the phone.

"Hi, you," Charlie said. He brightened as soon as I gave him the handset. "Yeah, I can't believe it either," he said, sipping his cider. "No, it's going great."

I wished I could hear the other side of the conversation. What Taylor was saying. The animation in Charlie's responses suggested he'd established an intimacy with her that I hadn't enjoyed in years.

"What? No, please!" Charlie yelled. Another pause.

"Girl? Were those yours or did they stuff that bra?" Charlie asked, then laughed, genuinely laughed in a way I hadn't seen him do once in the week or so he'd been in Providence.

They barely knew each other, I thought. Their connection was through me. And now I seemed superfluous. This was the familiar but long-lost jealousy, which I thought I had given up shortly before Ken and I separated. But then it popped up in almost every case where Taylor was concerned—when she spent all of her time with that coach Jill in high school, her other teacher at boarding school, her boyfriend in college. Then she stopped telling me altogether.

"I'll just decide for myself when you get your ass here," Charlie said, and then he paused again. "Okay, what? Shoot." He listened for a long while and his face grew serious. "Okay. Okay. Mm-hmm."

I watched the TV, trying to block out Charlie's conversation. Some band in glitter suits was singing a love song. The boys didn't look a day over seventeen. *What on Earth are they talking about?* I wondered.

"Okay. No, it makes sense," Charlie said. "I'd rather you be with someone than alone. No, I know. Okay, I love you. Can't wait to see you either," he went on. "Wait, do you want to say anything to your mom? Okay, I'll tell her. Drive safely."

Charlie hung up. "She said to say she loves you."

I reached for a smile, but it wasn't coming. "What else did she say?"

"Oh, nothing really. We were just joking around about the TV show, Hollywood, you know, poking fun at her expense."

"Taylor doesn't really do that with me."

"Oh, honey," Charlie said, looking at me. "I'm sorry, I didn't mean to–"

"No, it's not you," I interrupted him. "It's me. It pretty much always has been."

Charlie watched me with both hands cupping his champagne glass. I looked back at the TV, and as soon as I did, Charlie did the same.

"This guy's a trip," Charlie said, when Dick Clark was interviewing the boys who had just been singing. "What's the joke about him?"

"I don't remember."

I spent a lot of years not saying what I thought, a lot of those years just trying to figure out what it was I thought. Charlie didn't seem to know this, nor did Taylor. Nobody. I struggled with myself every day to figure out what it was with me and Taylor. Now to see my own brother seem to work something out with her, behind my back for god's sake. It was a secret I wasn't willing to let go by without trying to intercept. Secrets had passed practically invisibly, just over our heads, like darting mosquitoes, for all these years. Now maybe I could grab one and kill it before it sucked any more out of me.

"Charlie." I said it much louder than I had intended. "I want you here in my home, but I won't live with another family member who disregards me, shuts me out, and goes on with her life thinking I don't know the first thing about what's really going on."

He looked at me, surprised. It was, perhaps, the first time I'd been this blunt with him in our lives.

"I may be out of it," I continued, "but I do have some intuition, and I won't ignore it anymore, and also won't let any of you ignore it either."

"Arlene, what's going on here?" Charlie asked. "I thought we were all right?"

"We are 'all right,'" I said, making quotation marks around the words, the way Charlie did so frequently in casual conversation. "What were you talking to Taylor about on the phone, and why haven't you talked about it with me? What's wrong with me?"

"Nothing's wrong with you. I just didn't think you wanted to hear this kind of stuff. I mean, you never really have."

"I always have. Where did you get that?"

"I guess we just never, you know, really talked about some of these things," Charlie said.

"Well, I want to now."

"Okay. Well, she just said that she was driving cross-country with my friend Isak," Charlie began, hesitantly. "And she wanted to make sure that it was okay with me, since, well, you don't really want to hear all of this–"

"I do!" I exclaimed, maybe a little too eagerly.

"Well, since Isak and I kind of broke up, if you will, and we haven't been getting along."

"I didn't know you were a couple," I said, but even as it came out I wanted to retract it. I felt stupid, as though I was supposed to have known something I didn't, that I had missed it all yet again.

Charlie looked at me with disappointment, or maybe resignation. "We aren't. I mean, we weren't. It was just a figure of– forget it." He looked back at the TV. It was about eighteen minutes to midnight.

"Maybe we can talk about it in the morning?" Charlie asked after a few seconds. He looked tired.

"What? What'd I do? I'm sorry. What did I say?"

"Nothing," he said. "Let's just take it slow. Let it happen instead of force it, you know what I mean?"

I didn't, but I also did. And then I just wanted to be alone, like usual.

"I'm going to go upstairs to bed and read," I said.

"It's almost midnight," Charlie said, but I could tell he thought it was a good idea too.

"Are you okay, can I get you anything before I go up?" I asked him.

"No, thanks though." Charlie patted the dog on the rump,

and they both watched me get up and head for the stairs. "Happy New Year."

I couldn't believe there was a dog sitting on my couch.

"Happy New Year to you," I echoed. And then: "None of it's really easy, is it?"

"Mm-mm, no," he answered, shaking his head.

"Well, I love you."

"Me too. Goodnight."

"Goodnight."

It took me just a few days living under the same roof with Charlie again to see that I was acutely equipped to deal with both his life and death sentences because, I realized, mine were practically identical to his. Our crimes were just slightly different.

13

TAYLOR

"SO, DO YOU LIKE POP, or rock, or what?" Taylor asked, just as she pulled onto the 10 Freeway heading east. Probably for the last time in a long time.

"I like jazz—mostly stuff from the '20s and '30s," Isak said. "Whatever is fine, though."

"Oh, well, I don't really know any jazz stations," Taylor replied. She looked in her rearview mirror for the ocean, but she couldn't see it over the gentle rise of the Santa Monica foothills.

"We'll lose L.A. radio in an hour or so anyway," Isak said, pushing the button to roll down her window just a crack. Cool air exploded into the car and thumped in Taylor's right ear. The straps on their bags flapped violently in the back seat. "I think I have a couple of tapes somewhere, but we have plenty of time to listen to them," Isak added, rolling the window back up, sealing the car off from the city that raced by their windows, just a blur.

"Great," Taylor said, but Isak didn't make a move to get the tapes. She just sat there, calm.

Taylor adjusted her rearview mirror. She caught a glimpse of herself in it, and as quickly as she saw herself, she looked away. She wondered whether this escape from Los Angeles was accelerated by Isak's appearance in her life. But she didn't want to admit that it was. And then she thought of Robert, who had cried when Taylor pulled out of his huge, circular driveway that morning. She wouldn't miss him a bit. This was another one of those things, those situations, you just left.

Taylor tucked her hair behind her right ear and watched Isak shift in her seat several times. *Maybe she's uncomfortable,* Taylor thought. Besides "Here we go" and the brief discussion about her musical taste, Isak hadn't offered anything but one-word answers to Taylor's questions. Taylor could tell something was off with Isak, but she didn't feel like it was her place to inquire as to what it might be. Taylor was convinced that Isak's mood was a reaction to her, that Isak didn't want to be driving cross-country with Taylor, that it was five days of hell ahead in Isak's mind. Taylor had been looking forward to it: five days straight of Isak's undivided attention, while she'd have no choice but to take Taylor seriously, to let her in.

They sat in relative silence for the two hours it took to get to the outskirts of Barstow. Taylor was unnerved by all of the silence, but she kept telling herself that everything was okay; they just needed to settle into the trip. Isak stared out the window.

"I thought we'd take I-40, in case we run into any bad weather," Taylor said. "You know, stay south for as long as we can."

"Great." Isak opened up the map that was folded into the side pocket of her door. She looked at it quietly.

"Is that okay with you?" Taylor asked.

"Of course. Yeah. I like the old Route 66 towns."

"Okay, so then I guess I should look for 40 right after Barstow?"

"Yep."

"Oh-kay then," Taylor said, bobbing her head slowly and exhaling loudly. To her, this silence was ridiculous. It was ominous, foreshadowing something negative for the rest of the trip. Isak probably thought it felt just right.

After Taylor steered them onto I-40 heading east, Isak announced that she had to go to the bathroom. Taylor pulled off at the very next exit with a blue "services" sign.

"Want something to drink?" Isak asked, leaning into the car

the same way she had the night they went out to the pier and played air hockey. Her arms and hands were so sturdy, her movements so assured. Taylor forgot that Isak was a woman sometimes. Or when she thought of Isak, Taylor didn't really think of her as anything.

"Sure. A Diet Coke would be great," Taylor said. "I'll be out here stretching my legs."

Isak came back with two drinks, red straws poking out of the tops. Taylor rose from a stretch and pushed her pelvis forward with her palms on her hips. She moaned a bit from the loosening of her muscles and ligaments.

"Do you need a break?" Isak asked. "I can drive some."

"No, I'm fine." Taylor got back into the car and pulled the seatbelt across her chest. She took a sip of her drink, but it didn't taste like diet soda. It was syrupy and sweet. She didn't say anything.

Isak also took a sip of her drink, but winced dramatically. "Eew! This isn't mine. I *hate* diet."

Taylor laughed hesitantly and handed over her drink. Isak took a sip and said, "Much better. Much, much better. Real sugar. Now that's more like it."

"I'm partial to fake sugar myself," Taylor said.

"You know, you shouldn't drink that crap. It's full of Aspartame," Isak said, half-smiling. Taylor was happy Isak was talking. "I've read about studies with rats and people getting all sorts of neurological disorders when they're exposed to that stuff. Not to mention cancer."

"I think it tastes better," Taylor said. She still didn't quite have her groove on with Isak. But it was coming. Taylor tried to channel the person she was that night on the pier. The Taylor who is open to whatever happens, who listens, who wants to be a good person in somebody else's eyes.

"What the hell could taste better than a regular old Coke?" Isak asked.

"Diet Coke," Taylor countered, offering her cup to Isak.

Isak pushed it away playfully, then said, "I'm serious, you should stay off that stuff. I guess I've found my mission: By the time we get to the East Coast, you'll be off Diet and begging me for plain, old Coca-Cola."

"I don't think so," Taylor answered in a mock-bitchy voice. She finally felt comfortable enough to flirt a bit.

"We'll see about that."

"Fine."

"Fine."

The Mojave Desert flew by like television. Taylor started to feel the weight of fatigue, mostly in her eyes. The gas tank was on empty, so Taylor looked for the next gas station. Isak had fallen asleep with her ski hat on and her head resting against the window. Taylor didn't want to wake her up. She looked like a little boy there, passed out from too many games of tag.

Isak woke with a start when Taylor set the emergency brake.

"Gas," Taylor whispered apologetically.

Isak pulled off her hat and looked around. She shivered visibly. "I'll pump," she said.

"No, I've got it. You were sleeping, so let me do it," Taylor offered, but Isak was already halfway out of the car.

Taylor slid her credit card into the slot on the pump.

"No, you got the first tank," Isak said, and then pressed the red cancel button on the pump.

"Why'd you do that?" Taylor asked. "I said I've got it." She'd spoken more forcefully than she'd wanted. Isak seemed surprised; she waited for Taylor to swipe the credit card again.

Taylor started to reach for the nozzle, but Isak grabbed it before Taylor got there. Taylor stood and watched as Isak pumped. A sort of battle of wills had apparently begun.

Isak fumbled with the nozzle to see if she could get the lever set in an open position without having to hold it. But she couldn't, so she just stood there holding it and looking at Taylor. It was cold, and Taylor could see that Isak's knuckles were bright red.

"Here." Taylor handed Isak the gas cap. "Put this under the lever."

"Thanks," Isak said, wedging the cap into the pump's handle. She put her hands into the front pockets of her jeans.

Taylor watched the numbers race on the gasoline pump. "I don't need you to pay for this trip," Isak said, after about the seven-gallon marker. "That's not why I agreed to come with you."

"I know." Taylor didn't want to tell Isak why she could pay for the trip. But she would probably have to.

"I have money, and I expect to pay half of our expenses," Isak continued.

"Isak."

"What?" she replied, annoyed. She waited for the pump to click stopped, and then pulled the nozzle out of the tank. On the way out, the nozzle dribbled some gasoline down the fender of Taylor's car.

"Shit, I'm sorry." Isak rushed over to get a paper towel and dunked it in the dirty squeegee bin. She squatted and wiped up the gasoline with the soapy solution, but it just spread the gasoline further. The water beaded over the layer of gas.

"It's okay, it's okay," Taylor said. "I do that all the time."

207

"I can get it off with a little more soap."

Taylor went around to the other side of the car and tossed the keys over the hood to Isak. "Forget it. Let's go," she said, getting into the passenger seat.

Isak obliged, and then she was in the driver's seat, adjusting the rearview mirror and glimpsing over at Taylor periodically.

"It's not my credit card," Taylor blurted, as soon as they pulled back onto the interstate.

"What?"

"It's Robert's. He insisted I use his card for gas and hotels along the way. I figured I'd just do it, since he was offering."

Isak didn't respond.

Finally, Taylor asked, "Isak, what?"

"Nothing."

"What?"

"Well, I'm just not interested in freeloading off your sugar daddy. We're already using his car."

"It's *my* car."

"Well, he gave it to you."

Taylor felt stung by Isak's words. She seemed so bitter about Taylor's relationship with Robert–even from the beginning, when they first met for coffee in L.A.–but she never just came out and said anything. Just little digs here and there.

"I'm sorry," Isak said, much to Taylor's surprise. "I'm just saying I don't want to use his or your money. I'd like to pay half of everything."

"Fine," Taylor conceded. She played up the hurt in her voice. And she was hurt. But mostly she was pleased that Isak had apologized for something, had considered her feelings.

It was getting late, but they decided to drive on through Flagstaff. Taylor was driving again, with Isak sleepily answering her questions about where they should stop for the night. Taylor assumed that they were both avoiding the inevitable question of whether to get one or two rooms for the night. It would be ridiculous to get two rooms, Taylor thought. She hadn't asked Isak, but she took Isak's silence on the matter to be indicative of similar confusion.

"Isak? Isak, this one okay?"

"Yeah, fine."

They were coming up on Winslow, Arizona. The sleepy town twinkled with blue, green, and white lights in the wavy atmosphere to the south. Taylor pulled into the carport of a Budget Inn just west of the exit for Winslow's business loop. The bright yellow and white motel sign assaulted her eyes and made them ache. She turned off the car and waited for Isak to say something. But Isak just sat in the passenger seat, seemingly waiting to be told what to do.

Taylor sat. Isak sat. Taylor looked at Isak, then looked away as soon as Isak returned her stare.

Finally: "Do you want me to go in, then?" Isak asked. "It's probably better if you do."

"Oh. Okay," Taylor said. "Why?"

"It just is. Do you want some cash?" Isak offered, shifting toward Taylor so she could reach for the wallet in her back pocket.

"No. No, I've got it." Taylor fished around for her wallet in the console between them.

Isak just sat there. Taylor stopped.

"Isak?"

"Yeah?"

"No, nothing. It's nothing," Taylor said, opening the car door and heading toward the night-registration window. She looked back at Isak, who was reaching for something in the back seat. All Taylor could see through the windshield was Isak's butt in a faded pair of Levi's.

The attendant came to the window in her pajamas. She was Indian or Pakistani or something, Taylor figured.

"Single?" she asked, looking around Taylor toward the car. "Oh, no, double."

"Yes," Taylor answered, sliding Robert's credit card through the paper-thin slot beneath the glass.

"Thirty-four ninety-eight, plus tax," the attendant said. "Will that be a queen-sized bed or double?"

Taylor felt a sudden surge of relief. Double beds. That was it. The perfect option. Why hadn't she thought of double beds? She had just assumed: one room, one bed. But her anxiety quickly lifted, a passing summer storm.

"Double beds!" Taylor yelled through the speaking hole in the glass. The attendant looked up at Taylor, faked a sleepy smile, and then swiped Robert's credit card through the machine.

"Everything go okay?" Isak asked as soon as Taylor returned to the car.

"Yep. We're around back," Taylor said, pulling the car into the parking lot. She looked for their room number, 216, and parked in front of room 116, just a floor below.

"We should unload all this stuff," Isak said, nodding toward the back seat.

"Why?" Taylor asked.

"Why? Well, only because some people, their only job in life is to troll motel parking lots, ripping stuff off. We'll lose everything if they see this nice car with all that stuff in plain view."

"I think it'll be okay," Taylor said. "We'll be right upstairs."

"I'll do it. It's not that much."

"No, I'll help."

"No. Let me do it, Taylor." Isak loaded herself with three or four of the heaviest bags. She seemed annoyed. And then Taylor felt sick to her stomach.

Usually she knew the script. She knew what would normally occur: a shower, then sex, then some sleep before getting up and doing it all over again the next day. And the next. And the next.

But those were under normal circumstances. Nothing about these circumstances with Isak was anything resembling normal. Taylor was a bit unnerved, to say the least. She didn't know what to do but go into the bathroom, start the shower, and steam up the room while Isak finished unloading their bags. So she did just that.

210

In the shower, Taylor tried to get some lather going with the tiny square of dry soap provided by the motel. It was a useless endeavor, but Taylor nevertheless managed to clean her vital parts, including her feet and behind her ears. She heard the door slam, the deadbolt slide into place, and her car keys sliding across a tabletop. And then the TV.

Taylor grabbed an entirely too small towel and wrapped her body in it. Or as much of her body as she could cover. She noticed how the towel scratched her skin; she was used to Robert's plush bath-sheets. Taylor's legs were shaky and tensing up uncontrollably, in tiny fits. She didn't know why. Whether she was nervous, scared, turned-on, excited, what? *It all depends on Isak*, Taylor thought, but what good was finding out what Isak wanted when she didn't even know what she was feeling herself? She never really considered what she was feeling. It was always whether the other person was game, and if they were, great. But if they weren't, then it was Taylor's mission to make them want her. Which was never terribly difficult.

She took a deep breath and entered the bedroom. Isak was sitting on the foot of the bed closest to the TV. She was watching the Weather Channel, her face bathed in blue. Isak didn't look up from the screen as Taylor walked over to the bags to find something to wear. She had to squat with her knees toward Isak, so that her butt wouldn't hang out the bottom of the tiny towel when she bent over. She watched Isak the whole time, though still Isak didn't look up.

"What's the weather like?" Taylor asked.

"Looks clear, at least for the next day or two."

"Oh."

Taylor found a T-shirt and dropped the towel around her waist, folding it over itself like men always do in locker rooms, or after sex, or while shaving before work. Isak still didn't look her way, so Taylor didn't bother turning her back to Isak as she pulled the T-shirt over her head. When her head poked through the shirt, Isak was still staring at the TV.

Taylor pulled some flannel pajama bottoms out of a bag and stepped into them under her towel. Then she used the towel to dry her hair a little better. She walked back to the bathroom in front of the TV.

211

"Did you have a boob job?" Isak asked suddenly, and Taylor almost fell into the toilet.

"What? *What?*"

"Did you get your breasts done?" Isak asked again, matter-of-factly.

Taylor ran her hands through her hair and looked at herself in the mirror above the sink. She followed the shape of her breasts through the tight yellow T-shirt she had just pulled on. Her nipples were still hard against the shirt.

"Yes, I did," she said, as non-threatened as possible.

"I thought so." Taylor waited for Isak to say something else, but she didn't.

"Well?" Taylor asked finally.

"What?"

"Why did you ask me that?"

"I just had a feeling, and I went with it," Isak said.

"Well?"

"Well, what?"

"Aren't you going to ask me?"

"Ask you what? I don't really care; I was just wondering, so I asked. I hope it's okay that I asked."

"It's fine," Taylor said, shoving her toothbrush into her mouth.

She watched herself brushing her teeth and tongue—rather hard. Taylor couldn't believe Isak had the nerve to ask her that, when Isak couldn't even manage to take her eyes off the TV set as Taylor passed in front of it. She spit and rinsed, put some moisturizer on her face, hands, and elbows, and went into the bedroom. Isak still hadn't moved.

"Is that the bed you want?" Taylor asked.

"Not if you do."

"I don't really care. It just seems like you might want that one because you haven't gotten off of it since we checked in."

"What's wrong with you?" Isak asked, finally taking her eyes off of the TV.

Taylor stared at Isak. She had no fucking idea what to do or say. "Nothing," Taylor said, fluffing two anemic pillows up against the pressed-wood headboard, which slammed into the wall when she leaned against it. "Nothing's wrong."

Isak went into the bathroom and closed the door to the toilet. When she came out, Taylor could hear Isak brushing her teeth and splashing in the sink. Then she pulled off her jeans and stood in her boxer briefs while peeling the bedspread back and folding it neatly over the base of the bed. Isak left her T-shirt on, which was a soft, faded black color and hung off her shoulders in a gentle way. Her underwear was gray, with buttons down the front, but Taylor tried not to look. When Isak finally sat down on the bed, she pulled her arms into her T-shirt and fumbled around so that it looked like she was fighting with herself under the shirt. Then she pulled a black jog bra out from one of the sleeves and flung it onto the chair with the rest of her clothes.

"Well, if you must know," Taylor began, shortly after Isak

settled into bed, "I had very oddly-shaped, small breasts my whole life, and so when I moved to L.A. and met Robert, he heard me complaining about them and offered to pay to have them reconstructed for me."

Isak didn't respond.

"It wasn't a big deal at all," Taylor added. "And not that you care, but I feel much better about myself now . . . more confident and generally happier with my appearance."

Isak turned to look at Taylor. "Well, that's great, then. Okay if I turn off the TV?"

"Yep," Taylor said, pleased that she got that out of the way. *Off her chest*, Taylor thought, chuckling to herself.

Isak kept looking in Taylor's general direction, her eyes softening into little grins. She looked like the tired little boy again, and Taylor felt the warm feeling she had for Isak while she slept in the car with her cap on earlier that day, when they were somewhere in the southern California desert. Taylor watched as Isak dozed off in the line of light that sliced into the room from between the heavy drapes over the room's only window.

This cannot be all there is, Taylor thought. "Isak? Isak, are you asleep?"

213

"I was. I was just asleep."

"I'm sorry," Taylor said. "This just feels weird to me. Does it feel weird to you?"

"Why, because we're not fucking right now?"

"Jesus, Isak," Taylor said, her warm feelings for Isak vanishing once again, as quickly as they had appeared. "What the hell is your problem? I'm just trying to connect with you here, and I'm not talking about sex."

"Aren't you?" Isak asked.

"No. I'm not."

"Well, what is it then, Taylor?"

"I don't know. I guess I expected to, I don't know, *talk* a little more on this trip than we have been."

Isak sat up in the strip of yellow light with a huge sigh. Taylor could see half of her handsome face, the heavy frown across her brow.

"What?" Taylor asked.

"Taylor, it's been one day. I don't know what you want."

"I don't want anything. I, I guess I'm just saying I thought we broke through something on the pier that night, and then now, it's like, pow! Back to square one. No, even before square one. Back to like, square negative seven."

"Well, if you're waiting for my life story," Isak began, "I can start it right here, right now if you want. But I was sort of waiting until we hit the panhandle of Texas or Oklahoma, or something like that. It's a long trip."

Taylor didn't really know what she was asking for. Was it as simple as not getting what she wanted for the first time in recent memory? Too trite. Nothing was ever about what she wanted.

"Maybe you can start your life story tomorrow, somewhere just this side of Albuquerque," Isak continued, "and then when you're done, I can start mine. Where do you think your life story will get us? Tucumcari? Amarillo? Elk City? All the way to Oklahoma City?"

"Why do you get this way?" Taylor asked.

214

"What way?" Isak demanded. She was growing angrier by the second, it was clear to Taylor. "How do you know anything about the way I get?"

And then Taylor couldn't help it; she started crying, and she couldn't stop it from coming. At first it was silent–perhaps could've been concealed–but then she couldn't keep it back any longer.

"Oh, come on, Taylor," Isak said. "I'm sorry. I just don't know what the hell you want from me. I thought we were driving cross-country because we both needed to get there, share the driving, keep each other company. I thought that's what we were doing today, didn't you?"

Taylor didn't answer. Isak started to get out of bed, but Taylor said, "No," because she didn't want it to look like she was manipulating Isak into her bed. Or maybe Isak hadn't even been getting up to go to Taylor's bed. "I'm fine."

"Listen. I'm sorry. I'm just really tired. It's been a long day, and quite frankly, a rough month. I didn't mean to hurt you; I was just trying to say that everything seemed fine to me."

Taylor turned her back to Isak.

"Tay?" Isak asked. This was the first time she had called Taylor by that nickname, and it sounded sweet in Taylor's ear. "Do you want me to lie there with you? Would that make you feel better?"

There, Isak said it. The offer was both what Taylor was hankering for, but also the very thing that killed her. That is, being patronized or pitied by Isak.

"I'm fine."

"Come on, Taylor," Isak pleaded. "I feel really bad. I didn't mean to make you cry. I don't know what I–"

"Forget it. Let's just get some sleep."

"Okay. Good night then," Isak said hesitantly. "Are you going to be okay?"

"Fine."

Taylor faded in and out of a tired, teary-eyed state. She listened to Isak's irregular breathing until she was blitzed with the persistent image of Isak as the innocent, beautiful little boy again. Sleeping his fitful sleep so he can be rested for another day full of little boy activities.

And then Taylor wondered, until it made her shake again, what it would feel like to have Isak curled around her, with her soft, black faded T-shirt resting against the strip of exposed skin on Taylor's back.

Neither Taylor nor Isak mentioned the previous night's exchange. They woke up early and drove all day again, straight through New Mexico without much stopping, aside from gas (twice), food (once), and bathroom requirements (four times). It would start getting dark in an hour or so. Outside of Amarillo, Taylor saw a sign advertising the "Largest Cross in the Western Hemisphere," just ahead, in Groom, Texas.

"We have to stop," Isak said. "Do you mind?"

"No, sure," Taylor said, scanning the flat horizon for said cross.

"I see it!" Isak took one hand off the steering wheel to point up ahead and to the car's right.

"That's a telephone pole. It has to be bigger than that. It's the largest cross in the Western Hemisphere."

"No, that's it, I'm telling you," Isak insisted.

Taylor still scanned all around them. There was nothing out there, save for a few craggy, wooden entrances to ranches and some antiquated irrigation equipment. Nobody they saw was doing anything but driving I-40, which is what people seemed to do around those parts. That, and slaughter cattle.

"That's it," Isak repeated as they drew closer. "I knew it."

"Jesus," Taylor said, though she hadn't meant to use that particular expletive. The two laughed despite themselves. Despite the cool, guarded courtesy with which they'd been treating each other all day.

"This beats Cadillac Ranch by miles," Isak said. They had passed the ten graffiti-covered cars sticking out of the earth on the other side of Amarillo a couple hours earlier.

216

Isak pulled the car into the lot, as the cross, large indeed, loomed over their every turn. Taylor couldn't believe she was stopping to see this thing. Had Isak not insisted, Taylor would've been content to watch it pass by the right side of their car on the highway . . . First tiny, then small, large, small, and then tiny again, disappearing in the rearview mirror and blending in with all of the crooked telephone poles on the yellow plain.

Isak rolled down her window. "Welcome, friends," a man said, with his arms wide open like the cross, indicating that they could park anywhere. He was clean-shaven, a little chubby, with a square head of brown hair parted precisely down one of the sharp corners of his head. He was bundled in a big brown jacket.

After Isak parked the car, she looked at Taylor. "Ready?" The man had gone back into the obviously heated kiosk; it was freezing out there. A crisp wind whipped over the snow-dusted plains and up around the massive silver cross.

Isak took Taylor's hand, and together they walked across the parking area, the cold gravel crunching underneath their shoes. They stepped onto the massive concrete slab and finally reached the base of the monument, where Isak let go of Taylor's hand and looked up at the cross. Taylor followed Isak's gaze. The sky was ice-blue above them, and she could hear the wind blowing over the cross. Or maybe it was just in her ears.

"Why were you holding my hand?" she asked Isak.

"Shhh."

"Why were you holding my hand?" Taylor whispered, leaning closer to Isak.

"Because you have California plates, a German car, and that guy is staring at us from the window in that little kiosk. Not to mention the fact that there is a memorial to the unborn souls murdered by abortion right over there."

"Oh," Taylor said.

Isak guided Taylor toward the memorial. "We would never abort our baby if I accidentally got you pregnant before we were married, right?"

"Right."

They stopped in front of the memorial, which was more like a gravestone. "Probably microphones everywhere," Isak mouthed softly to Taylor. Isak smiled.

They knelt in front of the gravestone. There were bunches of dried flowers around it, one disintegrating bunch accompanied by a red note in the shape of a heart:

Dear Angel: Mommy and Daddy miss you very very much. We now [sic] we made a very big Mistake, but not a day doesn't go by [sic] that we don't think of you up there in HEAVEN with all the other Angels. We love you. xo

Isak and Taylor walked back toward the car, but before they could get in, the smiling man was back, welcoming them into the kiosk.

"Come on in for a spell," he said. "I can offer you free coffee and hot chocolate."

Taylor looked to Isak for a cue. A maroon minivan with

Oklahoma plates pulled into the lot, the gravel spitting out from under its tires. The man waved at them too.

"You in the military?" he asked Isak, once they had all squeezed into the tiny kiosk.

Taylor looked down at Isak's jacket, which was a green, thrift-store, army-reject type of a thing. She looked around at the pictures of Jesus, postcards of the cross, and fake gold trinkets all over the place. She wondered what the hell Isak was going to say.

"No, I mean, well, yes," Isak began. "I *was* in the military, and now I'm *not.*" Taylor thought it was as good of an answer as any. But she was getting creeped out nonetheless.

"Well, where're you folks heading?" he asked, eyeing Taylor. She noticed that his question was directed at Isak, and not at her.

"We are heading to Tulsa, to visit some family," Isak said. Taylor couldn't help but smile to herself. Isak continued, "So how tall *is* it? I mean, I'm sure you're sick of hearing that question."

"Hundred and ninety feet, to be precise," he said. "Coffee?"

Isak shook her head *no,* but then looked at Taylor to see if she wanted any. Taylor shook her head as well. There was a warm, stale smell to the place.

"Then you're the hot chocolate kind," he said, reaching for a red paper cup with reindeer prancing around it.

"No thanks. Nothing please," Isak said.

"You newlyweds?"

Taylor was dumbfounded, but Isak seemed to know what she was doing. She was more polite to this man than Taylor ever thought her capable of being.

"If she'll take me," Isak said, with a fake southern accent.

Taylor smiled at the man. "He's quite a charmer," she said. "Quite a charmer. You ready to go?"

"Sure, honey," Isak replied. She was flipping through a photo album with pictures of the cross at various stages of its construction. "Thank you, sir, for letting us come in from the cold. I see you're not quite finished with the stations of the cross there, but I wish you the best in their completion."

Taylor didn't know what the hell Isak was talking about, but she looked out the window and saw a couple of black statues of Christ with the cross, situated around the base of the larger cross. A semi pulled into the lot and parked, idling loudly. It was followed by an orange and white pick-up truck with empty gun racks installed in the rear window.

"Yeah, well, we're hoping to get the other five stations completed in the next year or so," the man said.

"Any other interesting tidbits about the structure?" Isak asked. "I'm really interested in the technical aspects."

Taylor felt what had to be fear grab hold of her throat from somewhere. She wanted Isak to stop. It was a fucked-up game she was playing. Taylor grew dizzy, her muscles tightening. She didn't know for sure what she was experiencing, because she didn't feel true fear very often. Rarely. Pretty much never. Everyone always took care that Taylor would never know fear. But this kind of fear seemed implicit in Isak, just waiting around the corner wherever she went.

"Well, one thing I always tell people, and they don't believe it, but she'll persevere in winds up to a hundred and forty miles an hour, if need be," the man said. "Engineered that way."

"Whew," Isak replied, shaking her head. Cool as she could be. "How do they measure something like that?"

"They just know."

"Oh."

"And she's got fifty thousand pounds of rebar in her," he went on, "seventy-five tons of steel."

"Honey, we should probably get back on the road," Taylor managed. "Thank you."

"Sure. Well, I do thank you for your time, sir," Isak said, opening the door for Taylor. A bell on the back of the door jingled, and the sound startled Taylor. Outside, the sky was darkening, a hint of purple reflecting off the cross. "Happy New Year and all."

When they got to the car, Isak went around and opened Taylor's door for her. Then she got into the driver's seat and put the car in reverse, waving good-bye to the man by the kiosk, who was by then chatting with the family from the minivan.

Taylor caught her breath.

"Doesn't it make you want to buy a lot down the road and build a cross that's, like, a hundred and ninety-*one* feet tall, just to piss them off?" Isak asked. She laughed at herself. "Wouldn't be the largest cross in the Western Hemisphere anymore, that's for sure."

Taylor didn't respond.

"And wasn't that freaky how he kept calling the cross a 'she'?" Isak asked after a while. "Like it's a boat or something."

"What?" Taylor finally responded.

"Wasn't that strange how–"

"I know what you said," Taylor interrupted. "What were you doing back there?"

"What?"

"Isak, come on."

"You said you wanted to know me," Isak said, cryptically.

"That wasn't you," Taylor started, "that was just, just *weird*. And dumb. It just felt like, I don't know. Damn you."

Isak took her eyes off the road to look at Taylor a few times. Taylor wasn't getting whatever it was Isak was trying to tell her. Or maybe she did get it. That feeling she got out of nowhere, standing there in the hot little kiosk, looking out the window at the massive cross above them. She blamed Isak for putting her in such a dangerous situation, and yet, had it even *been* a dangerous situation?

As though reading Taylor's mind, Isak said: "The scar on my head that you asked about?"

"So?"

"Well, whatever you're feeling right now, that's kind of what it's like a lot of the time for me."

"What do you mean? People aren't like that in New York or L.A."

"Well, actually . . ." Isak said, smiling. "At least I know what that guy back there's thinking. It's when I don't know what I'm dealing with that I get worried."

220

"But you were just fucking with him to, I don't know, just to fuck with him. He knew there was something wrong with us. I could just tell."

"Yeah, and the more I poured it on, the less he was gonna do something about it," Isak said. Taylor stared at the small strip of road that ran alongside the interstate. It was supposed to be the old Route 66. "You're not that monumentally naïve, are you?"

Taylor resented Isak, but she didn't know why. She didn't know how to describe it. She knew Isak could sense her frustration, but she didn't know whether there was reason to be as angry or upset as she was. There was nobody at fault. But she felt like kicking something.

Taylor wanted out. Away from Isak for a minute. To think. She saw a sign for a truck plaza in three miles. "Stop there," she demanded.

Taylor got out of the car and rushed to the bathroom before Isak had a chance to turn off the ignition. She felt tears coming, but she held them in. She had no idea what she would be crying about. Taylor went into the handicapped stall, put the seat cover down on the toilet, and sat on it. She felt better being there, as though calm and safety were coming. She just needed to sit there and wait for them.

221

She must've been there for a while, because a woman's voice said, "Are you okay in there?" as she knocked on the stall door.

"I'm fine. Thank you," Taylor answered in a sweet voice. The woman went away.

"Taylor?" It was Isak's voice, and Taylor ducked down so she could see her feet; Isak was walking down the aisle and stopping in front of each closed stall.

"Excuse me, this is the *ladies'* room," an older woman's voice said in a perturbed tone.

"I know, I'm sorry ma'am," Isak said. "Just give me a second here."

Taylor didn't know what to do or say.

"Taylor? Are you in here?" Isak yelled.

"Here," Taylor said quietly, and she kicked her foot under

the stall door to show Isak which one she was in.

When she saw Isak's beat-up, black leather boots at the door, Taylor opened it up and let her in.

"What's going on?" Isak asked.

"I don't know."

"Listen, I'm sorry if I made you uncomfortable," Isak started, whispering. "It's just kind of how it is. I'm sorry I put you in the middle of it."

"Did you hear what that woman just said?" Taylor asked, keeping her voice low.

"It happens all the time." A faint smile traveled across Isak's face. "Which bathrooms do you think I've been using for the majority of this trip?"

"Oh."

"Unless they're individual rooms or the place is empty," Isak said. "You just have to kind of laugh it off. I swear, it's no big deal."

"Right there," an angry woman's voice whined. "He's in there."

222

Taylor started to get anxious again, but Isak looked at her and made sure Taylor could see that she was still smiling. Isak winked at her and mouthed, "Ready?" Taylor nodded.

Isak opened the stall door. "I'm sorry, folks. My sister's diabetic, and I needed to bring in her shot," Isak said to the few women who were gathered around the door, including a security guard in a blue suit. Isak put her arm around Taylor and ushered her out of the women's bathroom.

"You okay?" Isak asked, once they were safely on the other side of the convenience store. Isak led them to the windshield-wiper, mud-flap, and reflector aisle, where everything smelled like plastic.

"I'm fine," Taylor said. "I'm sorry I freaked out."

"Don't worry about it."

"No, I'm sorry," Taylor went on.

"It's okay, it's okay . . . Here, want a Coke? Or, sorry, a *Diet* Coke?" Isak asked. "I'll get you a seventy-two-ouncer if you want."

"No, regular Coke's fine," Taylor said. "Especially with my diabetes."

Four days later, Taylor drove the last leg of the trip into Providence. Isak had never been there before, had just driven through she said, so she was leaning up and forward to take in as much of the city as she could on the route Taylor took into town.

"The architecture is beautiful," Isak said. "What's that?"

"The capitol. Or the train station. Which are you pointing at?"

"Both," Isak said. She was smiling wide, genuinely curious, which made Taylor relax. "What a beautiful old downtown."

"I guess." After a few more blocks, Taylor pulled the car up in front of her mom's house. "Well, here we are."

"This is a pretty swanky neighborhood."

"Well, my father bought the house when he was still with my mom," Taylor explained, "and we got to stay in it after he left."

Taylor looked up at the house and saw something she never thought she'd see there: a dog poking its head through the curtains and barking.

"Mary!" Isak yelled. Taylor could tell how happy just hearing the dog's bark made Isak. She looked at Taylor. "Can we go in?"

"Is there a choice?" Taylor honked the horn once.

Arlene opened the front door, letting the dog out in front of her. She followed the dog down the steps, arms crossed. "Well, hello," she said, while the dog ran full speed toward Isak, jumping up and down, spinning, whining, twisting, and wagging.

"Hi, Mom," Taylor said, moving to hug Arlene. They held one another sort of awkwardly for a few seconds before Taylor pulled away and said, "Wow, looks like Mary missed you."

"Well, he's a sweet dog," Arlene said, and Taylor looked at her mother as though she had just spoken in tongues.

"Mom, this is Isak," Taylor said, remembering her manners. "Isak, my mom, Arlene."

"Nice to finally meet you," Isak offered, trying to curb Mary's jumping with her knees. "Thank you so much for letting him stay here with you."

"Oh, please. He's been no trouble at all. And Charlie loves having him around."

"How about you?" Taylor broke in incredulously. "Do *you* like having him around?"

Arlene and Isak seemed uncomfortable with the pointed question, but then Arlene said, "Well, yes. It turns out I do like having a dog around more than I ever thought I might."

Isak laughed in a forced way, as did Arlene. Taylor looked over at Isak, and she was immediately seized with a hyper-awareness of Isak's appearance; she wondered what her mother was thinking. Had she seen a picture of Isak? Had Charlie mentioned anything? Taylor searched her mother's face for a sign, because surely Arlene would give herself away, but there was nothing but a benign smile on her mother's face.

As the three walked up the stoop, with Mary running ahead of them, Arlene said, "I'm sorry Charlie's not here now. He went to run a few errands. But he shouldn't be too long."

"No problem," Isak said. "I hope we're not interrupting anything." Again, Taylor noticed how excessively polite Isak was being .

"How's the store?" Taylor asked, once they settled in the living room. Isak was tugging at a tennis ball in Mary's mouth.

"It's great. Christmas was good this year," Arlene answered. And then to Isak: "I think his little rag doll I got him is somewhere around here. He seems to love playing with that."

Taylor looked around the house, which seemed different, although she couldn't pinpoint why. Except, of course, for the dog.

"How long will you be staying here?" Arlene asked.

Taylor wasn't sure whether the question was addressed to her, but she answered, "I don't know," kicking her feet up on the coffee table in front of her. She reached to pet Mary, who scooted under her legs to bring the tennis ball back to Isak.

"As for me," Isak started, "I'll be out of your hair by tomorrow, day after, at the latest–if that's okay with you."

"No, no, by all means, of course. I thought you were staying longer," Arlene said. "You're welcome as long as you want. You must be exhausted from the drive."

"Well, I just have to make some calls and then get back to New York and find a place to stay, a job, you know, the basics. I'll probably grab a train back down in the afternoon."

"Well, no rush," Arlene said, "really."

"That's very kind of you," Isak said. "Could I ask where the bathroom is?"

"Oh, it's just upstairs, first door on your right." Isak pushed Mary aside so she could stand up. He followed her upstairs.

"So, what happened with your job?" Arlene asked as soon as Isak closed the door to the bathroom. "I remember you hadn't told your boss that you were quitting when I talked to you. Was he upset that you left?"

"Yeah, but it was fine," Taylor said.

"Well, what now? I mean, are you planning to do any acting out here, or go back to the Cape, or New York, or–"

"I don't know, Mom."

"I was just wondering, because you coming back seemed so all of a sudden."

"You know what? I just came here for a break from it all," Taylor said. "So, do you think you could give me one?"

"Gosh, Taylor, I just wanted to know how you're doing, you know, what's going on in your life. Things that mothers ask."

"Well, thanks for being such a good mother," Taylor said, looking toward the windows. "I think I hear Charlie." She went over to look down at the street. Charlie was unloading a bunch of grocery bags from the back seat of her mother's old station wagon.

"Hi, honey!" Charlie yelled when Taylor emerged from the front door. He looked good, Taylor thought. She wanted to feel his energy, so she ran down, took his bags, and put them onto the ground. He was the only thing that felt remotely like home.

"You look so good," he exclaimed, embracing Taylor. "The

last time I saw you was on TV, and I thought you looked good *then!*"

"Don't remind me," Taylor said, letting go of Charlie so she could see him. "You're the one who looks good. I guess country living agrees with you."

"Please, it took twenty years of living in New York for me to realize Providence is cosmopolitan enough."

"Well, I don't know if I agree with you on that one, but . . ."

"No, really," Charlie said. "I have everything I could ever need here."

"Now you sound like a true suburbanite," Taylor replied, and they both laughed. She started picking up the grocery bags from the ground.

"Looks like you made it back in one piece," Charlie said, locking the car door behind him. "Isak wasn't too much of a pain in the ass?"

"She was . . . great," Taylor said, in her most earnest tone.

Charlie shook his head. "How great?" he asked. "I'm going to kick her ass."

"No, no," Taylor conceded. "Not like that."

"Mmm-hmm," Charlie mumbled. "Let's go up."

They laughed as they climbed the stairs to the house. As soon as they opened the door, Mary ran over and started the greeting dance for Charlie, although the dog still basically ignored Taylor. Arlene and Isak got up from the couches and came over to Charlie and Taylor.

"Hello," he said, rather coolly, to Isak.

"Hey," she said, and came over for a hug. They embraced in a loose, Hollywood sort of a way. Taylor didn't know it was this bad between them.

"I guess you guys made it," Charlie repeated.

"We did, we did," Isak answered. Taylor could sense how nervous Isak was around Charlie, in front of Arlene.

"Let me unload these," Arlene offered. She started picking up the groceries and heading to the kitchen.

"Here, let me help," Charlie said. "I really got a lot of stuff, because our population just, well, doubled."

"No, no. Stay and chat," Arlene insisted. "You all haven't seen each other in ages."

Charlie, Isak, and Taylor sat down in the living room after they each carried a grocery bag into the kitchen. There were four people for five bags. Arlene stayed in the kitchen, as did Mary for a moment, while he noisily lapped up water from his bowl. Then he ran out to the living room to try to entice either Charlie or Isak with one of his dirty toys.

Charlie stared at Isak while Taylor watched him. He didn't take his eyes off her, as though waiting for her to make the first move. Taylor felt like she shouldn't be there, like there was so much to be said—none of it to her.

After an awkward silence, Isak finally asked, "So, how are you doing?"

Charlie hesitated for a moment, and then answered Isak, though he didn't look at her. "I'm actually good. This new drug is really mellow." It was the first time Taylor had heard Charlie talk so openly in front of her about his status. She had (perhaps because of Isak?) been instantly let in on something that Charlie had previously deemed her too young or carefree to be privy to.

227

Charlie and Isak dished out meaningless small talk about Isak's ill-fated visit with her parents ("I told you so"), the move to Providence ("There's no Cock bar down the block, but still"), and Mary's bowel movements ("I think he's developed a food allergy"), but soon Taylor stopped processing their conversation. She sat across from the two of them, watching the dog shuttle back and forth, seemingly trying to lure them together in his own dog way.

Taylor pulled away from the scene, hovering above it the way she did sometimes. She thought about Robert, everything she left in L.A.–for this. *What was this, again?* She fought so hard to be the center of every world she entered, somebody's obsession. Or maybe it wasn't a fight; it just happened, and she couldn't help it. That was what everyone told her. They couldn't help themselves around Taylor.

But now, after almost a week of relating equally with someone, bullshit free, with no exchange of sex for something else, Taylor started to see how maybe it was a choice. You either stay or you go. And she always chose to go, which she was itching to do just now. How were things ever going to be any different than they were here, with her mother? But she would try, she decided, to stay. At least for a while. With no one person dominating her landscape. No Jill singularly obsessed with Taylor's soccer prospects; no Tom at boarding school, knocking Taylor up and risking his teaching career for some hot, young sex; no Jules to carry Taylor around like a trophy; no Robert–well-meaning as he thought he was–to shape Taylor's rawness and see how far he could take her in his crazy world.

And, apparently, no Isak as anything to Taylor but one of four bodies now. Or five, if you counted the dog.

14

CHARLIE

"YOU HAVEN'T SAID A WORD to me all night," Isak said, gently pushing the door to my room open.

"You haven't exactly been Mr. Communicative either," I replied.

"Can I come in?"

"Sure."

Isak walked in slowly. There was something peaceful in her movement, something that wasn't there the last time I saw her, over a month before. She came to sit on the bed next to me, but changed her mind when I didn't make room for her. So she patted Mary on his butt, and then swerved over to the dresser and leaned her back up against it, facing me. Some bottles of pills fell over behind her when Isak put all of her weight against the dresser. They rattled in their containers.

"Is everyone asleep?" I asked.

"I think so."

"Where are you sleeping?"

"On the couch," she said, crossing her arms. "It's sweet; Arlene set it all up for me with not one, but two comforters, and a glass of water on the coffee table."

"She's been good to me," I admitted.

"It's really nice of her to let me stay the night," Isak said, and then an odd expression came over her face. "Why is Arlene in that tiny room, and Taylor in the master bedroom?"

"Long story," I said. "That was Arlene and her ex-husband's old room together. I guess she finally wanted out. And now she doesn't guzzle downers at night anymore, so go figure."

"Oh."

"Are you going back to the city tomorrow?" I asked.

"I guess. Tomorrow, or the next day." Isak exhaled loudly. "First I need to make some calls and find somewhere to live."

"That Stacey girl keeps leaving messages on the voicemail," I said. "I think she thinks your leaving town had something to do with her. Either that or she misses you."

Isak shook her head. She probably hadn't thought about Stacey once during the time she was gone. There were always people who wanted to give Isak things. I don't know whether she knew that.

"I bet you could stay with her," I offered, but I knew it was ridiculous. "Or, I don't know whether the subletter has rented your room out yet. All your stuff should be there in the closet, I mean, I don't know if you'd—"

"No, I don't want to . . . I think that would be a little strange."

"Yeah," I mumbled, pulling my finger out of my book and putting a bookmark in its place. It seemed as though we were going to have a Talk with a capital "T." Mary stood up, turned a circle, and settled again at my feet. Then he sighed.

"Well, I can keep Mary until you get situated," I said, although what I really wanted to say was that I could keep Mary, period.

"Yeah, I don't know. Let's see."

I was growing anxious. What was this conversation supposed to be about? Us? Taylor? What? I had to ask.

"What happened with you and Taylor?"

"What?" Isak responded, surprised. "What the hell are you talking about?"

"Please, Isak," I started. It seemed as though she was nervous, because she kept glancing out toward the hallway as though Taylor, or worse, Arlene, might walk in at any second. Guilty behavior if I'd ever seen it.

"What?" she repeated.

"I can tell the way she acts around you."

"Oh, and how does she act around me, Charlie?"

"I don't know, it's how she *looks* at you or something."

"Nothing happened," Isak insisted. "And why do you care so much anyway? You don't trust me?"

"No, I trust you. You're just all wrong for her."

"Oh, I see. I'm all wrong for her," Isak said. I knew how to hurt her better than anyone. "Well, I don't think you need to worry about Taylor, because, trust me, that girl can take care of herself."

"I know," I conceded. "I know she can."

And then it was clear that Taylor was not what this conversation was about. Which left the topic of us.

Isak was giving me her "Ouch, you hurt me" look. It was working on me. But she still pissed me off. She wasn't just going to waltz in here after all this time and . . . I don't know, but whatever it was, she wasn't going to do it.

There was silence, then Isak began to say something, and stopped. Then she tried again, and this came out: "I'm sorry. I'm really sorry."

There was no way it was going to be that easy for her. Fuck her. Not this time.

"What are you so sorry about, Isak?"

She looked confused. "For everything," she said, softly, obviously. I missed her.

"And what, exactly, is everything?"

"I'm sorry I left like that," she began. I waited for more. "I didn't think I was leaving for good, I just, I don't know. I needed some time, and I wasn't getting it around you. In New York."

I didn't say anything. I wanted her to dangle.

"Charlie?"

"I'm listening."

"No, I don't know." She looked like she was about to cry, but that couldn't be the case. I'd never seen Isak cry once in all the years I'd known her, even on friends' deathbeds, at funerals, nothing. If she cried, she did it alone. And yet, her eyes looked wet and red, both of which are pretty reliable predictors of crying.

"I got scared," she blurted out suddenly, and then I knew it, I knew she would cry. I could just make out a single, tiny teardrop sneaking down the side of her nose.

I wanted to give in to her. I wanted her to come over and hold me, to let go of it all. We would lie there, catch up, talk about nothing and everything. Play with the dog, watch '80s reruns, fall asleep. But no. I didn't do anything wrong. I got sick. That's all. There were no promises broken. I offered to take her with me, to keep going together. She quit. Not me. Fuck her.

Ultimately, everyone leaves, and I always knew she would too. So when she did, I let her. That's why they say that thing about blood and water. Look who wanted me, and look who didn't: Jack left, Isak left (both water). But Arlene came around (blood). Ken left Arlene (water), Taylor did too, and yet one day, Taylor will come back around (again, blood).

"I didn't want to lose you," she went on (a very water thing to say). "I mean, coming up to Providence just seemed so, so final. I didn't want to hold you back from coming here, but then I didn't know what I was going to do. I mean, it wasn't my end, you know *the* end, for me, but . . . I don't know. I'm sorry, I can't say it enough. But I am."

"Why did you go?"

"I don't know."

"Yes you do."

"I guess I wanted to see what was there for me," she started, looking down at the floor like a little kid. "But there was the same thing there for me that was always there. So I figured I was supposed to be here, but I know I basically blew that, and you probably don't really care what the hell I think, but there it is."

"Isak," I said, putting an end to her rambling, mercifully. "You never were very good at apologies, were you?"

"What the hell is that supposed to mean?"

"I'm just saying you could always do the 'I'm sorry' part, but the rest of it—the believing that you'd actually done something wrong part—not so good."

Now I really got her, I thought. I didn't mean to; it just came out. I could see her few tears switching over to anger, as Isak looked at me, disgusted, shaking her head.

"You are unbelievable," she said. "I don't even know why I fucking bothered." She left the room, admittedly less peaceful than she had entered it.

Mary woke up and watched her go. He looked worried over her departure, and almost got up to follow Isak out of the room. He looked back at me, then at the door, and then at me again, before finally deciding to stay put on my bed. I felt vindicated that Mary had apparently chosen to sleep with me instead of her. But then I also felt utterly monstrous.

In the morning I felt hopeful. Almost every morning made me feel more hopeful than the night before. Then it was downhill the rest of the day. I awoke to a great deal of commotion downstairs, much more than Arlene created when it was only the two of us in the house. Mary wasn't on the bed; the door to my room was open just enough to have let him pass through.

I grabbed my pillboxes and headed down the stairs, which creaked and groaned with almost every step. A chill gripped me, all the way up into the back of my neck. So I went back up to my room and grabbed a sweater out of the closet before heading back downstairs again, re-awakening the chorus of creaks in the old hardwood floors.

Arlene and Isak were in the kitchen, Isak sitting on the phone with a notepad and a steaming cup of coffee in front of her. Taylor wasn't there. Arlene quietly washed dishes in front of the sink, clinking a few together only sporadically. It was sunny and bright in the kitchen, a cool, gray-green winter day.

"Coffee?" Arlene offered, as soon as she noticed me. She was whispering so as to avoid disrupting Isak on the phone.

I nodded. Isak looked up at me as I sat across from her at the small table.

"Okay, thanks so much for your help. Bye," she said after a bit, hanging up the phone.

"Good morning," Arlene said. "You're up late."

"Morning," I responded.

Isak raised her eyebrows at me as a greeting.

"Did Mary go out?" I asked.

"We went for a long walk this morning," Isak answered. "He's still in the yard."

"Did you find his choke chain?"

"No, he was fine with his regular collar. He didn't pull a bit."

"So, what happened after the little boy vomited on her lap?" Arlene asked Isak, chuckling. She placed a bowl of cereal and a spoon in front of me. And then she said, "Isak was just finishing up a really funny story about riding Greyhound."

"Aren't you supposed to be at the store?" I asked.

"Oh, well, Elizabeth opened up for me today. I told her we had company."

"Where's Taylor?" I asked.

"Went out for a run," Arlene said. "She just breezed in and then breezed out again."

"So, what's going on with your phone calls?" I asked Isak.

"I've just made a few. No luck so far."

Arlene set a cup of coffee and a glass of water next to my pills in front of me. Coffee was my last vice. I couldn't let it go too. I took a few bites of the cereal and started on the pills.

"You're full of questions this morning," Arlene said.

Isak picked up the phone but then hung it back up. "Hey, do you mind if I use that voicemail number for people to leave messages for me?" she asked.

"I don't really use it anymore."

"Do you know the security code?"

"It's our old address," I said. "You should change the outgoing message though."

"Thanks."

Isak picked up the phone and made another call. She punched in tons of numbers, but still seemed to get an operator on the phone.

"I just did try punching in my calling card number," she said into the phone. "No, I don't. No, I didn't know. Okay, thanks." She hung up, scribbling something onto the pad of paper.

"Why don't you just dial direct, Isak?" Arlene asked. "It's silly to dial in all those numbers for every call."

"Oh, no, it's no bother. I think there's a way to make multiple calls; I just haven't figured it out yet."

"What's the problem?" Charlie asked.

"Nothing. I just didn't have the new toll-free number, so some of my calls weren't going through."

"Isak, really," Arlene insisted.

"Are you kidding? I'm not dumping my hundreds of long-distance calls on your phone bill," Isak said. "This is fine, I've got it all figured out now."

Isak made another series of calls, all with the same outcome: Nobody had a room to sublet or knew of anywhere that might be available. I knew it was the last thing Isak wanted to be doing now–talking to people she probably hadn't talked to in ages, admitting that she wanted or needed something from them.

"Okay, thanks, John," she said. "If you hear of anything, leave a message on our old voicemail. Yep, take care." She hung up the phone and crossed another name off her list.

Arlene turned around and sat at the table, placing her coffee cup down next to Isak's. She had a thoughtful look on her face, and I wondered how I might be able to force her to leave. A false fire alarm at the store? Broken credit card machine? Elizabeth coming down with a cold, what?

"Isak," she started, "this is just ridiculous. You don't need to go rushing off to New York when you don't have anywhere to stay. Why don't you stay here for a while? You can stay for as long or as little as you need."

Isak glanced at me uncomfortably and pushed back in her seat. She looked back and forth between Arlene and me a couple of times.

"Arlene, that is such a kind offer," Isak said, "but I couldn't possibly–"

"Please, we'd love to have you around." Arlene was grinning like a school girl.

I couldn't believe what I was hearing. I had been sure

Arlene was going to be freaked out by Isak, that Taylor and Isak would be at each other's throats after a week in the car with each other. And yet, look who was having the most problems with her being around. Moi.

Arlene looked at me as though expecting me to add something. "That'd be fine," I managed.

"Seriously, Arlene, thank you so much, but you've already been kind enough. Maybe I'll stay a few days, just through next week, tops. Then I'll be out of your hair."

"Great, then, it's settled," Arlene said.

From outside, Mary barked twice.

"He wants to come in," I said.

"Oh, I'll get him," Isak offered. She got up from the table and left the kitchen. Arlene stared at me.

"What?" I asked.

Nothing.

"What?"

"What could possibly have happened between the two of you for you to be acting like this?"

"Trust me, a lot," I said.

"What, then?"

"Arlene, don't get in the middle of it, okay?" I snapped. "You can't resist taking in such a pathetic, handsome case, can you?"

"Oh, don't pull that with me," she said. Arlene was speaking like I'd never heard her speak before. With force, and some sort of empathetic knowledge and understanding. "I saw how you lit up as soon as Taylor called and told us she and Isak were on their way out here."

"That's because they're new blood in this otherwise dead house."

The back door slammed and Mary trotted into the kitchen to find me. "I see," Arlene said. Isak followed Mary into the kitchen.

Arlene stood up. "So, Isak, since you don't have to make any more phone calls, do you still want to come see the store with me? I thought we could head over in a few minutes."

Isak looked at me. She could tell I had just been talking

236

about her. It seemed as though she wanted my permission, but I just looked away.

"I'd love to see it. Let me get my coat." Isak went into the living room.

"I guess you won't be coming?" Arlene asked. I shook my head, and then I was alone at the kitchen table.

There's this place I sometimes reach, when I feel something strongly for someone. It could be love or anger or attraction. It doesn't really matter—anything strong. At the height of my emotions, it seems that I want to extract something from the other person, to see them hurt, to be loved by them, or I want them to miss me. But then I look up, and I'm doing the exact opposite of what I should be doing, being the exact opposite person from the one I wanted them to see, to miss, to love. With Jack I became even more needy and clingy during the times he took more space from me; with Isak now, well, this was not me. I was not acting like me. Not the Charlie I usually was when I was with Isak, when we were together on all things.

237

I would never admit it, but I was as sorry as she claimed she was.

By the time Taylor got back from jogging, I had zoned out in the kitchen. I hadn't even finished swallowing my morning line-up, as I liked to call them. There was nothing "cocktail" about it.

"Oh, Charlie, you scared me," Taylor said, heading for the refrigerator. "I didn't think anyone was home."

"Just me."

"Are you okay?"

"I'm okay," I said. "But your mother and Isak seem to be better."

"What do you mean?" she asked, pouring a glass of orange juice.

"No, they're just getting along better than I ever thought they would."

"I know, it's strange, right?"

"Did anything happen with you and Isak?" I blurted suddenly. Taylor and I didn't usually speak of serious matters. Especially not sex or love, or whatever they were calling it these days. But I was still fishing for something with which to convict Isak.

"Honestly?" she asked, her eyes glazing over in that way they seemed to do whenever Isak was around or being discussed.

Christ, what the hell was she about to tell me? "Yes, honestly."

"Nothing happened like you're thinking, nothing sexual or anything."

Breathe, breathe.

"Why do you want to know?" she asked.

"I just do."

"I would've," she started, "I mean, I still want to, but she didn't—doesn't."

It felt like we could've been veering into the too-much-information department, but Taylor seemed to be opening up to me in a new way. Anytime we'd talked of any of her romantic interests in the past, well, she wouldn't tell me much about the many men—only the few women. And even then, she always sounded so in control and detached. This time though, speaking of Isak, she sounded different.

"You know, sometimes I get thinking that things could be so perfect between us," Taylor started. "But then I do something, or say something, and then there's something wrong and I think I caused it, so I stop entertaining that idea of perfect, and I move on."

"I know exactly what you mean," I said. And I wondered where this kid grew up, because I knew it wasn't in this house with my sister. I realized then that Taylor was probably one of us.

"Isak thinks she screwed things up with you for good," Taylor continued. "She seems wrecked over it."

"She said that?" I asked.

Taylor nodded. "What happened?"

"Nothing. She left, that's all. She basically just left."

"But she came back."

"This isn't coming back."

238

"Oh, really? How so?"

"It just isn't," I said. "It's one of those impossible, inexplicable things that most independent films are about."

"Oh, Charlie, that's a load of crap."

"So? Since when are you so wise?"

"I'm not, trust me," Taylor said. "I just have the benefit of having spent a little bit of time with her, and I listened for once."

I stared at Taylor then, and I would've never said it aloud, but she looked like a grown-up. A woman, with tits—she must've gotten a boob-job out in L.A., because nothing real is that perky—and this sense about her, a knowing quality. About how people are, how they could be if you played them the right way. I could see Isak not falling for it the way everyone else had.

"I'm going to take a shower," Taylor said, "but I'm really happy you're here."

"Me too."

"I don't know if I'm necessarily happy *I'm* here, but . . . that's another story," she trailed off. And then she went upstairs after touching the side of my face with her fingertips. I was alone with my medication once again.

I listened after Taylor left. I listened to everything. The refrigerator's low hum, the wood and glass crackling from the late morning sun pouring through them. I imagined that Taylor wasn't even in the house anymore, but rather a ghost of her was floating around, making the noises she would make. After just a short time in this house, I could tell the difference between the toilet flushing (like a sewing machine that runs on water), and the shower being turned on (more of a popping sound with an echo). Taylor had flushed the toilet before starting the shower. But ghosts don't take showers or use the toilet, so I knew it had to be Taylor up there. Sometimes I pictured places when I wasn't there anymore. Where my ghost goes around doing things silently, making sure not to disturb anyone or anything.

I moved into the living room, wondering where Mary was. If Arlene and Isak had taken him without telling me, that would have been really inconsiderate, I thought, because I would worry. Like I was worrying now. What if he had gotten out and I didn't know. He could've been hit by a car. Or stolen. Maybe he was stolen for medical research. Or poisoned by some sick person who soaks steaks in antifreeze and then feeds them to dogs and watches them die from the inside out.

"Mary?" I yelled. But he did not come. "Mary, come here this minute."

I listened. Finally, I heard him hit the floor upstairs, the ghost of him getting off of my bed and padding through the house upon my demand. He was at the top of the staircase, I could tell by the sound of the wood. Then he was at the bottom, heading into the living room. He came and stared at me on the couch. He looked resentful that I had interrupted one of his fifty naps of the day. I patted his head. He was not dead, or poisoned, or even tied up in a laboratory with wires attached to his brain and tubes stuck into his penis.

Later that night, Isak and Arlene were in the kitchen and Taylor and I were on the couch watching TV. Arlene insisted, over Isak's protesting, that she cook dinner for the four of us. Isak conceded only under the condition that she be allowed to cook dinner the next night. Taylor and I sat in the living room listening to their mock argument, accompanied by a great deal of laughter. More laughter than the jokes seemed to warrant.

"That's not flirting, right?" I asked Taylor.

"Don't even," she shot back.

"It's not though, right?"

"No. Stop it."

We laughed. Mostly because we both knew how charming Isak could be—we'd obviously both been taken in by it at one point or another—and now Arlene was simply falling prey to it in her own strange way. *M*A*S*H* reruns were on cable TV.

"Only the best television show ever," I offered. "I mean, aside from *Beverly Hills, 90210,* of course."

"I've never really seen it," Taylor admitted.

"What? *What?*" I exploded. "Subversive anti-war humor, rampant sarcasm, and don't forget male-to-female cross-dressing?"

Taylor shook her head.

"You call yourself a television actor and you've never even seen an episode of *M*A*S*H?*"

"I do not call myself a television actor," Taylor protested. "Let's get that straight."

Hawkeye and Hot Lips Houlihan were kissing on the screen, terrified and alone during heavy shelling. "This is one of my all-time favorite episodes," I said.

Nothing.

"I think Alan Alda was my first serious crush," I continued.

"Which one?" Taylor asked. She had a disgusted look on her face.

"Him," I said, pointing to Alda, looking dashing in a too-large green helmet, his arms clinging to Hot Lips as the camera shook and dust fell around them.

"Eewww," Taylor yelled. "That guy?"

"Oh yeah, I bet your director friend was really a looker," I teased.

"How do you know about him?"

"Your mother told me you were living in your boss' house," I said. "Duh."

"She doesn't know anything," Taylor insisted.

"Well, denial has its benefits, my dear," I started, "but don't think for one minute that passed me by."

Taylor smiled, and then sat back and watched the TV.

There wasn't as much noise as there was good food smell coming from the kitchen. I could hear the sounds of Arlene cooking, but nothing from Isak. I concentrated on listening and then heard Isak talking on the phone.

This was okay for now. It was most comfortable when I knew where everyone was, paired off like we were now, Arlene and Isak in the kitchen, me and Taylor in front of the TV, Mary on the couch beside us. Or three together and one alone, or even all of us doing our own things in the house separately. This must be what family dogs feel like, I thought, most content when each member of the pack is accounted for. Mary looked at me, then put his head back down and closed his eyes.

Isak came into the living room with no expression on her face. Or no expression I'd ever seen there before.

"You should check the voicemail," she said. "How long has it been since you've checked the voicemail?"

"I don't know, a week, two. What?"

"It's Bryan," she said.

"He called?"

Nothing.

"What, he's in the hospital?"

Still not a word.

"What? Tell me."

"He . . . passed. His mother called."

"He doesn't talk to his mother."

And then Arlene came in from the kitchen. She stared at me. And Taylor stared at me. Isak came over and sat on the couch next to me, very close, staring at me.

"Well, I'll have to go down for the funeral, then," I said. They all stared at me, still.

"You should listen to the message," Isak repeated, handing me the cordless phone.

"What?" I asked. "Just tell me."

"It was last week. It sounds like the service was last week."

"It *sounds* like it was last week? What the fuck does that mean?" I asked, dialing the voicemail. "Either it was last week or it wasn't last week."

I waited for the voicemail to pick up. I couldn't believe Isak had said, "He passed." It was practically the stupidest thing that she could've possibly said. I punched in the security code and the message played:

Hi, I don't even know if this is the right person. Anyway, I'm Bryan's mother, and I found your number in his address book, and we're having a service for him here in the city on Thursday. And so I thought you'd want to know. Well, I guess I should've said first, well, he passed away on Monday. Here's the information. I hope I have the right person; it just says Charlie and then this phone number. So this is for Charlie: eleven A.M. at Bryan's old apartment, and we're having it catered.

That was it. They were having it catered. No phone number, no date. So I pressed eight, to listen to the time of the call. Bryan's *old* apartment? What, had they already leased it? I knew real estate in New York was tight, but this? The voicemail barked the time and date stamp at me. It had been the Tuesday before. She called on Tuesday to tell me that he died on Monday and that the service was on Thursday. This made me angry, although it made sense. Then I felt a little lucky and even grateful that I had gotten a call at all. Grateful to this woman who, by all accounts, was pretty much Joan Crawford in *Mommy Dearest* incarnate.

I had always assumed he would die and I would be the only one there. Because who else would deal with him? He never spoke to his parents. That old girlfriend was busy with her being-taken-seriously-and-thus-interviewed-on-NPR type of music career. He didn't have anybody but friends. Your average New York-dwelling, self-involved, entirely too busy for death and dying friends. And ones who seem to recede when you get sick in the first place. And yet, here I was, missing his death and its various accoutrements for another reason: because of voicemail. She did call. Mommy Dearest happened to find my number in his book.

This never would've happened if he'd died of what I will eventually die of. It just wouldn't have. With no "community" (in quotes), people don't expect it. You don't expect death among your peers like you expect engagements, weddings, births, showers, and deaths of parents, sometimes. When we die, everyone knows, because it's built-in that way. When I go, Jack will know, and then everyone will know. Will be sad for me, will be sad for Jack (they hadn't been together in years, *years*), then finally sad for themselves, for everyone else before me. And then they would get to stop being sad until the next opportunity for sadness arises. (He's next, poor Jack.)

I hung up the phone. I don't remember whether I saved or deleted the message. The three of them were still staring at

243

me. It was getting intolerable. I replayed Bryan's mother's message in my head. She had also used the term "passed," as in "passed away." However, it did sound less strange to say "passed away," as opposed to just "passed," like Isak had said. She must not have been thinking. Or she was thinking. She was thinking: *How can I report this to Charlie in the kindest manner possible? I know, I'll say "passed." Bryan passed.* So if anything, she was trying to take care of me. She should've said, "He finally croaked," "He bought the farm," or, simply, "He kicked it." But she said, "He passed."

"Can I have a minute?" I asked.

Taylor jumped up, patting me gently on the shoulder before heading upstairs. Arlene knitted her fingers together, then apart, then together again. And then she went into the kitchen. Isak still sat close to me on the couch. Too, too close.

"You okay?" she asked. When I didn't respond, she added, "I'll be upstairs."

Jack would be the only one who would understand. He hadn't understood in years, but surely this, well, there would be a small corner of him that would get it, would be what I needed when I didn't even know what I needed.

I dialed his number. Our old number. He still had it.

"Hello?" Or, apparently, he and *Edward* still had our old number.

"Is Jack there, please?" I asked.

"Um, wait," he said. And then I heard him yelling, "Jack! Jackie! Phone," and then to me: "Who is it?"

"It's Charlie. Who's this?" I asked, though I knew damn well who it was. And *Jackie?* He hated when anyone called him that.

"Edward. This is Edward," he said, because once was not enough. "Wait, where's 401? It says area code 401 on the caller I.D."

"Providence. Is *Jackie* there?"

"Hold up. Jackie!"

I waited. Arlene poked her head out of the kitchen at me. Mary pushed against me on the couch. He was stretching his legs.

244

"Charlie? I am so sorry, but he's right in the middle of something. Can he call you back?"

"It's sort of urgent."

"Right back. Right back. I swear. What's your number? Wait, I have it here in the I.D. box."

"Okay, tell him I'll be waiting for his call."

"Will do. Bye."

"Bye," I said, but he had already hung up the phone.

That stupid, fucking little fuck. I spent the better part of a decade with Jack—Jackie—and now I have to deal with Edward the muscle-head gatekeeper? I have to go through him? I gave Jack fifteen, no twenty minutes to call back. After that, I don't know what, but I wasn't giving him more than twenty-five or thirty minutes.

I remembered then what Jack said on the day I moved the last of my things out of our (his) apartment. He said that we had a battle of sorts to fight together, simultaneously, but we couldn't do it if we were always battling each other. Something like that. Something stupid and ridiculous and empty and meaningless like that. And brilliant and honest and true and real if it were so. If it had only been so.

"Don't get on the phone!" I screamed into the house. To everyone. I hoped my voice would travel into every room, corner and crevice of that old house. Into the floorboards. Arlene poked her head out of the kitchen at me again. *"I'm okay,"* she probably expected me to say, but I didn't.

Then I thought of Bryan, dead. I couldn't picture a time when he wasn't with brain tumors. I had known him longer without than with, but brain cancer was just one of those things that erased everything else. It did. He, too, had been there for me when I found out. He listened without flinching, without dodging me. He never took his eyes off me, even though Bryan always had so many things going on in his life.

When he got sick, it was quick. There was a seizure, which got him hit by a car on Houston. A CAT Scan in the ER, then, whoa, a golf ball–sized tumor in there. Golf ball–sized, but when he told the story, before the first surgery, when he didn't

245

quite grasp what he was about to go through, he held out a fist in front of him to show the size of the tumor. Which made me wonder how something that big could fit into such an already tightly packed space.

After the first surgery, there was a thick purple line traversing Bryan's bald head, practically ear to ear. And then three more surgeries. And a permanent indentation, with a square flap of skin like an attic door, and many, many staples to hold it all together. After the second surgery, he didn't work anymore. And he also forgot about my virus, my status changing from sick to not sick in his eyes, virtually overnight. And I never reminded him. It was a treat to go back like that. Erase it all in someone else's mind, because everyone else's memories were so good, would never let me forget. Would never take those stupid fucking pathetic sorry looks off their faces.

Everyone was sneaking around the house. Arlene kept peeking at me from the kitchen. And then Taylor tiptoed into the kitchen, ostensibly for a drink. Isak called down from the top of the stairs, "Charlie, okay?"

I looked up at her. Only Mary sat still next to me, usually so intuitive when things went wrong in the human world, only this time seemingly oblivious to my pain. Probably because I was oblivious to my pain as well, seeking more by calling Jack, by abusing Isak, by putting the "Closed" sign on the door. And still I kept doing it even as I knew what I was doing. Oh I wasn't stupid, no. And then the phone rang, and there was no time to think better of it, to stop–

"Hello?"

"Hi, may I speak to Charlie, please?" It was Jack.

"Jack, it's me." Had my voice changed or was New York really that far away? I wondered.

"What's wrong?" he asked, panicked. What was he afraid I'd say? And was Edward in the room to see his fear?

"My friend Bryan. He . . ." and I was going to say passed away, passed on, something (certainly not simply "passed"), but changed my mind mid-sentence. "He died."

"Gosh, Char, I'm sorry," he said, with a hint of relief. I wondered if he even remembered my friend Bryan, or if he had been too over it–over me–by then to care. "What was it?"

You prick. You stupid prick. Cancer. Brain cancer, the worst kind of cancer, you die sooner, your mind is blown, you don't just live and live and live with it until you then get to die slowly. The little tumors everywhere like stars in his brain. We talked about this, you knew how much I liked him, my cute, straight friend Bryan, the only good part about my job.

"Brain tumors."

"Oh, that guy, right. God, that's just tragic," he said.

"Jack?"

"What? Can I–"

"No."

"You're in Providence?"

"I am, but–"

"How is it? How's Arlene?"

"Fine, it's fine," I said. *But there are no good bars, no really high-quality drag queens, no twenty-four-hour gyms.* (I cared about these things before? When?) *There's no you.*

"Are you staying up there for good now?"

"Yes." *I am. For good.* "I have a family here. My sister, my niece. Isak." *I have this, at least. And what about the battle we're supposed to be fighting together, remember?*

"Well, what else?" he asked. "Are you okay?"

"I'm fine." *I thought it might count for something that I called you at this particular juncture, and yet you don't see it as anything but tragic. Isn't that what you said: "God, that's just tragic." It is tragic.*

"_"

"So that's all you can manage?" I asked.

"What do you want from me?" By now he was whispering. Perhaps because Edward was dressed and standing before him, ready to go out to some nice restaurant on Eighth Avenue, where the cheapest entrée is twenty-seven dollars and doesn't even come with a salad.

I want . . . What I want is–

"Charlie, I can't do this," he said. "I will always have a place for you in my heart, but. But not like this."

He didn't just say what I thought he said.

"Charlie?"

"You did."

"I did what, Charlie?"

"Have a nice dinner, Jack."

"I'm not having dinner," he said. "Charlie, is everything . . . okay?"

He paused before "okay," because he knew I knew what its opposite, "not okay," would mean. Is this it? Is it happening? You seem to be out of your mind. Is this how it starts? Do you begin to say odd things that make other people uncomfortable? He had the nerve to wonder, the gumption to think that he would be doing so much better than me.

You put me here. I am not saying I might not have ended up here on my own, but you did this, to be sure. And you can't even grant that I might be okay, might be better than you.

"Oh yeah, I'm okay," I said.

"Listen, Char, I'm sorry about your friend. I'm glad you wanted to call and share it with me, and I truly am sorry for your loss. Good luck up there, okay?"

"Good luck down there," I said. *My loss?* "Good-bye."

"Bye," he echoed, but I was already hanging up.

I realized then that Isak had been standing there behind the couch. Her presence startled me. She hadn't made a sound.

"Oh, it's you," I said, turning around.

"He's still Jack," she said. Just that.

"I know. How long were you standing there?"

"A minute or two."

"Oh, well. I'd still like to be alone."

15

ISAK

SOME INDUSTRIOUS RACCOONS and neighborhood strays had overturned the garbage cans and ripped into the bags in front of Arlene's house. She left the house in a hurry to make an appointment with her accountant at the store. But she came back inside in a tizzy, complaining about the smelly mess outside.

"I'll clean it up," I offered.

"No, Isak, you're our guest," Arlene said.

"No, I'm a freeloader is what I am. Go on to your meeting and don't worry about it."

"Are you sure? I just feel horrible letting you do that."

"Go," I insisted, pointing toward the door.

"Tell Charlie where I am when he comes down," Arlene said, picking up her purse and keys. "Or, what are you supposed to do when he's like this?"

"Just leave him for now. He'll be fine."

She hesitated at the bottom of the stairs, as though she were thinking about going up to see Charlie. But then she looked at me and headed to the front door. "Thank you."

When I went out to examine the mess, I located the source of the problem immediately. The garbage bin didn't have a working latch, so the animals could just nose their way in, tip over the cans, and then *voilà:* an all-you-can-eat buffet. I got to work picking up the trash, stuffing it into bags Arlene had pulled out for me.

By the time I cleaned up all of the garbage and recycling, I had worked up a sweat. It was an unseasonably warm day and I was overdressed. I looked up at the sky; a few white–blinding white–clouds raced across the blue screen above.

I decided to try to make myself useful. I went into the garage, looking for any tools Arlene might've had. There was a drill, surprisingly, and some screwdrivers and a hammer. In an old margarine tub, a big handful of rusty old screws.

I planned on remounting the same latch that was swinging by one screw from the doors, so I wouldn't have to go to a hardware store. I didn't even know where a hardware store was. I ducked into the bin to see what the wood looked like from the inside, and the rottenness that comes from years upon years of things that have been thrown away wafted into my nostrils. The doors were off their hinges too. When I pulled my head back out of the bin to get a breath of fresh air, I saw Taylor jogging up the hill toward me. She stopped in the driveway, spread her legs, and bent down into a stretch. She was breathing hard.

"Good morning," I said. Taylor looked up at me.

"That was a mess," she said, out of breath. "Did you have to clean it up?"

"Yeah, well, I wanted to. I'm going to try to fix it."

"I think raccoons do it."

"That's what your mom said."

Taylor swung her arms back and forth across her chest. "Is Charlie up yet?"

"I don't know, I don't think so."

"I'll go knock on his door after I take a shower," Taylor said. "Hey, do you want to play some pick-up soccer with me today? It's warm enough that a bunch of us are going to be out."

"I guess this whole global warming thing's for real," I said.

"I guess. So you'll play?"

"Okay, if you drive me to the grocery store so I can buy some stuff for dinner."

"Deal."

"What time?" I asked.

"People show up around one."

"I'm way out of shape," I said, "haven't played in years."

"There's all different levels." Taylor looked across the street, then whispered, "Uh oh, Boorman alert."

"What?"

"Hi, Mrs. Boorman!" Taylor yelled, and then she was gone, sprinting up the stairs and into the house.

I looked across the street, and an older woman with a yellow scarf tied crookedly around her head was making a beeline toward me. She walked like she was swimming, with her arms paddling through the air, doggie-style.

"You can't be Arlene's brother too," she said, once she was close enough.

"No, ma'am," I answered.

"Are you Taylor's beau, then?"

"No, not that either," I said, smiling.

"Well, I'm their neighbor, Mrs. Boorman," she offered finally, holding her hand out toward me. I took it in mine. "George is my husband, but you probably haven't seen him around. He's a pilot. Only five months 'til he retires . . ."

"I'm Isak," I said. "It's nice to meet you."

"It is," she repeated. I nodded and picked up the drill, slowly untangling the extension cord. "Are you visiting, or doing work on the house, or . . ."

"Oh, well, I'm just trying to fix this bin so it'll close properly and the animals won't get in," I said, looking back at the garbage cans. "This was a mess."

"It was. You know, I saw it first thing this morning," Mrs. Boorman said. "I had to shoo away the Wilsons's dog because he was eating coffee grounds."

I didn't say anything.

"You know, George and I, we just keep our garbage in the garage instead of keeping it in its own little house like that," she began. "I mean, we don't wake up to our garbage strewn about the street, but it sure doesn't seem quite right to keep your trash inside, does it?"

"No, I guess it doesn't."

"It smells up our house, sometimes all the way into the kitchen," she added.

I nodded my head, while Mrs. Boorman looked like she was getting an idea.

"You know, I've just been begging George to make us one of those bins like Arlene's. But he's been ignoring me for years." She laughed. "Do you think you might be able to build us one? I mean, I don't know whether you do that kind of work, but we'd pay you and, well . . . We have space right over there at the base of the driveway."

"I–"

"Well, actually, I don't know if you can build out that close to the street," she continued, ignoring me. "They have codes around here. I mean, it really preserves the flavor of the neighborhood. It's historic."

I put the drill down and looked at the houses across the street.

"What do you say?" she prodded.

"I didn't know it was historic."

"The whole neighborhood is."

"Well," I started, wondering how many days it might take me to build a home for Mrs. Boorman's trash, "I'm not quite sure I'll be in town."

"Oh?" She looked disappointed.

"But if I'm here for any length of time, I suppose I could do it."

"Great. Great," she said, re-inspired. "Well, you just let me know if you can, and we'll get started right away."

A teal SUV drove by, the woman in the driver's seat leaning over a toddler and waving at Mrs. Boorman, who waved back. I thought for a moment: I could probably charge four or five hundred dollars to build something like that.

"It would be great to surprise George with it," she said, after the SUV turned into a driveway up the block. "Or, well, how long do you think it would take?"

"As I said, I don't know if I'll be here to do it. But probably no more than four, five days."

"Okay, then."

252

"Should I take your phone number?" I asked.

"Honey, don't be silly. Arlene has my number. Or just knock on the door."

"Thanks, I will."

That night, I prepared a Thai meal for the four of us. Charlie had always loved my Penang curry, so I decided to try to resurrect the dish to surprise him. It had been years. I also threw together some coconut soup with tofu, and coconut rice. Lots of coconut, all around.

"This is so delicious," Arlene said, wiping a spot of grease from the side of her lips.

"Yeah, Isak, this is really good," Taylor added.

"Where's Charlie?" Arlene asked.

"I tried to call him, but he didn't want to come down," I said. "He didn't come out of his bedroom all day."

"He came downstairs when you were walking the dog," Taylor corrected me. "And I talked to him for a while in his room earlier this morning. He's doing okay."

"I swear, he's like a teenager," Arlene said.

"Well, his friend just died," Taylor said. "Give him a break."

Arlene didn't respond. We ate silently for a few moments. I wondered whether I'd made the soup too spicy.

"Thank you for fixing the garbage bin," Arlene said. "It looks great."

"It's the least I can do around here. And you know your neighbor, Mrs. Boorman? She wants to hire me to build one of those bins for her."

"That's great," Arlene said. "She's very sweet."

"She's very nuts," Taylor said.

"Taylor!"

"What? She is."

"She's just getting older," Arlene said. "Are you going to do it for her, Isak?"

"I don't think so," I answered. "I told her I didn't think I was going to be here long enough to get it done."

"Well, you might be," Arlene said. "Maybe you could do a

253

few things around the store too. I've been meaning to get someone in to do some general maintenance and cosmetic stuff."

"Ah, well," I said, trailing off. I looked over at Taylor, who seemed to be in a quandary. I could see right through her there: caught between so many different worlds. She reverted to being a snotty kid around her mother, but I could relate to that dynamic, having just come off a month under my parents' roof. Then there was the specter of Taylor's glamorous Hollywood life, not really her, but something she was at least the inventor of. And there was this other family life here, with Charlie and Arlene, and I could tell she wanted to live up to it. To do the right thing. Just to be at ease for once.

I knew exactly how she felt on almost all counts.

"Taylor took me to play soccer today," I said, trying to jump-start the conversation. "But I'm going to be sore tomorrow."

"And you're playing again tomorrow morning," Taylor said. "Everyone comes out on Sundays. Plus, it's supposed to get up to fifty tomorrow."

"Great," I said, exaggerating my lack of enthusiasm.

With a little work, exercise, and food in me, that night I slept better than I'd slept in months.

We crossed Brown to get to the playing field the next morning. I had to admit that the campus was beautiful, as much as I hated to. It was annoyingly perfect. I drove, and Taylor wrapped the laces of her muddy cleats around her feet and tied them.

"If you play fullback again today," she began, "don't forget, I'm right behind you when you get in trouble, okay?"

"I know," I said. "I don't know what happened yesterday."

"He was all over you," Taylor conceded.

"Whatever. I gave up the goal and lost the game."

"Just communicate with me a little better, and I'll know when to come out of the box."

"I know." I hated being told what to do.

When we got to the field, Taylor jumped out and grabbed

her bag from the back of the car, ready to play. I pulled the emergency brake up and thought for a moment before getting out: I needed to get better at being worse than Taylor at this. That is, better at pulling in the reins of my ego enough to allow that she was by far the superior athlete. I was used to being the best at things, especially in the informal pick-up game arena. I should've known when she kicked my ass at air hockey back in Los Angeles.

We stretched, formed teams, and I decided to play left full, with Taylor starting in goal. It was a good game, evenly matched. Each team picked off a goal apiece in the first five minutes. These people took their pick-up games seriously. I was up against a heavy right forward, who did get around me once and managed to take a clean shot at the goal. Which, of course, Taylor saved, no problem. But that forward kept grabbing my upper arms when we tangled, which pissed me off, and did more to disturb my game than motivate it.

I did end up tapping the ball back to Taylor a few times when I got in trouble. I hated doing it. Obviously because she had told me to. I remember back in high school, when Scott coached me to do the very same thing and I resisted so much. It felt like I was giving up, saying, "Here, take this; I can't handle it on my own." But it was a team thing, I eventually learned, though I wouldn't hear it from anybody but him. And apparently now, Taylor.

At the half, I walked to the car to get our bottle of water and my jacket. I was exhausted. When I came back, I noticed Taylor was talking to a woman, forty-ish, with hair that was just turning gray and a body that looked like athletics used to encompass a large part of her life, but didn't anymore.

I walked up to them, holding the bottle of water out to Taylor. The woman looked at me as though I had no right to be there.

"Jill, this is Isak," Taylor said, holding her hand out toward me like a display. "Isak, Jill. Jill used to coach me in high school."

Taylor seemed unsettled, and Jill looked like she was waiting for me to go away. I unscrewed the cap of our water bottle and took a few gulps, then handed it to Taylor, who took it, but didn't drink.

"So," I said, "are you gonna play?"

"No, just watching," Jill replied coolly. She scrutinized me closely. I could feel it even when I looked away, across the field at a guy throwing a tennis ball with a lacrosse stick for his quick black dog. The breeze had picked up, with a few more clouds gathering in the sky, which I hadn't noticed while we were playing.

The three of us stood there in silence. Taylor finally took a drink of water from the bottle. It dribbled down the side of her cheek, and she wiped her face with the back of her glove, which she hadn't taken off from the game. Her cheeks were flushed red and she left some dirt across the left one.

She was beautiful.

Jill turned toward Taylor, offering me the better part of her back. "What were you saying?" she asked.

"Oh, nothing really. I was just saying that I'm really enjoying getting back into this," Taylor said, motioning to the playing field in the same way she motioned to me just seconds before. "It feels, well, right. I'm thinking about maybe training again, I don't know."

"Well, honey, it's not too late," Jill said.

"I don't know about that," Taylor admitted.

"How long are you in town?" Jill asked Taylor, who looked to me before answering. As though I knew something she didn't.

"We'll see. But for now, indefinitely."

"I can work out with you if you want," Jill offered enthusiastically. "We'll get you back in shape in no time."

"I bet you will," I interjected. Taylor looked at me like I was the crazy one.

"I don't know," Taylor said, turning back to Jill. "I'm looking for a job, so I'll just see what happens."

"We're looking for a J.V. coach at school," Jill persisted. "I'm sure they'd hire you in a flash. I mean, well, you'd have to work under me." She laughed. As though it was the funniest thing in the world.

I coughed and rolled my eyes. They both looked at me and then back at each other.

"That is, if I still have the job next year," Jill continued. Then she lowered her voice and said, "You heard my big news?"

Taylor shook her head.

"I came out at school."

"Wow, I didn't know," Taylor said. "How'd that happen?"

"Well, it just got to be a little ridiculous, you know what I mean?" Again she shot a look at me that said I was invading her space. "Everyone knew anyway."

"Well, that's great," Taylor said. "I hope it's working out for you."

"It is. Listen, can we talk alone some time? Maybe grab some dinner?"

The guys at the center of the field yelled at us that the half was up.

"Yeah, that might be nice," Taylor said.

"So, are you two, uh–" Jill asked, looking back and forth between Taylor and me.

"No, *no*," Taylor insisted.

"We should go," I said, nodding at the field. "Nice meeting you, Jill."

"Yeah," she answered. "Taylor? Call me; my number's the same."

"Sure, bye."

Our team switched everything up for the second half. Taylor came out of the goal and played up front. I, too, moved up to halfback. We were ahead by two, so our team was goofing off a little, still playing hard, but maybe taking more chances and running plays we might not have been attempting had we been behind or tied. Taylor scored a goal with a header, off of a beautiful corner kick.

There were a few minutes left in the game. I switched back to fullback, because I was getting winded. I stood there in the backfield and watched Jill, who was watching Taylor's every move up the field. I noticed Jill was looking my way, which made me realize that the ball must've been heading toward me as well, when I'd been thinking it would stay at the other end of the field for the remainder of the game. I was wrong.

A big guy on the other team was taking the ball all the way upfield toward our goal. He outran Taylor and a couple of the other women playing half and forward. He had that determined look that comes from the frustration of losing. He came at me, dribbling the ball just a few feet in front of him and ignoring his teammates' calls for the ball. I put myself in front of him and went for the ball, but my body wasn't ready to make such a move.

My right ankle–the same ankle I injured playing high school soccer and then again in college–turned over with a pop. I went down in front of the guy, tripping him, and the ball went out of bounds.

"Fuck, what the fuck are you doing?" he yelled.

I caught my breath and rolled over onto my butt, looking down at my foot. I gingerly peeled my sweat pants up, my sock down, and there was a small egg developing there already, just above my ankle.

"Shit, you okay?" the guy asked, rolling over and standing up.

"Time's up!" the time-keeper yelled. "Game!"

"Hey!" the first guy called toward Taylor, waving her over.

I sat up and held my ankle. "This has happened before," I said. "It'll be fine."

Taylor sprinted over and knelt beside me. A few of the other players came over and stared down at me.

"What happened?" Taylor asked. "Let me see."

I pulled my sock down again.

"Shit," Taylor said. She looked behind her. I could see Jill slowly walking over to us. I tried to stand up, put some weight on that foot, but it was all jelly and I fell back down again.

"Are you crazy?" Taylor asked.

"No." I laughed a bit, managing to extract at least a hint of a smile out of Taylor.

"Can somebody get some ice?" Taylor asked, with high-pitched urgency in her voice.

"You want me to call an ambulance?" Jill asked.

"I think so," Taylor said, carefully untying my shoe.

"No!" I insisted. "I've done this twice before, worse than this. I just need to ice it."

"Maybe we should get it checked out," Taylor said. "You don't want to mess around with these things." Jill leaned over me and looked at my ankle. She nodded her head in agreement with Taylor. I wanted her to go away and not look at me. Ever.

"I'm not going to get it checked out."

"Well, let's get you home then," Taylor said. She asked the guy who fell on me to help lift me. I felt like a fool—worse than when I got hurt in peewee football. Jill was just standing there staring at me, hands in her vest pockets. God, she had a bad haircut.

"I can walk," I insisted.

Taylor pulled my arm around her shoulder and I slowly put my foot down. It hurt, but it wasn't broken. We started walking that way, Taylor taking my weight whenever my right foot was down on the ground.

259

"Can you get that blue bag over there?" Taylor asked. Jill did as Taylor requested, though she lumbered slowly, seemingly making the point that she could've cared less about what happened to me, and that she was only helping out because Taylor had asked her to.

They loaded me into the passenger seat, and Taylor pulled my jacket around me before I leaned back. I felt like such an idiot, getting hurt like this. Jill came back with the bag; Taylor fumbled around inside for her car keys and then went around to the driver's side.

One of the other players came back with a bag of ice. "Thanks," I said. I placed my ankle against it on the floor of the car. It stung like mad.

"Feel better," the guy said. A couple of other players waved at me, and then Jill leaned into Taylor's window and said, "Good luck," although it seemed to be directed at Taylor as opposed to me. What, again, did Taylor need luck for?

"We should go to the ER," Taylor said, putting the car in gear.
"No."

"I think we should get an x-ray, just to be sure."

"It'll be fine. Just get me home."

"What if it's broken?"

"It's not," I said, "and I don't have insurance anyway."

"So, they'll still take you at Rhode Island Hospital."

"Seriously, I had this same injury twice before. Same exact thing. I swell up real quick, but it's not broken. It'll go down with some ice, I swear."

"Fine," Taylor said, making a quick right turn. I recalled her face when she first came over to me on the field. In the brief time I'd known her, I'd seen Taylor upset, sad, cocky, angry, flirty, frustrated, scared, shunned, what else? But I hadn't seen her genuinely concerned. She had just been really worried about me. So, she was capable of that. Again I was struck, somewhere under the ribs, by how attractive this Taylor was: dirty, sweaty, pretense-free. Guileless. This was her world, not one she had to fit herself into.

260

"I'm going to pick up a bag of small cubes," Taylor said, pulling the car in front of a grocery store. "Mom has those big ones, and they'll hurt."

"It'll be fine," I said. She got out of the car anyway.

Taylor came back with two big bags of ice. "Wait, do you have any painkillers?"

"Yep, I'm set."

"I can go back in and get some."

"No."

"What do you have?" she asked.

"Is this a test?"

"Well?"

"Ibuprofen."

Taylor didn't seem satisfied, but she started the car anyway. "You okay?" she asked after a moment.

I nodded. I stared at her.

"What?"

"Nothing."

"Why are you staring at me?"

"I'm not," I lied, turning to look out the window. After a few more blocks, I decided to ask, "What's up with that Jill character?"

"What, why?"

"Is that the woman from high school?" On our drive cross-country, Taylor had said something about being with an older woman when she was in high school. She hadn't mentioned that it was a frigging teacher, though.

"Yeah."

"Well, what's her story?"

"What do you mean?"

"I don't know, she just seems really protective or something around you."

"She's just Jill," Taylor said. "I feel kind of sorry for her."

"Why?" I asked. "What could you possibly feel sorry for?"

"She's just kind of stuck," Taylor began. "I mean, I'm surprised she came out to people at school—that was a big move, but still."

"Oh, so she can be involved with more students now, but openly?"

"No, it was only me."

"Right."

"Why are you so freaky about this?" Taylor asked.

"I'm not," I insisted. "But don't you think it's kind of twisted? I mean, how old were you, fourteen, fifteen?"

"Yeah."

"Which?"

"Fourteen, then fifteen."

"Well?" I said, looking at Taylor as though I had just rested my case. My ankle was getting numb from the ice.

"You don't understand," she said. "It wasn't like that."

"What was it like, then?"

"Listen, can we talk about anything but this?" Taylor asked. We were almost home; I was starting to recognize houses in the neighborhood. "I still think we should get an x-ray."

"I don't."

261

* * *

Arlene and Taylor fussed over me when we got back. I hopped over to the couch and sat down. Taylor stacked up a few pillows for my leg, while Arlene fixed a fresh bag of ice. I hated drawing attention to myself in this way.

"I feel like a king," I said, and Taylor and Arlene looked up at me from what they were doing. Arlene spread a soft dishtowel across my ankle, then gently packed the ice around the swelling. I worried that my foot smelled.

"It looks horrible," Arlene said.

"I told her we should go to the hospital," Taylor added.

"Do you think it's broken?" Arlene asked, but she directed the question more to Taylor than to me.

"I would say yes," Taylor started, "mostly because it swelled up so quickly, and when I've seen that happen, it's usually been broken. Did it make a sound?"

"Yes," I admitted, "it popped." Arlene winced as though she could hear it.

"See? Broken," Taylor said to Arlene.

"It's not broken. Trust me, I know what broken feels like, and this isn't it."

"I hope you're right," Arlene said. She and Taylor stood over me. It seemed as though they were relieved, just to have something tangible to do. Arlene reached over and pulled some dead grass out of Taylor's hair. I think it was the first time the two of them had touched since the day we pulled up to the house. "You're a mess," Arlene said to Taylor, and then she licked her thumb and wiped away some of the dirt on Taylor's cheek. Taylor didn't pull back or wince at her mother's touch.

"Can I get you anything else?" Arlene asked.

"I'm fine," I said. "Do you know where Mary is?"

"I think he's upstairs with Charlie," Taylor said. "I'll go get him and tell Charlie what happened."

"No, don't bother him," I said.

Taylor went upstairs anyway.

"You must be hungry," Arlene said. "Can I make you some lunch?"

"No thanks. I'm fine."

"I'm making it anyway."

"Well, okay. I'll come in there in a minute."

"Don't be silly, I'll put it on a tray and bring it out to you," Arlene offered. "You don't need to be hopping around on that." She went into the kitchen.

I reached down and picked up the ice bag and towel to get a look at my ankle. Purple now. It was still swollen as hell, but it was going to be okay. Clearly, just a little reminder of my limits. Mary slowly plodded down the stairs. He came over and put his head on my thigh.

I heard the shower upstairs being turned on. The plumbing was so loud in that house. Taylor must've been getting undressed then, a stack of sweaty, muddy clothes in a heap on the clean tile floor beside her. And then Charlie came down the steps. He looked tired. Mary picked up a tennis ball and ran over to Charlie with it.

"Taylor told me what happened," he said. "You okay?"

"Yeah."

"Did you break it?" he asked, sitting down on the couch next to me. "Taylor thinks it's fractured."

"No way, nope. Just a sprain."

Charlie reached over for the remote control. He switched on the TV, but kept it on mute. He flipped through the channels quickly. We listened to the sounds of Arlene in the kitchen and Taylor in the shower. Mary kept trying to get one of us to play with him. He nudged his big wet nose against my arms, my legs, Charlie's hands, his feet.

"I know you get the brunt of my shit," Charlie said.

I looked at him. He was watching the TV, flipping through all the programs without stopping on any of them. Then I looked at the screen too, where the channels flew by, all of the faces and scenes and different shades of things. It was an entire life, flashing in front of us. And for a second there—it was only a second—my busted ankle was the worst thing that could happen to us. Ever.

Mary climbed up and put his two front paws on the cushion

263

between us. The tennis ball rolled off the couch and bounced onto the floor. He pushed off and rummaged around for the ball, which had disappeared under a chair. So he ran around behind the couch and came back with the rag-doll toy in his mouth, shaking it like a small rodent.

Then Charlie said, "I'm forty and I collect disability checks."

"What?" I asked.

"Age and occupation," he said. "Duh."

"Oh, now you want to play?" I teased him. "And that's not even how it's supposed to go. You can't be reality." But I knew exactly what he meant.

Mary shook the rag doll some more. It was a new toy, almost like that of a child. I didn't even know what the hell it was supposed to be–a boy, a girl, human, scarecrow? Maybe a monkey. Arlene had bought it for Mary after Charlie moved in. I would never have given him a toy like that. But he loved it.

Mary shook the ratty doll against the floor and then threw his head up and back, launching it into the air. I watched the doll hovering, its arms outstretched, legs split wide open, hair fanning wildly. And for a moment I worried it might never come down. Or worse, that it would land (splat!) on the hardwood floor. But the next thing I knew, Mary had caught it in his teeth, gently, and then placed the doll safely in my lap, damp with saliva.

I knew then that all of this would be brief. But it would be good.

264

Also from AKASHIC BOOKS

Kamikaze Lust by Lauren Sanders
2000 Lambda Literary Award Winner
287 pages, trade paperback
ISBN: 1-888451-08-4
AKB05 - $14.95

"*Kamikaze Lust* puts a snappy spin on a traditional theme—young woman in search of herself—and stands it on its head. In a crackling, rapid-fire voice studded with deadpan one-liners and evocative descriptions, Rachel Silver takes us to such far-flung places as a pompous charity benefit, the set of an 'art porn' movie, her best friend's body, Las Vegas casinos, and the psyche of her own porn-star alter ego, Silver Ray, all knit together by the unspoken question: Who am I, anyway? And as Rachel tells it, asking the question is more fun than knowing for sure could ever be." —Kate Christensen, author of *In the Drink*

Hell's Kitchen by Chris Niles
279 pages, trade paperback
ISBN: 1-888451-21-1
AKB19 - $15.95

"If the Olympics come to New York, apartment-hunting should be one of the events . . . Niles's fast-paced *Hell's Kitchen* plays with the city's famed high rents and low vacancy rate to put a new spin on the serial-killer novel. Taking aim at contemporary romance, the media, the idle rich, and would-be writers, Niles has written a thriller that's hilarious social satire." —*Detroit Free Press*

Synthetic Bi Products by Sparrow L. Patterson
341 pages, trade paperback
ISBN: 1-888451-18-1
AKB16 - $15.95

Sparrow L. Patterson's debut novel follows a nineteen-year-old bisexual girl on her whirlwind journey of sexual escapades, drug-induced hallucinations, shoplifting sprees, and other criminal behavior. Sexy and romantic, a fast-paced story of lust, deception, and heartache, *Synthetic Bi Products* is a compelling and original novel narrated in a bold, fresh, funny voice.

Adios Muchachos by Daniel Chavarría
2001 Edgar Award Winner
245 pages, paperback
ISBN: 1-888451-16-5
AKB12 - $13.95

A selection in the Akashic Cuban Noir series. ". . . [A] zesty Cuban paella of a novel that's impossible to put down. This is a great read . . ." –*Library Journal*

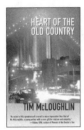

Heart of the Old Country by Tim McLoughlin
Selected for the Barnes & Noble Discover Great New Writers Program
216 pages, trade paperback
ISBN: 1-888451-15-7
AKB11 - $14.95

"Tim McLoughlin writes about South Brooklyn with a fidelity to people and place reminiscent of James T. Farrell's *Studs Lonigan* and George Orwell's *Down and Out in Paris and London* . . . No voice in this symphony of a novel is more impressive than that of Mr. McLoughlin, a young writer with a rare gift for realism and empathy."
–Sidney Offit, author of *Memoir of the Bookie's Son*

Boy Genius by Yongsoo Park
232 pages, paperback
ISBN: 1-888451-24-6
AKB21 - $14.95

A selection in the Akashic Urban Surreal series, *Boy Genius* is a powerful identity satire, the picaresque odyssey of a child seeking to avenge the wrongs perpetrated on his parents. Park renders his vision of late-20th-century global culture with the bold, surreal strokes of Pynchon and the wild political sensibilities of Godard; the painful, largely unmapped narrative territory of *Boy Genius* creates a gripping, harrowing read.

These books are available at local bookstores.
They can also be purchased with a credit card online through www.akashicbooks.com.

To order by mail, send a check or money order to:
Akashic Books
PO Box 1456
New York, NY 10009

Prices include shipping. Outside the U.S., add $3 to each book ordered.